MAGIC CITY

GO THERE.

OTHER TITLES AVAILABLE FROM PUSH

MAGIC CITY

DREW LERMAN

SCHOLASTIC INC.

NEW YORK   TORONTO   LONDON   AUCKLAND   SYDNEY

MEXICO CITY   NEW DELHI   HONG KONG   BUENOS AIRES

No part of this publication may be reproduced, or stored in a retrieval system or transmitted in any form, or by any means, electronic, mechanical, photocopying, recording, or otherwise, without written permission of the publisher. For information regarding permission, write to Scholastic Inc., Attention: Permissions Department, 557 Broadway, New York, NY 10012.

ISBN-13: 978-0-439-89027-4
ISBN-10: 0-439-89027-6

All rights reserved. Published by PUSH, an imprint of Scholastic Inc., 557 Broadway, New York, NY 10012.

SCHOLASTIC and associated logos are trademarks and/or registered trademarks of Scholastic Inc.

12 11 10 9 8 7 6 5 4 3 2 1   7 8 9 10 11 12/0

Printed in the U.S.A.   40
First printing, February 2007

To my mother and father

ACKNOWLEDGMENTS

Oh, there are a bunch of these.

I'd like to thank my family—the Whitebooks, the Corcias, and the Tachés. Also, of course, the Lermans: my parents, and my sister Elizabeth.

I'd like to thank Jake Nelson, Andy Gaber, Josh Malina, and Ryan Sprechman for everything. Logan Jaffe, thanks for your help at the beginning. Jordyn Ostroff, thanks for your help toward the end, and for telling me about the Scholastic Art and Writing Awards. And Jenna Abrams, thanks for your inexorable faith in my writing.

Lacey Friedman, your awesomeness and ambition never cease to amaze me, and I want to thank you for being the optimistic half of our two-person writer's support group.

I'd like to thank Eric Garcia, who is not only a brilliant writer, but also the nicest guy in the world.

Thank you to Damon Halback, a great teacher, mentor, and friend.

Thank you to Barbara Zitwer, my relentlessly wonderful agent.

And thank you to David Levithan. A better editor could not be imagined.

MAGIC CITY

O

IT'S A TRICKY THING, GROWING UP. You spend your whole life believing the world to be one way and then, out of nowhere, everything changes. You realize that maybe your parents don't know everything, your government is corrupt, your ancestors are murderers. You discover one day you're going to die — and after that, who really knows? In small doses, you learn that the world is absolutely nothing like it's been described to you. The brainwashing wears off, and all you can hope is for it to wear back on.

Charlie Brickell tells me all this.

I tell him that sounds about right.

He tells me the real question is, what do you do? What do you do so you won't find yourself thirty, forty, fifty years down the road, wondering what you've just done with your life?

I ask him what he thinks, because that's the point. I'm just here to keep the rhetoric conversational. Call me Tonto. Igor. Sancho Panza.

He asks me if I want to spend my whole life being a pawn. If

I want to take the risk of playing their game for my whole life, letting them define virtue.

Right now I don't really care, but I can gather that the answer he's looking for is no. Talking to Charlie, sometimes I feel like I'm answering the questions they ask on those late-night info-mercials. Do I want freedom?

Happiness?

Do I want a better life?

All this, and Charlie's telling me that there are three kinds of people in the world.

It's midnight and we're sitting out on the beach. Charlie's leaning back on his elbows; I'm resting my arms across my knees, and my chin on my arms.

And I ask him, "Only three?"

A soft wave crashes up onto the sand and slips back into the Atlantic Ocean.

"Three, and I guarantee you everyone you know can fit perfectly into one of these three groups."

It seems like Charlie has a built-in drumroll, and he says he's talking about losers, assholes, and cool people.

"Name anyone," he says. With Charlie, every conversation is pick a card, any card. He knows it — and you know he knows it — but you figure maybe you can learn the trick if you pay close enough attention. If you play along.

So I do. And ask him, "Keith?"

"Asshole."

"Keith's our friend, though."

"Keith is *your* friend. And anyway, it doesn't make a difference. He's still an asshole."

"Phil."

"Loser. Come on, I'm waiting for a challenge here."

"Well, how do you come up with it? How do you decide?"

And he tells me it's a fairly simple equation: If they're too lame to hang out with, they're losers, and if they're too obnoxious to hang out with, they're assholes. Everyone else is cool. This number is smaller than you might think.

I laugh, and he doesn't. He looks up at the sky, then out to the ocean. For a long time, we stare at the reflection of the moon floating on the water. It's a few days away from full, and I can almost make out the shadow where the rest of the white will fill in.

Just to fill the air with noise, I tell him his system is bullshit. It's not a universal system. It's just based on his own opinions, and who is he to make such absolute statements?

And he says, "Fuck you. I have good judgment. If I say someone's an asshole, he's an asshole. If you don't like it, you can make up your own fucking system."

I lean back and feel the cool sand on my palms. The sky is a dark watercolor blue and the water never ends. This night should be perfect. And I guess it is.

But for some reason, the only thing I can think about is Rebecca Tuttle.

And Charlie's asking me, do I want to go back to the hotel?

He's saying, "Come on. Let's head in."

And I say, "Just hang on one second."

I'm trying to enjoy this.

PART ONE

FAT ONES, QUIET ONES, AND TALKERS

1

WHAT YOU HAVE TO REMEMBER about post-traumatic stress disorder is that it can take time for your symptoms to improve. What you need to know is that getting better can be one of the biggest challenges in a person's life. What you don't want to forget is that people with PTSD can recover.

At least, that's what the doctors will tell you.

It's storming again, which means I'm sitting up in my bed at three-thirty in the morning, shaking and sweating. They put me on pills, but it doesn't stop the rain. And the way the rain is — I don't care how stupid this sounds — I think of cats and dogs. When the bubonic plague was going on in London, cats and dogs were always dropping dead in the middle of the street. After a bad storm, their corpses would float around or wash up in the gutters, and you know how medieval people were — one thing led to another, and it's raining cats and dogs.

My teeth chatter.

I want to look at the box in my closet, but I don't.

I hear the storm outside, and it's almost as if it's inside my house, inside my room, just pouring all over me. It wouldn't be the first time.

Every sound in the house is magnified by the silence. The wind blowing on the sliding glass doors. The relentless ticking of a clock. Lizards or cockroaches scuttling around on the floor. Sounds are good, because if it's too quiet I'll actually think, and if I think, I'm going to be thinking about the rain.

So I turn on the TV.

ABC, CBS, NBC. CNN, FOX, BET, MTV. This is life. After global warming or nuclear holocaust or whatever does us all in, this is what they'll find. Eighty million hours of archived television footage. *I Love Lucy. All in the Family.*

The Fresh Prince of Bel-Air.

Seinfeld, Friends, Cheers, Happy Days, Three's Company.

When they dig up our remains, at least they'll think we were laughers.

In the TV's hypnotic blue presence I can totally zone out and not worry about everything. I can close my eyes and not think of anything at all.

What I'm definitely not thinking about is the box in my closet. The box, which is just some old shoe box from three foot-sizes ago, is nowhere near close to being on my mind.

And I remember what the doctors tell me.

There are all kinds of criteria that they give you to determine whether you have post-traumatic stress disorder. They fall into three basic categories: intrusion, hyperarousal, and numbing.

They arrange the symptoms so that if you have four from this category, or five from this category, or three from this category, they can figure out how the disorder affects you personally. You get papers with checklists, and they make it like one of those fun little magazine tests. They have the symptoms all listed with the little boxes on the left.

Intrusion — this is re-experiencing. This is when you find yourself up in the middle of the night plagued by visions and memories and flashbacks. This is when you can practically feel the rain pummeling you into the ground.

Check.

Hyperarousal is how you jump every two seconds when it's nothing at all. How you're suspicious and paranoid. This is your twitch. Your nervous tic. Your wary eyes.

Check.

And numbing. This is you leaving the past behind. Moving on. Letting go and saying there is no fighting what's happened. There is only giving it up. Throwing it away. Putting it in a box.

The trick, if you ever want to get anywhere, is to skip the first two and go straight to numbing. Intentional amnesia. Because how can the past repeat itself if you can't even remember it?

What they'll tell you over and over again is that these symptoms aren't just in your head. You're not crazy.

You remember all this while downing your pills. Two orange, round, film-sealed fifty-milligram Desyrels.

The pills the doctors give you, they're for depression. Adapin to Luvox to Zoloft, none of it is unfamiliar territory. These are all the fancy name brands of more generic medicines, but if you're going to have a mental illness, at least do it with style.

You take twenty-five milligrams of Asendin.

Fifty milligrams of Effexor.

A hundred milligrams of Pamelor.

Everything's done in metrics.

After they have you all sedated on these drool pills, they sit you down and tell you real slowly, enunciating every word, the way all non-crazy people talk to one another, that PTSD is a real live illness just like diabetes or arthritis. It is never, ever a sign of personal weakness. That's why you have to take *these*. And you can feel free to slow them down if they're going too fast.

Still, with all the pills in the world, it's hard not to flash back on a night like this.

Lightning, thunder, and the pouring rain.

And a drip, drip, drip. Where it's coming from, I don't know. Probably the ceiling. Just a few drops at first, plinking softly against the shingles, and then the whole roof gives and the ceiling caves and you die.

Or maybe it's just the sink.

I breathe in hard and close my eyes. Exhale.

My parents are out of town again, because these days they always are. They're off at work, at conventions. I'm home doing the whole high school thing. It's our dynamic. Them, sleeping alone in hotel rooms across the country; me, flopping around on my mattress like a suffocating fish.

Counting sheep gets old, so I rattle off some trivia — all those PTSD fun facts. Like when you wake up from a tormented sleep, screaming or muttering to yourself or crying — this is your limbic system at work. The dreams, the flashbacks, the way you remember every detail perfectly. You can thank your *hippocampus* for this. It's all written in these books the doctors have. It's all there in black and white. In your *temporal lobe*, where your brain makes memories.

People who get Alzheimer's disease, their hippocampus becomes damaged and shrinks until they have no short-term memory. The disease spreads to eat away at the rest of their limbic system and eventually their frontal lobe. Sooner or later, they can't remember anything.

Right about now, that sounds like heaven.

And this wasn't a big scheme of mine or anything. I never meant to be this fucked up. Really. All I ever want is what everyone else wants. To be happy. To be successful. To be loved. And, at this moment, sitting up here in bed tonight, my major goal in life is to just sleep.

What they tell you is to take comfort in the fact that you're not alone. A little more than 3.5 percent of Americans experience post-traumatic stress disorder in a given year. Be comforted, you're nothing more than a statistic. There are a million others just like you and, when you die, there will be a million more.

2

THE WAY BECCA DRESSED, a funeral would never catch her unprepared.

Black shirt, black eyeliner, black sunglasses, red lipstick.

It's the next night. We're sitting in the park on a bench. Becca's head rests on my lap. I look up at the sky and can make out a few stars — planets, maybe — and the moon.

"It's a pretty night," I say. She smiles, so I keep going. "It's so cool when you can actually see any stars around here. It's just like you look straight up and there's this tiny speck of light, and around this little insignificant nothing, this little dot of white in the sky, there could be a whole entire system of planets. People there could be looking at us right now, thinking the exact, exact same things, looking right back at us, wondering what we're thinking about. It's incredible."

Becca's eyebrows contort in disbelief. "Jesus Christ, Henry — don't be such a fucking cliché."

I nod. My mistake.

She closes her eyes and starts whispering, a low, beautiful

hum. Her mouth barely moves, but every so often I can glimpse her teeth shining bright white between her red, red lips.

And she says, "It's okay. I have a pretty nice cliché if you're interested."

"Sure."

She breathes in. "It's this city. I've got to get out of here. It's such shit . . . it's so boring and fake and *stupid*. It's like it's contagious too. I feel like one day I'm just going to wake up and turn into everyone else. Like it's just a matter of time." She stops, harvesting something from her mind. Then she picks back up. "Everything's so artificial — like we're living in this giant mall. I need to go someplace cold, or someplace with seasons. Where there's snow and a fireplace. And everything there will be totally honest and real." She closes her eyes for a few seconds and they are motionless under her lids. She opens them and looks at me. "I don't want to die here."

Becca thinks Miami should never have been a city. People should never have been brought here. Miami is a marsh playing dress-up, trying to fit in with the other cities. "Where we live," she says now, "is just a cultivated swamp."

She says that this is what death would be like if everyone got too lazy. This is what it would be like to die, if nobody actually wanted to go through the trouble.

Becca wants to leave the city, and I can't help but think of the whole thing as some huge personal attack. Because aren't I enough? Can't she get what she needs from me? Maybe not. She wants me to think not. I'm supposed to think — everyone is — that she doesn't need anybody and that she's fine on her own, because she's such a goddamn individual and way too fucking unique to be bothered by the concerns of other human beings. That's strength. Need is weakness, desire is weakness. So Becca sighs and grins and rolls her eyes and wears black. Any other color would be weakness. Fine. She knows that I want her to say — *Oh, Henry, oh, won't you come with me to my magical winter wonderland so we can live together there because you and I are all that matters* — but she won't do it. And I want to say something. Something witty and brilliant — something that proves in a single casual remark that I know what she's doing, and that I want her to know I know it.

"So —" I begin, but already she's cutting me off.

"Why do you always tell me about other girls you think are hot?"

"I don't."

She leans back. She can't even look at me now. "Yes, you do."

"Okay, I said one thing about Rachel Flagler —"

"It's not just one thing, Henry." She stops. Finally, her eyes condescend to connect with mine. "And anyway, why did you say that?"

"I don't remember. I wasn't really thinking about it."

"Yes, you were. You said it specifically to get a rise out of me."

I tell her, "I don't think so, Becca."

"You did. I heard the pause in your voice after you said it. To wait for my reaction. You actually paused."

"Why the hell would I go out of my way to say that?"

"To make me jealous perhaps."

"That's absurd."

"Is it?"

"Of course."

"Well," she says, "I guess I disagree."

"It's not a matter of agreeing or disagreeing — I *wasn't* trying to —"

"Well, let me ask you, Henry, if it's so absurd, if it was so unplanned and inconsequential, why did you bring up Rachel Flagler when I was only talking about girls in general? Clearly, you haven't forgotten what you said and, clearly, you know it was important."

"You're being stupid."

And she says "whatever" and leaves me there.

I sit for a couple minutes. I feel tired.

I realize, probably way too late, that I need to chase her. That I need to find her and tell her everything's my fault.

Part of me is begging: *Forget it! Let her fix this for once! If she even cares!*

And then I realize where I am without Becca.

Alone.

Or playing cards with the guys at Bill's house. And with all the liveliness there, I might as well be alone.

On the sidewalk, everything has these long shadows. The night hides everything. Shattered beer bottles glimmer from the streetlights. A squirrel scurries into the center of the road and then climbs up a mammoth oak tree. A stray dog pisses on a fire hydrant. I'm walking and there's no sign of Becca anywhere.

Finally, I see her sitting on the side of the road, and she's crying. Right out, crying. And I can't understand how she's just *crying* like this. Her eye makeup is everywhere. She looks up.

Oh, her smeared eyeliner is telling me. *It's just you.* And with her lips, she says, "Please go away," softly and sincerely.

I am punched in the stomach by nostalgia and a little guilt.

She never used to push me away like this. Not so completely. She would be on the couch, her hair and her mind everywhere, desperate, depressed, for no obvious reason. She would whisper, *No, Henry, I understand you're trying to help, but stop. I don't want to talk about it.* I'd say okay and sit next to her, put her hand in mine. And that would be talking about it. Because sometimes catharsis is bullshit. Sometimes you just need a hand to put yours in.

And I say, "Becca, would you please just talk to me?"

I know, I swear I *know* she's saying something really important right now, and I cannot stop looking at her lips.

Her red, red, red lips and her white, white teeth.

Her lips, the way they stick to each other for that split second while she's opening her mouth to speak. And then open. It's fantastic, my God.

And she's saying, "Henry, are you even listening to me?"

I say of course I'm listening to her.

Some guys stare at their girlfriend's breasts, but with me it's these lips.

I tell her that I just want stuff to be okay with us. That I don't want it all to be ruined because of some stupid, insignificant thing.

She asks, "Do you really think it's stupid and insignificant?"

And I say, to comfort her, "Yes."

Now she's standing up, so I must have said something wrong. I stifle a yawn, not wanting to ruin the drama. It's just getting good. My every move, I analyze and judge and laugh, because I am just so far away from all of it right now.

"Jesus, Henry! That's so fucking typical of you. When *I'm*

upset about something, it's stupid!" I want to say *and insignificant,* but just to prove to myself that I can exercise restraint, I don't.

I say, "No! That's not what I'm saying at all. You're twisting my words." I hope I sound as shocked and appalled as I think I should be. "The situation is stupid, I mean. My reaction to what you said."

"Well?" she's asking me. "Which is it?"

"Can't it be both?"

"Goddamn it, Henry!"

And this yawn, it's just begging to get out.

"My comment!" I say. "My comment was stupid. And insignificant."

And I'm saying, "Becca." I'm saying, "I don't want to be in a fight."

So sincere. So genuine. Hell, *I'd* go out with me.

How much longer I can keep this act going, I don't really know. But I'm not in any kind of hurry. I don't have anywhere I really need to be. Argument with Becca? Sure. Pencil it in. If there's anything I've got, it's time.

And you know, I say I don't care. I say it's all the same to me. But things used to be so different. Where did we get lost? Making things fine was completely natural — a few simple, honest gestures. No questions, no explanations. Now it's all so planned, some boring million-year-old teen drama. I want to take her hand in mine and sit next to her. I want a moment of well-timed silence as we both look slowly up and up until our eyes meet and connect, locked, golden light blazing all around, overcome with astounding clarity. And as we kiss, a bellowing auditorium of applause, the whole world, clapping and shouting and crying tears of uninhibited joy, so pure and perfect, and the curtains roll down and the credits roll up and, God, I wish I didn't know what a bunch of bullshit that is.

And she's saying, "Fine. Whatever." She breathes in hard.

No credits, no climax. The real world being its usual drag.

She's had enough, I've had enough. We're a perfect match.

Now I tell her that everything will be fine, but she already knows what a liar I am.

She's learned how to play along, though. She says, "Good. Let's go home."

So I walk her home.

The trick to being in an argument with your girlfriend, if you really do care about her, is to always know when to stop. Because the idea isn't to win; you can't win. The idea is just to tell her what you're upset about and hope she does something with that information.

You're not telling her this in search of comfort. The things you want to tell her — well, they're only going to lead to an argument. So get out what you need to get out, and just when you feel like she's going to get *really* mad, tell her she's right and that you love her.

You're not allowed to get angry. If you do, she's mad at you for being angry. So then you have to comfort her for being mad about the fact that you were angry.

Every time you're mad, if she knows about it, it's all over for you, so you sure as hell better have a reason to let her in on it. Once she figures out that you're mad, she'll decide to get upset at you over this, and then you'll have just lost all your power.

Poof.

Like it was never there.

And the truth, obviously, is that it wasn't.

Rebecca Tuttle. She used to be everything I ever wanted. It wasn't anything specific so much. I guess it *was* the way she rolled her eyes. The way she didn't want anybody's help. Maybe it was the guard she kept up. Or maybe it was her lips or the way her eyes looked sometimes or the way she smiled when it was real. Because it used to be. And now — well, now I don't know.

Why we're still together, I don't think either of us knows. I guess it used to be that the world was shit and we needed someone on our side. Not to fight it — fighting shit was too messy, too exhausting. Just to avoid it. To distract each other from everyone else. It went on for a while, but pretty soon the tricks ran out, and then you're just two clowns with air fresheners in a septic tank.

Still, I feel she may be the answer. I feel that if there's anything that could save me, it might just be Becca.

Because it would be so much easier that way.

3

THE DOOR TO BILL'S IS ALWAYS UNLOCKED on poker nights. I stand there for a second, paralyzed, listening to the sound of chips moving, flipping, sliding on the wood table, everyone possessed and silent inside. I don't know who'll be there, but I don't really feel like being around anyone but Bill. I certainly don't feel like talking. It'll be the same bullshit if it starts up — who got a blow job from whom, who got drunk and did what, who got blazed and did what. It gets exhausting.

It shouldn't matter though. We usually don't have to talk.

I drift in and enter the game; a few rounds pass. I've never had much trouble keeping a poker face. My face is a poker face.

And against the sound of poker chips and grunts, there is just the quiet, something out of place but comfortable — like the last few moments of clarity as sleep creeps over your body at night. A more specific, more important kind of silence. I was looking for somewhere to just exist, and this is where I found it.

Here. Between Phil and Evan, across the table from Keith and Bill, with other less familiar faces spread around. With a two of hearts, a three of diamonds, a seven of clubs, a queen of spades, and a four of spades.

I guess I zoned out for a second because now I find myself surrounded. Bill's saying, "Henry?" He looks tired. "Henry, are you in or out?"

"Out." And they all shrug, maybe because I took a while to respond, or maybe because I'm usually out. I drop my cards and decide to head home. I tell Bill I'll see him tomorrow. He nods without looking up.

Before I leave, I glance back. Bill's looking at me now. Just for a second. Then he looks to the table and says, "Guys, let's call it quits for tonight."

"Yeah, I'll bet you want to quit," someone says.

"Whatever, dude, I'm not even losing that much."

"Yeah, all right, Bill," someone else says. "See you next week."

"Yeah, Bill, see you in school."

The cards are shuffled away into packs, the chips stacked up in ivory towers and blue cylinders. The tables, the chairs, everything is abandoned.

The silence stops. Everyone's off. To smoke or see a movie or play video games or grab some food at a twenty-four-hour pizza place with red flickering lights.

"Later, Bill. Later, Henry. Take it easy."

"Later, Keith."

The clunk of the front door closing reaches the living room with finality.

"Are you okay?" Bill asks.

Oh, these questions. I could say:

"Yes," which would mean, "No."

"No," which would mean, "No, but I'm probably not going to tell you what's the matter anyway."

"Yeah," which would mean, "I've been better."

"I guess," which would mean, "If you press me, I will probably give you some information."

"I don't know," which would mean, "I am breaking down, take what you want — it's all lying in piles of smoky, burning debris on the floor anyway, and I want you to take some pleasure in it. Rub it on your body, you bastard. Love it. Yes, I have post-traumatic stress disorder. Yes, my relationship with Becca is falling apart. Yes, I am spiraling downward. Yes, yes, yes, okay? Everything is fucked up! Is that what you want to hear? Is it? *Is it?*"

"I don't know," I say.

"Well, you should know you can talk to me about it," he says. "Whatever it is."

We go down to the park to throw around a baseball. We walk past all the rich houses, and at the end there's this big patch of grass that in fifteen years — no, in five years — will be nothing but more rich houses.

Bill's about five foot seven, with skin that seems like it would tan easily. He's got glasses on, but they're not bad. His hair is dirty blond and cropped short. He's drawn in simple, curving lines.

He tells me, "Rachel Flagler, man. She is just totally amazing."

At the name, my breath gets lost somewhere in my chest. It doesn't make sense to hear that name coming out of Bill's mouth. Not that I care or anything, so I say, "Cool," and throw the ball back.

He goes, "No, dude. I don't know. She's just so real and so down-to-earth. Just, like, wow. I didn't even know girls like that existed."

"Neither did I," I tell him. This is a mistake for two reasons (and a side note).

1. The *Bill Actually Listens* Factor. Because to be honest, I'm just talking out my ass here.
2. The *This Means I Think Something Bad About Becca* Factor. Because as much as I want my relationship with Becca to be good, I'm not an idiot like Bill. If there's one thing that should not be romanticized, it's my relationship with Becca, and this is something Bill refuses to learn.

Side note: Did I not tell Bill about Rachel? Ever? I guess I never did. Do I mention it now? No. Not now. If I mention it now, then after I tell him he will say, "Oh, well I won't get involved with Rachel, if that's how things are." He will say that to make a point to me about how friends don't do things like that to each other. Like I did to him. And I don't need him making that point. And *also* I kind of like the idea of Bill trying to get with Rachel. Not that he could. Just him trying to get with her is a nice idea.

"What about Becca?" he says.

"What about Becca?" I say.

"She exists."

"Well observed, Bill."

"Are you guys even still going out?"

"Yes."

He throws the ball at me and squats with his mitt forward. "It doesn't seem like it."

"We are."

"I'm just saying, like, every weekend you come over to play cards and stuff —"

"Do you not want me to?"

"Of course, it's fine with me, but Becca —"

"Fuck off, Bill. Enough about Becca. I can't fucking play a game of catch without getting railed by you about my relationship. You're like a girl about these things."

"Dude, I'm just saying I think you should talk things out. I don't hang out with Becca like I used to and I don't want either of you to get really hurt when all of this blows over."

"Okay."

I drop my mitt on the ground and walk away. Because I don't feel like dealing with this anymore, and also because Bill knows about my PTSD, which means I can just walk away from him in the middle of conversation and he can't be mad at me. You're not allowed to be mad at people with mental disorders. You have to be understanding.

I'm walking away, and Bill's calling after me, saying, "Hey, man, I'm just saying that because I think you and Becca really have something special."

And I start walking faster, thinking, *Yeah. Special like a rare form of cancer.*

"Seriously," he's shouting. "You should try to fix things. Don't do anything you'll regret."

And I'm running, faster and faster down the street, and he's yelling, "I used to really envy you guys."

And he's yelling, "Why do you want to throw it all away?"

And he's yelling, "Can I at least have my ball back?"

But already, I'm gone, running, lost in the mechanical

motion. I run down the street and past the guard gates and the guardhouses. My feet land rhythmically against the pavement, the concrete, the grass.

I run until it hurts, and then I run until it doesn't hurt anymore. My muscles, my joints and bones, everything is about to crack and come down. I sit down against a fence. Just for a second. Just to get a breath.

When I wake up, it's dark out and I see a face right up to mine. I see sunglasses, a plaid hat, and a black leather jacket. He's been leaning over me for I don't know how long.

"You're liable to get yourself killed here," the lips tell me, still right up in my face. "Passed out on the side of the road like this."

I guess I make a face, because the guy wrinkles his brow and stands up straight.

I ask him who he is. He says if I take this road south for about five or ten miles, I'll be home. He places a cigarette in his mouth and lights it. He shakes the match out with his arm and tosses it aside.

Then I recognize him. It's a guy from school. A grade ahead of me. That would make him a senior. But that's not exactly right, I don't think.

"Five or ten miles?" I ask.

I study his face as he speaks. He doesn't seem to notice.

"Just about. You know how to get home?"

"No." And I figure it out. He's the guy who got expelled at the beginning of last year. The guy everyone was talking about. The school paper tried to run a story about it, but the administration withheld it from distribution. Charlie something. I can see the headline vaguely. The journalism kids passed around the paper, the few that they got out before the princi-pal pulped the rest. I remember there was a picture of Mr. Englewood smiling and the headline: BRICKELL EXPELLED FOR PUNCHING TEACHER. The picture was from the yearbook. Englewood wasn't smiling after that punch. Not for weeks. His nose was broken.

A lot of people loved Mr. Englewood, although he's strictly a douche bag. In the article, Charlie said he had reacted out of irrepressible rage. Old Englewood had said something about Charlie's dead parents, had gotten all up in his face.

Mr. Englewood wasn't quoted, but Charlie said Englewood took offense to a few "pointed remarks during a particular lecture."

"Punching him in the face probably wasn't the best idea," Charlie said, "although it probably wasn't the worst one either."

Anyway, he was expelled.

Now he's here and he's saying, "Yeah. You're just off U.S. 1. You want to take it that way till you reach the intersection, and then turn left. It's straight that way till you get home, about fif-teen minutes." He points. "And I think you dropped this." He puts his cigarette in his mouth and takes Bill's baseball from his jacket pocket. He tosses it up, catches it, and tosses it to me.

I look around. There are a bunch of barbed-wire fences and old buildings, and a little farther down the street I see some car dealerships and fast-food restaurants. It's dark enough that I can see maybe twenty or thirty stars.

I tell him I don't have a car.

"Oh," he says.

He starts walking away, and I debate whether to ask him for a lift. He picks up a beer bottle from the ground and holds it by the neck, the liquid splashing around inside. With his other hand, he takes a drag of his cigarette.

I stand up, wipe off my jeans, and crack my neck. I rub my hands together, getting off most of the dirt. When I look back, he's gone.

So I walk.

My cell phone is somewhere in my bedroom. I pass a pay phone and realize I could just call Bill, and he could take me home. Just ten digits and thirty-five cents, and I wouldn't have to worry about this ridiculous walk. He's probably at home now watching some soap opera with a tissue in one hand and some Nora Roberts novel in the other, leaning the phone between his ear and shoulder, bitching to Rachel about how he's so lonely, and she'll be there saying no, it's going to be okay, blah, blah, blah.

Another pay phone pops up. I keep walking.

One day Bill will learn that what girls want isn't a sweet, caring listener. Girls don't want a nice guy. Because what's more boring than someone who treats you nicely and respects you and thinks about you all the time? That's considered leechy. And no one likes a leech.

Another pay phone.

I try to remember how I met Bill. It was in elementary school. We were in second or third grade. He had buck teeth and what looked like a really ridiculous comb-over. He was sitting on the swings. I was talking to someone who I can't remember, and we just looked at this kid, this dumb little baby of a kid, and in our elementary school way, we thought: *What a douche bag*. We knew the deal with him. He was Toolsville. A geek. Doomed to spend the rest of his life sliding glasses up the bridge of his nose and associating with all the other losers, because that was just the way things were and, we figured, the way they ought to be.

How I got to be *friends* with Bill was a different matter. We got some group project assigned so our teachers could feel like they were teaching us about teamwork and *sharing*. All my friends ditched me and went to work with one another, and there, sitting by himself, with his stupid glasses and stupid greasy hair, was Bill. And I thought, *Oh, great.*

I pass another pay phone.

So I told this kid, this little puny pathetic doofus, "I guess I'm with you."

And he said, "Yeah," reluctantly, as if it was somehow the end of the world for him. And I just rolled my sarcastic eight-year-old eyes and said, "Come on."

The project was called *Miami: Magic City*, and it was supposed to be about how Miami had changed over the last century. How it started, and how they brought the railroad here, and how the city exploded. We showed up to school with the project and found Randy Kirkman standing there.

Randy Kirkman was one hell of a big kid for a third grader. Not tall so much, but just huge shoulders, like he'd been doing the military press since he was in the womb.

He pushed Bill and asked him, "Hey, shrimp. What's that you got there?" or some such bullying cliché. Then he took the poster we'd worked on all week, threw it into the mud, and stepped on it.

That about did it for me. I figured I was a pretty big kid, so I just looked the bastard straight in the face and pushed him, saying, "Hey, man, just lay off."

He kicked both our asses.

And there's something in that, something singularly and powerfully bonding about getting your ass kicked with some other kid.

We were wimps, with two soon-to-be-black eyes apiece and a torn and muddy poster between us. We trudged to school with our heads down, too ashamed to look at each other or anyone else. Hating Randy Kirkman. Hating each other. Hating ourselves.

And Bill looked up at me, and put out his hand, and asked me if I want to be his friend.

And I smiled, real big, and thought, *What a baby.*

But I said, sure, and we shook hands, real businesslike, and from then on, we'd been friends. It took time for me to get used to him. Yet slowly but surely, it turned into what we have now.

And what is this, Payphoneville? Should I just call Bill? Swallow my pride and get a lift?

Or keep walking?

I'm walking home with my hands in my pockets, and the PTSD is coming on hard because I haven't taken my pills since this morning. It's the circus of imaginary things. Little flashes juggle and dance in my eye. I start walking faster, which gets my heart going faster, which makes the images flicker more, which makes me start panting, which makes me close my eyes, and soon I'm running blindly in the street. I know the rain isn't really there. Society says it's not, and these pills are so I won't get confused. I trip and fall. I look around me. What the hell am I doing?

I walk back to the last pay phone.

I grumble a little in protest of myself, and — long story short — I call Bill and he drives me home.

*   *   *

I get to my house and open the door. I guess my parents have returned home because there are two cars parked in the driveway. They weren't there earlier today. It's two in the morning.

I walk in and the living room light casts a strange shape onto the foyer. It's accompanied by a soft cacophony of static. I say, "Hello?"

My mom is up watching TV. "Henry?"

"Hey."

"What are you doing home so late?"

True story: I've been home this late every day this week and she's never said anything until today. I guess it would have been hard for her to notice from New York, Seattle, and then New York again.

"What?" I say.

"What do you mean, 'what'? It's two o'clock in the morning." There's an emptiness in her anger, too much rehearsal. Like every half hour, her brain has been updating the time at the end of the sentence.

"I had to stay after school to make up a test."

"Oh."

"I'm going to go to bed."

"All right," she says.

As I'm on my way out, she says, "What?"

"I didn't say anything."

"How are you doing in chemistry?"

"Okay." I'm holding on to the doorway of the living room.

"You got an F on that first test," she says. Trivia like this is her proof that she qualifies to be a mother.

"I remember," I say.

She looks back at the TV. I turn to leave.

"Henry," she says.

"What?"

"Making up a test? On *Saturday*?"

"No, you caught me. I was hanging out with Bill."

"Don't lie to me anymore."

"Okay," I say. I leave and go to bed.

4

IT'S ABOUT A WEEK LATER, and I wake up in class with everyone staring at me. It's always like that, because the teacher hears you snoring or sees you drooling all over your desk and then calls your name about fifty times, until the entire class is staring at you.

Then someone on your left taps you and you wake up, wiping your mouth and blinking a lot.

All last night I couldn't sleep, so now I can. They can wake me up, but they can't make me pay attention and they definitely can't make me care. Still in my post-awakening state, I'm thinking about how it might not be a bad idea to kidnap Mr. Black and take him home and force him to lecture me until I can fall asleep at night.

I'm awake, but everything seems so distant, I'm back in the shadow puppet world. Everyone around me is taking notes, scrawling away. Identical notebooks, identical desks, same words on the same thirty-two-lined college-ruled notebook paper. They all care and I don't, so it's either everyone else is wrong or I am. I look up and start writing down a few sentences, just as I hear them. This way it will be Mr. Black's fault if I do badly.

The trouble is, it's pretty easy to tune out chemistry teachers. The easiest teachers to tune out by far are foreign language teachers. My Spanish teacher, she has no chance at my attention. She's speaking in Spanish the whole time, so she's really not even trying.

Math teachers aren't too hard to tune out, either. They're talking in numbers the whole time, so it might as well be a foreign language.

Two skinny girls in front of me are laughing about some joke. Something hilarious about a penis. You can always tell this by the way they laugh, like they're in on some fantastic secret. I'm not exactly sure how the system works for these girls, but it seems to be something like this:

Penis: Scientific; nice, comfortable *Oprah* word.

Vagina: Questionable; can only be used by girls, unless when talking about sexually transmitted diseases.

Testicles: Hilarious! For example, "Oh, my God, Jen, it was *hilarious* when you kicked Todd in the *testicles*." (*See also* Balls).

Dick: Nice, versatile word. Can be used when talking about a celebrity whose *dick* you want, or when talking about a hot guy. (i.e., "It's okay, Nicole, John is just a *dick*. That's why he finds you boring and unattractive.")

Cock: Good for use if you're in one of those slutty moods on a girls' night out.

Balls: A good time, as far as words go. Nice for

description of weather, for instance, "My word, Peggy, it's hot as *balls* out here."

Cunt: By far the most offensive word ever to be created. Surely invented by chauvinists as a way to keep women from voting or earning equal wages. Must never be used.

Pussy: Another vile creation of the oppressive masculine capitalist insensitive war machine. Not as bad as cunt, but should also never be used.

I yawn. Mr. Black's up there going on about specific heat and heat of fusion. I want to just raise my hand and say, "Look, I appreciate it, but I am never, ever going to understand or use this, so can I just go take an early lunch or something?"

The lunch bell rings, and half the class is already out the door. I pack up my notebook and hoist my bag over my shoulder.

In the hall, my eyes are already darting around for Becca. If I see her, I don't know what I'll say. This search for her is just habit.

And there she is, in her usual cemetery garb. Seeing her walk by herself like this reminds me of everything I love about her. Her skin is like milk against her black hair and dark eyes. Her head has this apple shape, with some freckles scattered around her nose. She has on those thick black eyeglasses that got trendy when dressing nerdy and vintagey became hip. The muscles in her forehead seem to be taking great pains to keep her eyelids up; her expression is tired, borderline unconscious. She could pierce her whole face and tattoo herself up and down and she still would have this incredible innocence. She has one of those messenger bags over her shoulder, resting at her waist, sliding back and forth with her hips.

Suddenly, I'm alive again. I maneuver around the herds and sprint over to her, asking, "What are you doing tonight?"

This takes her by surprise. Her eyes slant a little and a small smile curls her lips. These smiles are the ones that mean I'm an idiot, but right now I love her too much to care.

She doesn't have lipstick on, but her lips are still as amazing as ever.

And they say, "Nothing, I don't think."

I ask them if they want to do something. "Tonight? It will be fun."

"This sounds suspicious," they say.

"Suspicious? What's suspicious? Can't a guy hang out with his girlfriend on a Friday?"

And she raises a thin eyebrow and says, with her tongue sticking out a little, that okay, sure, she'll see me tonight.

I kiss her and run off.

Lunch. You take fifty milligrams of Tofranil. These are reddish brown and sugarcoated, so you can eat them like candy. The word *Geigy* is written across the capsule in white

I try to imagine this Geigy character. It seems like he should be a little man who inscribes his name on everyone's pills, snickering to himself. Black mustache, top hat.

Geigy. The bastard.

Fifty milligrams, three times a day, or twenty-five milligrams, six times a day. You can split it up however you like.

Phil and Keith are sitting next to me, talking. I think they keep trying to include me in the conversation, so I nod a couple times.

I'm distracted, I'm confused, I don't know. I can't concentrate.

I mumble something at my shadow friends and leave the freezing cafeteria.

Out in the Miami heat, I can thaw out. I put my hands in my pockets and wonder why Becca hasn't broken up with me yet.

I show up at Becca's house at around seven-thirty. I knock twice on the door and, when it clunks open, Becca's head shoots out like a cork attached to her long, slender neck.

Her eyes look confused and she says, "What do you want?"

And I say, "Aren't we doing something tonight?"

"I'm exhausted," she tells me.

I don't know if I look as disappointed as I feel. Maybe because she's taking pity on me, or maybe because she really does like me after all, she goes, "Do you want to just hang out here tonight?"

And I ask her, "Would that be okay?"

"Sure," she says, and tilts her head toward the interior of the house. "Come on in."

We walk to her room, and I pet her cat on the way in. Her parents aren't home.

"My parents think whenever you come over, we're having sex," she says.

How depressing. I'm getting more action in her parents' minds than I am in real life. She rummages around in her drawers. I stand off to the side, unnoticed. All the lights in her house are off, and she's wearing red lipstick.

"I'm tired," she says.

"I'm Henry," I say, and smile.

She yawns and says, "That's funny."

"Oh, come on." I follow her from her room to the hall where she grabs a book off a shelf. She brings it to her room and I follow her back there. Finally, my presence is acknowledged and she says, "Okay, I'm taking a nap."

"Okay," I say.

"What?"

"Well, what do you want me to do?"

"I don't know," she says. "Do whatever you want. You can take a nap, too."

"Okay."

She walks into her living room and falls really clumsily onto this massive black leather sofa. There's something about girls falling clumsily that I can never get over.

I go back into her room and start looking through her stuff.

There's the regular stuff. A couple notes I wrote her, some pictures of the two of us, some drawings and poems of hers. The whole routine.

Then there are her journals. They're really diaries, but she doesn't want to be a girly-girl or anything, so she calls them journals. She has about a million of them, some stacked up vertically, some scattered, some opened, some closed. They're those hundred-sheet composition books with the black-and-white covers and space on the front to write your name and school and stuff.

Just because one happens to be open, and just because I happen to glimpse the name *Henry*, I can't help myself.

henry looked kind of hot today.

So far, so good.

but what the fuck is his problem? he's the most stupid, narcissistic, insensitive asshole that i've ever known. he doesn't even realize it, it's absurd. i swear it's like dating a small child who you always have to care for and look after.

ugh, why am i still going out with him?
does he want me to break up with him?
why?
why?
why?
i'm going to sleep.

So. She thinks I'm hot.

I close the journal.

I don't get too worked up about this. I'm not particularly surprised, to be honest. First of all, this entry could have come from whenever, and it's not like I had some kind of doubt she'd ever felt this way about me.

I walk into the living room and she's lying there, alone and angelic on the leather couch. I lift her head and she opens her eyes a little. I sit so the back of her head can rest on my lap. I comb a thin strand of her black hair behind her right ear. She has two earrings there. One in the regular place, and one through the cartilage on the top.

She looks up at me and tells me, "Henry, this isn't going to work."

And I tell her I know.

I tell her I've known that for a long time now.

She smiles a little, which is unusual, because it looks really genuine. Her lips are so red, and I lean over and I want to kiss them, but I kiss her forehead instead. I don't know why; it just seems like the right thing to do.

She smiles again.

And she says, Really.

Henry.

Really.

This really isn't working.

The third group of symptoms is called denial. Numbing. Not facing the truth.

And what has Becca been thinking? All this time? When she smiled and laughed, when we first met, the way her mouth used to curve up sideways. What was she thinking? Was she thinking that this was what she wanted? And then later, after the meds started and the pills, when she was asking me all these questions — when she wanted to know what was wrong, what was going on, and I wouldn't let her know and I wouldn't say a word — what was she thinking then? Did she care? She had her own shit to deal with, her own depression. Over the last year, when her eyes moved from distance to focus against the up and down of the weeks and the months, the downward spiral to college and adulthood and responsibility and death — was she indifferent to it all? As indifferent as I'm supposed to think now?

I just wish, more than anything, that Becca would spend the rest of her life happy. Of course, I also wish more than anything that I would spend the rest of mine happy. I'm not entirely sure whose happiness is more important to me, but I'm not going to lie — it's probably mine.

Sometimes you just have to wonder: Who do you want to die more? You or your loved ones?

It's tricky.

The whole world should be able to be fixed in little hundred-milligram tablets. Once they cure depression and insomnia, I say everyone will be ready to take on the world.

Twenty-five-milligram tablets, three times a day at first, and eventually up to around a hundred-fifty milligrams a day.

Or you can take the kind you put under your tongue for instant relief, this way it dissolves straight into your bloodstream.

Allow fifteen minutes for results.

The way the world is going, we need those fifteen-minute pills.

The instant-gratification tablets.

I say we get Earth on meds, and fast.

I look down at Becca and smile. I breathe in until the air fills my lungs, never wanting to let go. Never wanting to move from this exact position. Like that first escaping twilight in the park when I kissed her for the first time.

I don't know how long we stay just like that, but it feels like forever and it's not enough. I get mad at myself for being stupid like this sometimes, but it's the truth. I can't help it.

Slowly, Becca's couch encompasses me, and I feel lost in the huge, fantastic cosmos. It's just Becca and me, and I am warm and peaceful and happy. I don't know what it is, or why. I feel the cold comfort of leather against my skin, my bare arms, my neck. I feel Becca's body, warm — scientifically, biologically warm. Her movements, the flutter of her eyelids, the tiniest little twitches of her lips, everything works and she exists as an entity against the world, connected somehow to me. She doesn't breathe as a display of consciousness or of force or of anything spiritual or true. There is nothing behind her to account for her existence, only her existence itself. She is not a rift in being and consciousness, but a unity of the two — her every action a precise manifestation of her every thought. She doesn't exist for me. But here she is. With me. Thinking, probably, of nothing. I've learned when you ask people what they're thinking of, not to get annoyed when they tell you it's nothing. That's probably the most honest answer you'll ever hear from them.

Everything is clear for the moment. For the present tense. Within the half-second of life that is the now — after the two-minutes-ago of ancient history, and before the two-minutes-forward of the distant future. And that is the longest length of clarity I think I can ever hope for. And it is so clear. Maybe I haven't explained it the right way. It's too much to know where to begin. When so much is understood in so few words, it's suspicious to attempt to tack on syllables, streams of vowels and consonants. All I know is that right this instant, everything makes sense. I have my whole life ahead of me. I have everything in the world to look forward to.

I just wish the whole thing wouldn't be so damn depressing.

5

BECCA LOOKED PRETTY MUCH THE SAME in ninth grade. Her eyes and her teeth were a little bigger in her face. Her neck was a little longer.

Bill was on the phone with her. His house was always dimly lit. In the square room, I was sitting on the carpet two feet away from the TV screen with a controller in my hands. Bill was on the couch.

"Come on, get off the phone."

"One second."

My thumbs sped around the controls, and my body shifted to add leverage to my character.

"Come on," I said.

"Fine, fine." He muttered some crap to her and clicked off the phone.

"Throw me a control."

I chucked one at his face and he dodged it. "Watch it," he said. I started a new game.

After a while he was doing so awful that I looked at him on the couch to see whether he'd turned into pudding or something, but it was the same old Bill, only happier.

"What the fuck are you so happy about?"

"What? Nothing."

"It looks like something. Did they present you with some award for sucking at video games?"

"No."

"Well, pay attention. And stop smiling like that."

I knew Becca vaguely. She was quiet. The first time I really saw her was at Bill's one day after school.

The doorbell rang and he said, "Hang on." I had to pause the game. I sat in the living room and listened to them talk. They were laughing and flirting maybe. Some girl flirting with Bill. I wasn't happy for him. I figured she had to be a beast.

Becca walked into the room. She was wearing dark pajama pants and a big gray sleeping shirt that hung like a dress. She said, "Hi." Her hair was longer then. She wasn't wearing lipstick, and her lips were light pink. She smiled.

"Hi," I said.

There were bookshelves on the wall. She thumbed through a few before Bill came back. I didn't unpause the game. Bill walked in with a textbook.

"Thanks very much. I'll get it back to you tonight."

"Don't worry about it."

"All right, well, 'bye." I was looking at her as she left. She turned and waved lukewarmly, I waved back the same way. She let herself out.

Bill sat down and we started the game back up for a few minutes. Nobody talked. The noise from the screen was too quiet to fill the room. "What do you think of her?" Bill finally said.

"I don't know. How should I know? I don't even know her."

"I think I'm going to ask her out."

Then neither of us said anything again until the pizza came.

She said no, of course. I think it was awkward after that. We were so good at those stupid games.

I said, "Would you care if I went for Becca?"

My eyes didn't move from the screen and neither did his. We were casual.

"What?"

"I don't know. I mean, you don't still like her, do you?"

"I mean . . ."

"Well, if you don't want me to go for her, I won't."

"No, you can. I just didn't know you liked her."

"Yeah."

"Since when?"

"I don't know. I just wanted to ask you in case, y'know . . ."

"Yeah, thanks."

I don't know if Bill wanted to say, *You fucking asshole, of course I mind. Of course if you get with her it will kill me. Of course it will.*

I don't know if he wanted to, because he never did, and he never said anything about it. Except that he was happy for us when it all did happen.

Liking a girl gives you a sense of purpose in ninth grade. Something to do. Becca occupied my time.

And the conversations started like they do. Online.

hey

hey.

sup

not much, you?

nm

Twenty-five-minute pause.

ok gtg bye.

bye

And I would think, Goddamn it! I should have I should have I should have. But I don't, except to ask her for the —

hey whats the hw

i dont know.

whatever im not doing it haha

haha.

Sigh.

And did I mention that I'm in love with you?

No, I don't believe you did.

Ah, I can be so absentminded.

Let us run off together?

Yes, let's.

At least, that's how it should have gone.

My mom said to call when I needed a ride home from school, but I never called that day. Becca walked through the crowded, swarming hallways, her shoulder a magnet to the wall. Her face was red and muddy, her eyes dark, unconscious. I passed her, walking in the opposite direction, unable to pause against the moving, unified mass. She looked breathless, defeated. Something in her eyes, in her eyebrows and her forehead, something in the crimson anguish of her cheekbones — God, I just wanted to hold her, for it to be that simple, for her to understand and to let me.

I turned back.

"Becca."

She didn't react. I touched her shoulder.

"Becca."

She turned to me. Smiling only with her mouth, she said, "Hi," and turned back, walking faster, away from me, through the broad, ugly doors of the school.

She walked through the student parking lot, through everyone. I followed behind her and she knew it and I called at her to hang on. I thought this was it. This was my movie shot at Becca's heart. This was my chance to capitalize on her sadness and twist it to become her hero. It made sense . . . but thinking back now, maybe not. Maybe — to avoid sentimentality, to preserve my exalted cynicism — I've convinced myself this was more calculated than it actually was.

She stopped short and said, "What?" I stopped with her and the crowds surged past us in a constant stream.

"What's wrong?" I said.

"Nothing." She opened her red eyes wide, as if to say *Anything else?*, and brushed an index finger to her tear duct. Her hands fell back to her sides. "Thanks," she said, "talk to you later," and she began to walk away.

"Wait," I said. "Please." She stopped and turned slowly and gestured at me to proceed. "I just — I know, you don't really know me. I don't expect for you to tell me everything — or anything. I guess . . . I don't know. I'm really — you really — I really like talking to you. And maybe sometimes it helps to talk to someone who doesn't know about the situation. I can be a very good listener. I mean, I know you said it's nothing, but I'm not an idiot."

She nodded. "So, what, you want me to tell you what's wrong?"

"Well, I mean —"

"My parents are getting divorced. Good? Happy?" She swallowed and her eyes shone wetter.

"No, Becca —"

"So just pat me on the head and tell me it's not my fault and that it happens to lots of people and, y'know . . . just — I mean, *fuck*." She turned her head from me and let out a cry of stifled anger. "Let me ask you, Henry — did your parents ever get divorced?"

"No."

She nodded to herself. "Well, looks like we won't be able to empathize much. So, what do you want?"

I didn't know. I guess I wanted to kiss her. But could you say that? It seemed so shallow.

"I want to kiss you," I said.

She looked surprised, then laughed. "I'm not going to kiss you."

"Okay, then I just want to be your friend."

Now she laughed bitterly, quietly, looking away. "You want to be my friend?"

"I mean . . . yeah."

She looked back at me and smiled. "All right," she said. "I'll be your friend."

We walked to the park and talked. Her parents weren't home. I don't know where mine were. For a long time, we didn't mention the divorce. We talked about school — the absurdity, the pointlessness. We shared a skepticism, an implicit pessimism. We enjoyed our disillusionment. We both used it to avoid existence. To avoid getting too attached. Becca couldn't help crying, but she saw it, I think, as a vulgar self-indulgence.

That afternoon I fell in love with her. I didn't mean to, but I didn't mind. It was nice. I scoffed at it, but it was nice. And in the end, she let me kiss her. I knew I was supposed to save her, but somehow it felt reversed. I kissed her and her lips were so soft and so warm, so completely immaculately warm.

Becca and I were sitting on the beach a few weeks later. We wore thick jackets. It must have been winter. We squinted against the breeze and didn't talk for a little while. The air and water were both loud. The waves crashed with the wind. The tourists were gone, and Becca's mom had dropped us off here.

I asked Becca if she wanted for us to be going out, and she asked me, "What's wrong with this?"

"It's fine," I said. "I was just wondering."

"I don't know. I need to think about it. What would the difference be?"

"If there's no difference, what is there to think about?" I asked.

"I didn't say there was no difference. I just asked what the difference would be."

"Well, I thought you were implying there wouldn't be any."

"If I was implying that, I would have said it."

"All right, it just sounded like that."

I looked away. She wasn't looking at me when we talked. I shouldn't have said anything.

"Sorry," she said.

"Don't worry about it. Sorry I brought it up."

"Okay, let's just forget it."

"Okay."

Around June we started going out, whatever that meant. Right around when school ended. Then there was all of tenth grade, and then there was the beginning of eleventh — the end.

Once I had said "I love you," and she hadn't known what to say. Then she started saying it back. I believed it for the most part. It's easy to believe the things you want to.

6

SATURDAY, THE DAY AFTER THE COUCH, I'm wondering what the hell just happened.

On the one hand, Becca and I shared what could have been our most beautiful, most intimate moment.

On the other hand, I'm not sure, but I think she may have broken up with me.

I don't know whether to ask her or not. I really want to, so I can have some peace of mind. I have enough trouble sleeping as it is.

I decide to call Bill.

It rings a couple times and he picks up. I can almost hear the 7*th* *Heaven* music playing in the background.

"Hey," he says.

I ask him, "Are you guys playing poker tonight?"

"Yeah."

"Oh."

"Yeah."

"Can I?"

"Of course."

"I don't really know why I just called."

"Why did you call?"

"I don't really know. Like I said."

"Is something wrong?"

"Yes."

"Do you want to talk about it?"

"Not really, no."

"Are you sure?"

"Yeah, pretty much."

"Okay."

"All right. Well, 'bye."

"'Bye."

I hang up the phone. I can't bear to tell Bill he was right about Becca — that I need her and that I may have lost her. I call him again.

"Hello?"

"Bill, hey, it's me again."

"Henry?"

"Yeah."

"What's wrong?"

"What? Oh, nothing, nothing, okay, well, kind of, I think Becca broke up with me."

"Shit."

"Yeah, I mean. I don't know."

"What do you mean you *think* she broke up with you?"

"Well, she said it's not going to work. What does that mean?"

"I don't know."

"Well, she said that. She said it's just not working or something."

"So what did you tell her?"

"I don't know. I can't remember. We were like sleeping on her couch, or at least she was, and she was kind of drifting in and out of sleep, and she was smiling and telling me that it just wasn't going to work out. I guess I said that I know she's right or something."

"Jesus, why did you say that?"

"I don't know. Just seemed like the thing to say, I guess."

"Well . . ."

"But she *is* right."

"So did she break up with you or not?"

"I'm really not sure."

"Well, ask her."

"I'm afraid if I ask her, then she *will* break up with me."

"For asking her?"

"No, for kind of like mentioning it or whatever."

"That's stupid. Go ask her."

"I don't know, I think if I bring it up . . ."

"Listen, guys are starting to get here for poker. I'll talk to you about this later. Save this, though. Hang on to it."

"Okay, I'm coming there."

"Okay."

I hang up the phone. I walk over to the kitchen and fumble through the massive pill pantry and open up a bottle. It makes a plastic popping noise. They have those child-safety caps on the top. I empty some pills into my hand and down them, dry.

I don't go to Bill's house. I walk to my room, my footsteps are loud on the cold wood floors of the hall. I walk to my room and lie flat against the carpet and put my hands behind my head. Right now, Becca is somewhere, doing something.

Monday after school, Bill and I go to the gym. Bill had been telling me about how he wants to get some tone or tone up or whatever he says, and wanted to know if I'd come with him. I said yeah, what the hell.

We get into the weight room and there's already a lot of guys in there, all sweating and lifting. Some girls are there, too, on treadmills.

As soon as I walk in, I want to leave. The weights bob up and down, and the room is moving like a factory machine. Everything is in place, breathing and beating like an organ, and I have no idea what I'm doing here. A group of three girls stands by the water fountain, laughing. The laughter is harsh and desperate, louder than it needs to be. I don't want to exist in the same room they do. It's so easy to judge everyone, standing doing nothing. I don't want them to see me. Knowing I shouldn't care at all what they think, I'm trying to decide how much I do. Enough to sustain this mental conflict, I guess.

Next to me, Bill doesn't say a word. To Bill, the world around him is an exciting new place to be every day. It's disgusting to watch. I've never seen eyes sparkle quite the way Bill's do.

On the bench in the middle, a guy our age is lifting a bar with no weights on it. He's going up and down with fluid motion, calm and casual, surrounded by a dozen other guys huffing and straining and putting up all they can. If he doesn't need to prove himself, why is he here?

Bill walks over to do some curls or something, smiling. I see the fountain girls walk up to the guy. I walk toward the center and realize it's Charlie Brickell.

He's just finished his set, so he's hunched over, leaning off the edge of the bench with his legs spread out, his feet facing each other on the floor, his arms resting over his thighs. These girls, in the most expensive workout clothing, with eyes vicious and stupid, are all giggling at him.

He glances over, his eyes buried beneath his brow.

The girls are still laughing and talking at one another.

"Can I help you?" he says, looking up from the ground. He's wearing a button-up black shirt and shorts.

"No, it's just that you must be pretty strong," the talker says. With girls like this, there are always three of them. There's always a fat one, a quiet one, and a talker.

And the talker goes, "You know. With all that weight."

"That's really witty," he says.

And the talker goes, "Don't get all pissy with me. I was just saying that's a lot of weight you're doing. I was *complimenting* you." The other two girls laugh.

"Ah. You've discovered sarcasm. That must be very nice for you."

He leans back on the bench and starts lifting again, but the girls are still talking to him. He does a couple reps as the talker's saying, "All that weight, you must get strains in your back. Really, it's seriously impressive."

Charlie rolls his eyes and drops the bar hard against the pegs on the bench. It falls with a metal clang.

The girls jump a little, but manage to keep up their laughing.

He jumps up off the bench and looks at them, not flinching, and without a waver says, "First of all, this is a chest exercise, so I wouldn't strain my back. Second of all, if I were trying to impress you, I'd pop my collar and wax my eyebrows and buy pre-ripped jeans. I'd wear all name-brand designers. I'd go to football games and slap cheerleaders' asses. I'd go to parties and drink one beer and then tell my friends how drunk I am, and how cool that makes me. But the fucking fact of the matter is, I'm not trying to impress you, and the longer you stand here, the more I want to tell you that nobody is impressed by your stupid blond highlights or your braces-straightened teeth or your clothes or your car or your house. Nobody gives a shit who your father is, and nobody gives a shit what kind of shoes you're wearing. So will you *please* just fuck off. Please."

Beautiful. The most beautiful thing I've ever seen. I'm almost inclined to hate him. Because why can he say that? How can he? Of course, I'm not questioning his right to. Certainly, he has the right. Anybody with a brain has the right to say what he did. But to do it. It seems unfair that he could be able to say what I should have — what should have been mine and should have given me pleasure and superiority. But he didn't take it away from me. I wouldn't have done it.

I lie beneath a bench and try not to be noticed.

A couple minutes later, I go to the locker room to take a leak, and I see the talker chick walk out of a stall with Charlie, all over him. His face is expressionless. No. He smiles without his mouth.

I wash my hands.

A couple days go by.

You take five hundred milligrams a day, that's thirty-five hundred milligrams a week. Fifteen thousand milligrams a month. A hundred eighty-two thousand milligrams a year.

Give or take.

I get home again, and it's Thursday. Becca's been out of

town all week. Of course. She's visiting her family in New York to make my life difficult. I'm doing some project for Spanish class, and it reminds me of the first time I met Bill.

I take out the glue and all the other arts and crafts supplies for the project. What a massive waste of time and paper and energy. If this were teaching me Spanish somehow, maybe I'd care, but even then probably not. But I do it anyway, because that's what you do.

The next day, school is excruciating.

The way they do our classes is this thing called "block scheduling," where you're in three two-hour classes a day.

This is to get you ready for college.

Everything for school is to get you ready for something, apparently. In elementary school, they told us they were getting us ready for middle school. In middle school, they told us they were getting us ready for high school. In high school, they tell us they're getting us ready for college.

Biology, they're preparing you for chemistry next year. Chemistry, they're preparing you for physics.

Pre-algebra prepares you for algebra prepares you for geometry.

Geometry prepares you for algebra II prepares you for calculus.

Every year they make up new excuses for why you need to learn what you're learning. Eventually, it all leads up to preparing you for college. And then what? I don't even know why I want to go to college. I guess to justify these last twelve years of school. Everything leads up to this huge, ridiculous thing called *college*, and if you don't go, then why the hell did you waste your entire childhood busting your ass in this place?

Teachers, they're always finding new systems to shut you up and make you do your work. They don't know why you have to do it. They just work here. They didn't invent the education system.

But come to think of it, a card-counting class would have been nice; that's got to be some math skill. Because it's Friday and I'm almost broke.

I get to Bill's house and it's packed. I've never seen so many guys there. Four or five tables of people are playing; others are sitting around on couches bullshitting or watching the Marlins game on TV.

Eventually, I get to a table with Keith, my neighbor Phil, and two other guys who I've never seen before. We play a couple hands, and I do okay. Phil and Keith are both down, and these two other guys — one's a tall, skinny guy and the other's kind of puny looking, with red hair — they're both up a couple bucks. Nobody's getting hot.

By the end of the night, most people have slowly cleared out. I'm at the table, playing with Phil and the tall, skinny kid. The skinny kid, Adam or Aaron or something, says that he's leaving, so it's just Phil and me.

I look over at Phil, and we both look over at the other table. Over there is Bill, this guy Evan, some guy I don't recognize, and Charlie. I must have missed him coming in.

There's something odd about the way he looks. His jaw is defined without being substantial. He has a thick brow, and his eyes are sleepy and sunken in. His sideburns are thick down his jaw and shaggy.

I ask Phil if he wants to go over there and play with those guys.

He says sure, so we walk over and sit down in the two empty seats.

"Hey," Bill says. "Didn't see you come in."

I say, "Yeah."

Charlie smiles a little at me. It's not exactly sarcastic, just vaguely insincere. I wonder if he recognizes me from the side of the road.

Bill deals Phil and me in.

While Bill's throwing around cards, I scan the table. Charlie seems to have some ridiculous lead. No surprise.

We all ante up a dollar.

In the first deal, I have an eight of hearts, a nine of spades, a ten of hearts, a jack of clubs, and a four of diamonds. This could be a straight, no problem. Queen of hearts, clubs, spades, or diamonds. Seven of hearts, club, spades, or diamonds.

Any one of eight cards and I'm gold.

Fifty-two cards in a deck, so this gives me about a one in six-and-a-half chance of a straight. Real-life applications for mathematical principles. Fractions.

I throw in a dollar. Everyone else throws in a dollar.

Bill throws in a dollar. Everyone else throws in a dollar.

Charlie throws in two dollars. Everyone else does.

Bill goes back around. He takes three cards for himself.

Phil takes two.

Evan and the other kid take three.

I pick one up.

Charlie stays.

I look around the table and Charlie is just the epitome of nonchalance.

Bill asks, "Does anyone want to bet?"

And Charlie says — just Joe Fucking Cool here — he's saying, "Sure."

And he throws in five chips. Five dollars.

Phil hesitates and throws in five.

"I'm out," Bill says.

The other kid throws in five chips, and so does Evan.

I have the straight with the seven of hearts.

Eight, nine, ten, jack. This is so good it's stupid. So I throw in the five. This leaves me with ten dollars to my name. Any more bets and I'm out. This is one of those self-promise things, and I've come up broke one too many times from not knowing when to quit.

Phil says he has to go home. The kid, I think his name's Steven, he's in. Evan hesitates and he's in. And Charlie is in.

Bill's asking, "Raise?"

And I'm thinking please no please no please no please no.

Charlie says, "Sure. I'll raise ten."

And the Steven kid, he's out, along with Evan.

Seven, eight, nine, ten, jack.

On the table, there's got to be at least sixty bucks or so. Risk my last ten dollars to make sixty? That's logical. Perfectly.

But I can't do it.

So I'm out.

Charlie pulls the chips from the center to his side of the table. Bill walks into his kitchen to get the safe out, to cash them in.

And Charlie, the bastard, he's showing a three, four, nine, seven, and a king. Hearts, clubs, hearts, spades, diamonds.

He smiles and shrugs at me. "Shit," I say.

He walks into the kitchen with Bill. I walk in a couple

seconds later and Keith's sitting on the kitchen counter. "Sucks, dude," he says.

"Yeah," I say.

"At least it's not Becca's birthday."

"Yeah, Keith, good point."

He laughs. "I'm just kidding."

"What happened?" Charlie asks.

"Nothing," I say.

"Last time he blew all his money here, so he made us all promise not to let him do it again. It was his girlfriend's birthday and he hadn't picked up a present for her yet."

"Thank you, Keith," I say.

"Well," Charlie says, "now you see the trouble with absolutes."

"Yeah, maybe," I say.

Bill looks at Keith. "What are you talking about?" Keith asks.

Charlie looks at Keith but talks to me. "When you make an absolute statement, you assume a sense of personal integrity based on a pretense of moral objectivity, which exists only as a faulty heuristic to arrive at an easy conclusion, and deny yourself the responsibility of choice — it's more convenient not to acknowledge your freedom and settle for a less desirable outcome on the grounds that you had no choice, rather than risk acquiring the less desirable outcome by your own will, regardless of the possibility for a better one."

I try to process. Word for word, I'm not sure. I begin to piece it together in all its eloquence and pretentiousness, and it's annoyingly coherent, obnoxiously accurate. He's saying I'd rather lose by forces I believe to be out of my control. *Is* it accurate? Bill looks skeptical. Not of the statement, but just that it's being made.

"Dude, you're fucking high," Keith says, and starts laughing.

Charlie looks at me, and then turns to Bill to get the money. Keith laughs and asks me what's up, man. I don't know.

I realize Phil was supposed to be my ride home. I guess I curse or something, because Bill asks me what's the matter. I tell him, and Charlie pipes in, smiling like a bastard, saying, "I could take you home."

I say, "It's no big deal."

"Nah, come on," he says. "I figure I owe you."

"Funny."

"Don't worry, you're on the way."

I protest a little, but for some reason I want to go with him. So I say, "Sure."

He grabs his leather jacket off the coatrack and shuts the door behind us before I can say 'bye to Bill.

It's pitch-black and Charlie takes off his sunglasses.

We're in the car, and I'm wondering what he meant when he said that he owes me. Does that mean he owes me from the poker game, or from the time I saw him that night in the street?

He's asking me, "Don't you hate it when you're with some kid for a long time and you just don't know his name? So you wait around, trying to remember it, but then you realize, shit, you probably never knew it in the first place. So you try to figure it out, waiting for other people to say the name, or putting the guy in situations to use his name, but it never fucking works. So eventually, you just decide *the hell with it* and wait to ask someone else. But then there's always the chance that the other person you ask is going to tell the first guy, which would make your situation even more awkward, and you just keep figuring you'll wait longer and longer —"

And I tell him, very nonchalant, "Henry Fuller."

And he says, "I know. I was being hypothetical."

And I go, "Oh."

He pauses and laughs.

Then he asks me, "Do you like music?"

"Sure."

"Awesome. Me, too."

So I start laughing, sort of, and he's asking me, "What's so funny?"

"Nothing. I guess I just thought you were going to turn on the radio when you said that."

"You want me to turn on the radio?"

"No, it's just —"

"Listen," he says. "If you want me to turn on the radio, you just have to ask."

"No, it's not that. I mean it's not that I —"

"Jesus, do you want the radio on or not?"

I sigh a little and say, "Sure."

And he says, "No — what the fuck would you want to listen to the radio for? Doesn't the music piss you off? That is, if the watered-down, instrumentless, computerized bullshit that a corporation in Texas distributes to sell ads even *constitutes* music. Every fucking station, it's the same crap but with a different ethnicity — white, black, hispanic — click your thumb and index finger a couple degrees." He flips the radio on and spins the station dial as he talks. "And up next on ninety-four-nine: more repetitive, mind-numbing *shit* set to faster or slower tempos. And if you dig *this* — check out every *other* channel, 'cause it's all exactly the same! And stay tuned, for the *hilarious* DJ stylings of forty-year-olds who think prank phone calls are still awesome!" He turns it off abruptly. "Jesus Christ, you want to listen to the fucking *radio*? Get the fuck out of my car, dude."

The car stops short. "Get out." He looks at me. I start to talk a few times, open, close.

"I mean . . . I was just . . ."

He smiles with all his teeth and then laughs, starting the car back up and chugging forward. I smile at him for being insane. He scratches his neck and looks over to get a good look at me.

So I start trying to make regular conversation and ask him if he has a girlfriend or a band or anything, just to get off the subject of me looking like a moron.

"Not really," he says. And then he smiles again. The way this Charlie guy is, it seems like there's a huge camera crew in his backseat recording everything I say. I'm just waiting for him to start cracking up and tell me I'm on *Candid Camera*. I'm just waiting for the explosion of laughter. Ha-ha-ha.

"How about you?"

"I'm with a girl," I tell him. He gets a kick out of this.

"Right, the birthday one. What's her name?"

"Becca. She, um, we haven't been the best lately." As soon as I say it, I wonder why I did. But it's too late, I can't stop myself. "I mean most of the time I'm unhappy and I think she's worse. It just sucks. A lot. You know."

Finally, I stop myself. Why don't I just give him my social security number while I'm at it?

He yawns. "That's a tragic fucking story."

I'm annoyed to be playing so well into his hand. "I guess so," I say.

"Well, why don't you just break up with her? If shit's so bad and everyone's so unhappy?"

Well, I may have given him a lot, but I'm not going to give him an excuse to lose all respect for me. So I'm not going to say, *Because I thought my relationship with Becca would last forever.*

"I know if I broke up with her, I'd regret it," I say.

"Probably so," he says. "Probably so."

"What the hell's that supposed to mean?" I ask him. All indignant and whatever.

He smiles close-lipped at my little outburst and says, "Nothing."

We ride a few minutes in silence. I try to sit casually. Charlie flips on the radio and puts it on quiet. Finally, he says, "Is this your turn?" and I tell him it is.

He turns the car at the intersection, and we start heading toward my house.

I ask him how he knows those guys, Bill and all. But we're already at the house. So he tells me, "I guess we'll save this story for another time."

I tell him that's all right. I get out, and his car speeds off like he's chasing the sky.

I check my pockets and I can't find my keys.

I walk up to the door and it's locked. I jangle the doorknob for a while, until finally I give up and collapse on my front steps.

I wonder what time it is.

Suddenly, just as fast as it left, Charlie's car flies backward to the front of my house and screeches to a halt.

He lowers the window and calls out to me, "Let me ask you something. Are you a McDonald's guy or a Wendy's guy?"

I look up at him. "What?"

He's getting impatient. "Do you prefer McDonald's or Wendy's?"

"McDonald's."

"What are you doing sitting out in front of your house?"

"I lost my keys. Are they in there?"

"No."

"Oh."

"Want to go hang out somewhere?"

I look around. I shrug and figure, what the hell.

Ten minutes later, we're sitting in the park. I tell Charlie that I've been thinking a lot about what to do, that I know I'm young and that I don't want to miss out on opportunities, but that I really, really *like* Becca — I don't say love to him — and that I think it would be stupid to throw it all away.

"I'm upset about it," I say, "but I guess in the way you're upset when you lose count of something you've been keeping track of for a long time."

I say something about how it's nice to have someone to fall back on when you want to get some action — so, y'know, I'm just one of the guys, not some hypersensitive Romeo loser.

The whole time, Charlie sits there smiling like I'm a movie he's seen a hundred times.

I move my hands when I talk and I say, "It's not like we're in some huge terrible fight or anything, but nothing's ever really great or just perfect. The way it used to be, I mean."

"Why don't you just dump her?"

"Well, I mean, she hasn't dumped me, so I have to assume that she thinks there's still something salvageable in the relationship, you know."

He breathes in, smiling, and I can see his teeth.

"What?" I say.

"Oh, come on. That's got to be the most pathetic thing I've ever heard. You're in your fucking biological prime. So you sit around waiting for something to happen to you? Waiting for your girlfriend to break up with you? To avoid that kind of confrontation. That's fucking ridiculous, come on."

"It's not that simple. I mean I see her all the time, in school and everything —"

"It's exactly that simple. Simpler, maybe. I mean, it's pretty much a 'This isn't working out,' more or less. You don't even have to do it in person if you don't want to. How difficult is that really? And shit, from the way you describe it, she'd probably thank you anyway. But hell, I don't know you guys. I'm not that familiar with the situation. I could be totally wrong."

The way Charlie says he could be wrong is the way a calculator tells you it's not positive about two times two.

And I say, "No, I don't know. It's not that you're wrong, it's just that there's so much else that you're not factoring in. I know I'd regret it."

He nods and looks around the park, the empty swing set across from us, and says, "Yeah, probably would. And you know why?"

And I ask him why, sort of rolling my eyes and whatever.

And he says, "Because you're a McDonald's guy."

So we're back on that again. And I say, "What the hell does that mean?"

"McDonald's guy. Classic case. You're afraid of change."

"I see. And I suppose if I were a Wendy's guy I would *not* be afraid of change."

"That's right."

"That's stupid. It's just because you like Wendy's more."

As if he didn't already have an answer prepared.

A. I can ask anybody about the Wendy's vs. McDonald's conflict and hear the same thing. Studies have been conducted.

B. Wendy's is high-quality fast food, as opposed to the well-publicized detriments in McDonald's hamburgers and other products.

C. McDonald's is a major corporation that has been putting family-owned companies out of business for years and is bad for the environment.

"McDonald's is bad for the environment?" I say.

"It's true."

"Blah blah blah."

He laughs. "What?"

"God, I don't know. Everyone is so concerned with the environment. Look around. All those environmental campaigns. We're giving a heart transplant to a corpse. As if biodegradable burger containers are going to make up for the massive hole over Australia. Like using animal-friendly hair products is going to bring back the dodo bird."

I say all this, but what I'm really thinking is how none of this shit concerns me. Is Becca going out with me or not? I'm sitting here in some stupid park talking to a total stranger about the way fast-food conglomerates adversely affect society, and the real question is just: How much longer until I know what Becca thinks? Ronald McDonald and dairy farms and the oppressive system and the man? I don't care about it. It is a matter of profound indifference. Any emotional reaction has been imposed, and I understand it's wrong and, if it were up to me, I say free the livestock and give them weapons and blow up all the McDonald's you want. It's fine by me. Just leave me alone.

"Fine," Charlie says. "Fuck the environment. Fuck all the cultural implications. With reference to food alone, McDonald's still pales in comparison."

I say, "Well sure, Wendy's looks great from the advertisements. Burgers in these perfectly carved rectangular prisms. If you actually *go* to Wendy's, you'll see. They just slab a mound of ground beef and cereal onto your crusty seedless bun and tell you 'we don't cut corners.'"

Why am I still having this conversation?

Charlie says, "It's a good marketing campaign."

And I tell him I'm not criticizing the marketing campaign. I'm just saying if they advertise a square burger, then I want a goddamn square burger. Is that too much to ask? In these crazy mixed-up times is it too much to demand the simple pleasure of a square hamburger?

"Square burger or not, Wendy's is the newer of the two, and as such, managed to pull itself up from the trenches of small marketing in order to compete with the regressive, conservative industries, as a result of its radical geometric policies in regard to the shape of its goods. As this implies, and as is the point, a McDonald's guy is afraid of change."

God, this guy can really talk. It's a fucking sandwich. "Fine, whatever. I like Wendy's better."

"Aha! A McDonald's man who can't even stick to his convictions," Charlie says. "The worst kind. And now, the real question is aroused. Do you truly prefer Wendy's and were covering for it because you assume most people prefer McDonald's and you wanted to be accepted, or do you really like McDonald's more, but you're too scared of conflict to take a stand?"

"It's a lose-lose situation."

"It's a lose-lose situation," he agrees. "But isn't that life, really?"

I nod. "I guess so."

"And don't you forget it."

And I ask him, "Who are you?"

And he gets up, tips his hat, and says, "Charlie Brickell."

We're leaving the park, and I turn to Charlie Brickell and ask him, "Did you really just drive back to my house to ask me if I was a McDonald's guy or a Wendy's guy?"

And he says no, he drove back to give me my house key. He tosses it up in the air behind him, and I stumble a little to catch it.

Charlie Brickell.

We get in the car. "You got to be home any particular time?" he asks, putting the key in the ignition.

"No."

"Good," he says, shifting to drive and taking off. "Where to?"

"Wherever." I yawn. I'm exhausted. The clock on the dashboard says it's two forty-five.

He says, "Fuck."

"What?"

"Fucking tank's empty."

"Can you make it to the station?"

He shrugs, looking at the road. "Yeah."

We get to the station and he jumps out of the car, his boots hitting the pavement. I open the door and get out. He meanders over and grabs the nozzle for regular. He hits a few buttons on the machine, takes the nozzle out, and opens the tank of his car.

He gets close to me and says, "You know all three of these are the exact same fucking thing."

"Really?" This sounds like bullshit.

"It's true," he says. "Premium, ultra-premium, the ones that give your car a hard-on or whatever. It's all the same. I worked at a car dealership for a couple months, they tell you all this inside shit."

I nod. "Huh."

"Oh, yeah," he says, and flips on his sunglasses. The lights shine bright white from the overhang, and it's pitch-black on the street across the way and in the trees on the other side of the station. I squint up at the light. Right hand on the nozzle, he puts his left hand in his pocket and rummages until he finds what he wants. He throws a wallet at me. I catch it with both hands.

"Go inside and pay while I'm filling up, eh, Chief?"

"Sure," I say. I walk in to pay. There's an old woman behind the counter, and I walk up and open Charlie's wallet. It's all hundreds. About twenty maybe. I look up nervously and say, "Shit."

She looks at me. I hand her a hundred. "I'm, um, paying for the —"

I give her the bill and she looks at it. "I'm sorry," she says, "we don't take hundreds." She points at a sign.

I look out through the window, and Charlie has one hand on the car and the other on the nozzle.

"It's all I have," I say.

She bites her lip. I wonder how long she has been working here. "I mean, I can see if I have change in my purse," she says, and we both know she doesn't. She looks in her purse. In gas stations at night, or 7-Elevens or drugstores, I always imagine someone coming in and killing me. I wonder if this old woman is scared of it. She looks like she's scared of something.

Charlie finishes outside, replaces the nozzle, and looks in through the glass. He flips his sunglasses into his collar. He quickly and casually walks in through the door. The old woman looks up, startled. I guess this is why most places have a pay-first policy.

"What's the problem?" he says.

"They don't take hundreds."

He clicks his tongue. "Fuck. All right." He looks off and runs his fingers through his hair. He looks up and asks me, "You want anything?"

"Um."

"Whatever, gum, anything."

"Uh, sure." I pick up a pack of Extra.

"All right, good." He looks at the clerk. She's frightened. He grabs the wallet from me and the gum. He puts the gum and a hundred-dollar bill on the counter and says, "Um, the tank of gas and this gum. Is it okay if you keep the hundred and pay back the difference into the machine?"

Her mouth is open. She says, "Um."

"I know, I know," he says. "Gas prices these days, it may not even be in your best interest." He laughs. "No, but really, we got to get out of here, is that good?"

She doesn't say anything. She doesn't know what to say. "It's for you," he says. He gets close and looks at her name tag. "Come on, cheer up, Annie. It's a beautiful day."

He smiles and she smiles. "All right," he says. "Great."

7

IT'S SATURDAY. BECCA JUST GOT BACK from New York this afternoon, and I'm at the phone waiting to decide whether I should call to ask her.

I decide to call her. The worst-case scenario is she breaks up with me. Like it would make a huge difference in our relationship. Yeah, the couch was nice, but there are probably a bunch of girls I could be with right now if I weren't with Becca, and to be honest, the prospect doesn't sound all too terrible. I'm a good, decent guy. Probably tons of girls.

Rachel Flagler for instance.

So I pick up the phone and dial. This is going to be easy. If she wants to be with me, fantastic. If not, that's swell, too.

The phone rings.

"Hello." The *hello* has this throaty whisper to it. I breathe in; I want her again.

"Hi, Becca?"

"Yeah, what?"

"Um, you remember on the couch the other day?"

She's going to say no.

"No."

"When I came over." What was it, like four days ago?

"Oh, right." She's just trying to get me mad that she doesn't care. "What about it?"

"Um, remember how you said something, how things aren't going to work out?"

I hear her sit up on her comforter. The crunching noise of the cotton. It sounds like the kind of material that's cold when it's hot in your room, and hot when it's cold in your room. I really want one of those.

And she says, "Yeah, I remember."

I'm thinking, *Say it.*

No.

Say it.

No.

Stop being a jackass, just fucking say it.

"Did you want to, um . . . well, were we, did we break up just then?"

"I don't know, Henry."

She doesn't know. Good. That means she still wants me. If she didn't want me, we'd be broken up right now. I have control of the ball.

"What do you mean, you don't *know?*" I say.

"I don't remember."

"Did you want to break up?"

"I don't know."

"What do you mean, *you don't know?*" I ask her again.

"I just *don't know,*" she says.

"Well, how can you *not know*?" We're both getting pretty snotty by this point.

"It's hard to tell sometimes, Henry."

"Well, do you love me?"

"I don't know," she says. "Sometimes."

"Do you feel the same way about me that you used to?"

"No."

No.

No no no no no no no no.

What does she mean, no?

"What do you mean, no?"

"No, I don't feel the same way about you as I used to."

"Well, if you don't feel the same way, why don't you just break up with me?"

Yeah. How about them apples? Punk.

"I don't know. I still feel . . . emotionally attached to you, I guess."

"Emotionally attached? Like a person you're in love with or like an old blanket?"

"Old blanket, I guess."

Why am I so stupid? I'm arming my firing squad. I'm painting a target on my body. I'm begging her to break up with me. I'm down on my hands and knees, shouting, *please*, just a quick one right to the brain.

Fuck.

And she tells me, "Good metaphor, though."

"Thanks. But anyway, if you feel nothing more for me than you would for an old blanket, then I guess you should break up with me."

"Should I?"

"Yes." She should. I don't need to be someone's old blanket.

"Fine."

"Fine what?" Uh-oh.

"Fine, then I think we should break up."

"You *think* we should?" Wait, wait, wait. What the hell's going on here?

"Yeah."

"So . . . ?"

"I think we should break up."

"What?"

"I think we should break up."

"So, what then?"

"I want to break up with you."

The barrel is lodged up against my chin. The rain is pouring. The wind is racing. The world is in fast motion. Three-hundred-sixty frames per second. I have to think fast.

"So, what, do I have to say 'okay' or something?" I ask.

"No, I guess we're just broken up."

The dead air on the phone hangs and I see it all rushing away, the moments that a few words could have fixed, all the stupid shit I did. I see Becca's first impressions of me. The realization when I knew I had her. Fluttering around in my brain and my stomach and my chest, there's my attraction to her — physical, psychological. My conquest and my success. Failed.

"Um, do you think maybe we could give it another chance?"

I know I know I know I know I know.

I am the most pathetic human being alive.

"Not really."

Not really? I can just imagine her eyes rolling around in her head. No. It's over. Blah blah blah. I mean, it didn't *matter* to you, did it Henry? Our relationship wasn't *important* to you, right? Right, Henry?

Right?

I'm reaching. I say, "But. I mean. We've gotten into fights before."

"I know. That's kind of the reason I think it should end."

"Yeah, but they all resolved well."

"Well, not really, if you consider that it ended with this."

Ha-ha-ha.

I am so sick and tired of clever people.

"But, Becca. I mean —"

"Henry, what do you honestly believe will change?"

"What?"

"If I 'give it another chance.' What do you think will actually change in our relationship?"

"I'll be more aware of the stupid things I do. The way I act."

"Henry, it shouldn't have to be like that."

"It won't. Becca, come on. Think of everything great that's happened between us."

"You're not going to guilt me into going back out with you."

Why am I doing this?

Why? Why? Why?

Every word I utter is making her like me less.

"At least . . . at least wait until I can see you again."

"Wait for what?"

"To break up with me."

"We're already broken up."

"Well . . . can't we unbreak up until I can actually see you and talk to you about this in person."

"Why?"

"Just, come on. For me. For old times' sake."

"No. I don't think so."

In medieval times, wooden wedges were forced underneath the thumbnails to get a confession out of a criminal.

"But . . . but I really think things could be better."

I notice that I'm actually crying. Crying. This is so stupid. Who cries? I didn't even know I was capable of this.

"Henry, don't you think things would have worked out by now if they were going to?"

They had this thing called the copper boot. It was a boot filled to the brim with molten lead that caused first-degree burns when you put your foot in it.

"No. Maybe not. Maybe I was too stupid."

Oh no, would you *listen* to me? *Oh, Becca, I'm so stupid, I'm such an idiot, I'm such a blubbering, crying moron.*

Yeah. This is really what women want, Henry. I feel like Bill.

During water torture, the victim's nostrils were pinched shut and fluid was poured down his throat. Sometimes this was water. Other times this was vinegar, urine, or diarrhea.

What I feel for medieval heretics is empathy.

"Good-bye, Henry."

If the sun burned out right this second, it would take the earth eight and a half minutes to feel this. This has to do with the speed of light and the distance of the earth from the sun. Earth-space science. C-minus.

Eight and a half minutes would be way too long.

If the sun exploded this instant, it would consume all the inner planets, and then shrink into a white dwarf.

Then it would die, like everything you will ever love.

Thank you, Mr. Black.

Thank you, Becca.

Thank you, world.

"Please don't get all melodramatic about this," she says.

PART TWO

LOSERS, ASSHOLES, AND COOL PEOPLE

8

BECCA BREAKS UP WITH ME and I go to sleep. I can't do anything else. I sit up in bed, crying stupidly — there aren't really other ways — and decide I won't sleep. Something noble in that, I figure. So I sit there thinking about how I'll stay awake. The next day, I wake up and listen to some sad music to make me feel worse. I try to muster up memories of every good moment Becca and I ever had. I picture every scene. It seems that crying is good. Not as a way to vent, necessarily, but just as a way to justify everything. If what we had is good enough to make me cry, my life must be at least marginally worthwhile.

I get tissues from the bathroom and look at my face in the mirror. I look stupid. I stretch myself out across my bed. I think about Becca — one night when she'd laid in this bed next to me. The ceiling fan spun and she looked through the plaster. Her eyes were glassy and wet. We talked for a long time that night, some hot fleeting twilight between spring and summer. We talked about the future. And I thought things like, *I am a sophisticated human being and I know that Becca and I will not end up together, but these are just words, and I really think we will, despite any rationality, despite any logic, despite everything, and it feels good to think that, so why can't I?*

"What about a poet," I said. "You could do that."

"Too depressing. No one really gets to be a poet, anyway." Her head on my chest, I inhaled her completely, a smell of lemons, strong coffee, and ice water. She yawned into me and put her arm across my stomach. She was my blanket; I was so warm.

"If you love it, just do it — that's the most important thing."

Her fingers slid slowly onto my back, beneath my shirt, cool and calming. "I may love financial security, and I don't know if poetry will cater to that."

"I think you're good enough."

She laughed. "How can you say that? You've never even read anything I've written."

"Well, you won't let me."

"I know."

"Can I?"

"No."

"Why?"

"Because it's all shit."

"Fine," I said. She kissed me on the face and put her head next to mine. The blinds were drawn and pieces of light laid scattered on the carpet. Soft outside noises, owls, stray cats.

"What are you thinking about?" I said.

"Nothing."

"You always say nothing."

"I know."

I leaned over with my head resting on my hand. "Well, why won't you tell me?"

"I think there's only one thing in the whole world that really makes me sad."

"What?"

"I can't tell you now. I don't want to think about it too much. It will just make you feel horrible if you understand it."

"Well, now I have to know. With all that buildup."

"Not now, Henry."

"But you'll tell me one day?"

"Yes, I'll tell you one day." Everything was flowing out of my reach until I just gave up trying to grab at the loose ends.

Months passed, and now it's all over. Eventually I can't cry anymore, so I just put myself in black-hole mode. Oh, you know. Life is futile. Throw on some shitty clothes, don't eat. And what does Becca matter? Even if it lasted, we were both just going to end up dead anyway. I make myself lots of coffee so I can sit around drinking it, brooding. It feels secretly cool — to be beyond emotion. I feel like sitting around in cafés with a leather jacket, smoking cigarettes.

A day after the breakup. I'm in my room with the lights off. The phone rings. Probably Bill, I think. I pick it up, preparing a wretched, guttural hello.

"hello," I say.

"Yo, motherfucker. It's Charlie."

"Charlie? How'd you get my —"

"What are you doing right now?"

I look down at my coffee mug and across the room at the TV.

"Nothing."

"Good. I need you to do me a favor."

"What?"

"Come downtown."

I sneer to myself. I will not be seen in public. "For what?"

"I thought you said you weren't doing anything."

"Well, I mean, it's such a far —"

"Look, I know: I don't really know you, you don't really know me. If you're busy, hey, don't even think twice about it."

"It's not that, it's just —"

"Hey, listen, forget I even called. You're probably pretty wrapped in some good sitcom, or maybe you're tying things up with your girlfriend. Take it easy, though. Maybe I'll see you at Bill's —"

"Wait, wait, wait."

"What? You want to come?"

"I guess. It's just —"

"Good. Meet me at the Starbucks on Miami Avenue and Second Street. Hurry, though, or it'll be too late."

So I drive downtown. I get in the car and wonder why I'm going. If it's to distract myself from Becca, or to become friends with Charlie, or out of sheer boredom, I don't know. Eventually, I lose myself in the rhythm of stop signs, traffic lights, lane changes. I get there, have some hassle parallel parking, and start walking to Second. Distantly, I see a mob parading in the street, loudly, with a lot of signs, posters, banners. Some TV people are around with cameras and microphones.

I walk quickly to the Starbucks across the street and find Charlie sitting at a café table. There's a popcorn bag open on the table, and he's drinking coffee and smiling.

"What the hell's going on?" I say and sit down next to him.

"Protesters."

"I see that, what are they protesting?"

He gestures at their signs.

NO MORE IMMORALITY!

"They're protesting immorality?"

"Evidently," Charlie says, and stuffs his face with some popcorn. "Hey, there's a funny one."

DON'T SHOVE YOUR SEXUALITY DOWN OUR THROATS!

Some of these psychomoms are being interviewed by some stock standard microphone man. They're all screaming. Charlie takes a sip of coffee.

KEEP SIN OUT OF TAXPAYERS' SCHOOLS!

"So what is this, some school hired a gay teacher?"

"Yeah, City of Miami Middle School — but the outrageousness doesn't end there," Charlie says. "Popcorn?"

"No thanks."

"This *craaazy* lesbian has the unmitigated temerity to teach their elementary school children about this thing called evolution by natural selection."

"Jesus, they protest this shit in Miami?"

"We *are* a red state, don't forget."

"So we are."

I strain to hear.

Charlie says, "C'mon," and we cross the street. We blend in among the noise and the bodies. Charlie finishes his popcorn and drops the bag on the ground.

Some fat woman with a sign that says KEEP OUR CHILDREN OUT OF IT is saying, "This woman is a menace! Since the beginning of the *school* year, it was obvious! Not everyone caught on at first, but I knew. It was perfectly obvious to *me!*"

"Obvious that Ms. Reynolds was a lesbian?" this reporter says to the camera.

"No! She — she just admitted *that*, openly! *That* was already a *fact*, sir. What I knew was that she was trying to convert our kids to her ways! Kids are so impressionable! But then when I found out what she was *teaching* them! It went too far!"

"Goddamn it," I say to Charlie. "It's Sunday. Shouldn't these people be in church?"

"God would understand."

The reporter is saying, "And you, ma'am?"

"I think it's okay if they want to teach evolution, but the fact of the matter is, it's just a *theory*. If they don't teach it alongside with Biblical creation — well, that's a biased system of education. There's no equality there."

"*I'm* not sending my son back here until *she is gone!*" someone else says.

Charlie pushes his way to the anchorman and grabs the microphone from some woman. "Hi there, I'm Charlie Brickell." He puts an arm over the shoulders of two hostile women. The reporter tries to assert himself.

"Hey, hey, don't worry — I'm with you here. I'm a young man, so I have to put up with more of this super-liberal hogwash than you can even imagine. I mean, the fact that this *woman* can just teach evolution while completely *dismissing* the idea of creationism is absolutely absurd! Where is a good, solid education where just one side of the picture is presented? The kids have to be able to make the decision for themselves!"

"Exactly," one woman says, and Charlie aims the microphone at her and winks at me, so over-the-top, so insane. She says, "That's just the sort of thing I was talking about."

The reporter looks slightly relieved. The protesters are still shouting around the school.

"But that's not all —" Charlie says, "take the school clinics for instance. They're basing their treatment of these little children on some crazy, radical drugs. Tylenol, Advil! All this chemical rubbish!"

The women nod slowly, looking at one another.

"Everyone *knows* that their headaches are just the result of demons flying around in their brains for being sinful! And everyone knows the only way to let demons out: boring holes in their skulls. Just little holes, but the demons have to come out somehow."

I can't stop laughing. The women are onto him, backing away, angry, offended.

"And of course, there's this nonsense about the world being round! I mean, how do we really *know*?" Charlie's looking around now, talking to the camera and to the women. "I'm not saying don't teach that the world is round, but we have to at least present the full picture and give the Flat World Theory an equal shot. I mean, did these teachers *take* the satellite pictures? Anyone can make those things up on Photoshop in a half hour."

"All right, we get it," the reporter says, hands on his hips.

"Hang on, hang on! I didn't get to these insane elementary school math teachers! They present two and two is four, two and two is four, driving this crazy number propaganda into these kids' heads. Maybe two and two is five. What *is* a two, anyway? Just some abstraction made up by those crazy, sexually confused Greeks thousands of years ago!"

The reporter grabs at the microphone, but Charlie holds fast and says, "See — evolution, math, it's all interrelated in a left-wing conspiracy to get kids to use *logic*. Once they start in with that, it's all over! Then they'll realize there's not a fucking thing *wrong* with accepting people's differences, and then where will we be? Back in the Stone Age with the sodomizing Greeks!" Charlie throws the mic in the air, and the reporter stumbles to catch it.

"Save our children!" he yells as we walk away. "Get this menace out of there!"

I laugh and can't believe it. The protesters regain their composure, and the screaming and parading starts again.

He says, "See, that was better than *Boy Meets World* marathons."

"I don't know, it was just getting to Corey and Topanga's wedding."

"Let's get something to eat," he says, "I'm fucking starving." And we walk down the block to get some food.

9

THERE'S THIS RESTAURANT on Ocean Drive called Ender's. It's a real scream. The kind of place they give you really small portions of food for like eighty dollars a meal, no free refills on your drinks, all that.

Charlie works there, if you can call it work. Wearing a tuxedo, he goes up to the maître d' and says that he's with a party inside. Then he just goes to the bathroom and stays there for a couple hours with a cloth napkin over his arm. He steals all the soap and paper towels from any kind of general access and dries all these rich hands all night.

"These places don't actually *have* bathroom attendants," he tells me. "But it wouldn't be a big surprise to anyone if they did."

Charlie tells me the first important thing to know about being a bathroom attendant, fake or real, is that everyone wishes you weren't there. This is because, as a patron:

1. Drying your own hands is easy.
2. You feel social pressures to leave a tip.

3. It's a sort of uncomfortable thing, to have someone drying your hands for you.

"I mean, no one wants an ass-wiping attendant," Charlie says. "There are just certain things you'd rather do yourself, no matter how rich you are."

I ask him how he makes any money doing this if no one wants him there. He says that it's all a matter of bullshit and capitalistic exchange. If you feed these rich guys the crap they want to hear, they provide monetary compensation.

"And always put a few twenties in your basket first," he says. "Makes them think it's the going rate."

Monday after school Charlie asks me if I want to join him. I shut off the TV.

On the wall of the handicapped bathroom stall, there's a little cord you can pull during an emergency. I guess if you fall and you're handicapped they come in and save you. I'm in here because Charlie's outside bullshitting with someone, listening to a story about the American dream. Then comes the next customer, from the stall next to mine.

"Evening, sir."

"Hi."

A click of metal and then faucet water. I peek through the crack of the door.

"So how about this real estate explosion?" Charlie says, standing straight against the wall.

"It's something else, boy. It is *something else*."

"I know that a lot of these economists, they talk a lot about bubbles and depressions. I don't know much about it, I obviously don't have much investment ability, but it seems like real estate — it's always going up, y'know?"

"Exactly! They try to scare you, but as long as you hold on to your investments, real estate is the one thing that is always, always going up. God, I remember when I first bought property here on the beach. Not even *on* the beach, just in this area. I was a kid — thirty, thirty-five."

"I hope to do the same someday."

"Sure. And let me tell you — it was no easy fight. When I was, well, about your age I guess — what are you, seventeen, eighteen?"

"Yes, sir," Charlie says, handing him a paper towel. "Please allow me." He dries off the man's wet hands.

"God, when I was your age, I was working every single day — after school, when I went to school. Every day I would come into work fifteen minutes early and I'd *work*. Let me tell you, I would *work*. None of these long lunches, this talking on the cell phone business. And they *knew* I was going someplace. *I* knew I was and I let them know. But I was respectful and courteous. And most important: I got the job done."

"Not many people share that work ethic today."

"I know it. I know it because I work with these hot-shots — young guys, cruise in with the Mercedes their fathers bought them and think they own the world, think they know more than I know after forty years in the business. It's nice, actually — to see a young man actually *working* for a living."

"Thank you, sir. Hopefully, this job is only temporary. I know people say this a lot, but I mean it: I want to work my way up in this world. I want to make progress."

"That's good. Keep it up." The old man pauses quietly, distracted. "Anyway, I better head back to the family."

"It was nice talking to you, sir."

"You, too," he says and looks into Charlie's tip basket. Then he nods and drops in a twenty.

"Thank you very much, sir."

The way these restaurants are is the way that you can buy a Snickers bar at a 7-Eleven for sixty cents, and just as much chocolate from Godiva for fifteen dollars. It's just stupid to pay that much, unless you want to tell people about it. I'd rather have twenty-five Snickers bars, personally.

"It's not that hard to get them going," Charlie tells me. "Real estate is generally a good springboard." A couple minutes go by and someone else comes in.

These men in business suits have their Jacuzzis and their penthouses and their money. *But you know*, say they, *money doesn't buy you happiness.* Oh, yes, of course. I know that, good sirs. Certainly, though, it cannot hurt. And maybe it even *does* buy happiness. Were I given one billion dollars to spend the rest of my life in pursuit of hedonism and enlightenment, I think that would buy me happiness. If I had enough money to never face a forty-hour workweek or worry about food or necessities, I should be very happy. *Ah!* exclaims the communist, *this, then, is why we should smash the system and provide all with food, shelter, and income! Happiness would be ensured to all!* No, no. That's all wrong. I would still have to work. And if they were paying me some fixed wage, there's no *chance* I'd do anything — there'd be no motivation. *Ah!* exclaims the capitalist, *you understand the joy that comes with hard work and its rewards! Happiness would be ensured to all who worked hard for it!* Good God no. I don't want hard work and rewards. I just want the rewards. It's the same with school. If I could cheat on every test and get straight A's, I'd feel no guilt or shame. What difference does it make how I earn my grades? They're meaningless. They're at best indicators of who is the most effective cog. The truth is, there is no great nobility in wealth *or* poverty. There is no great nobility in anything.

And I wonder: Does Charlie think these things? If the conscious thoughts never cross his mind, he lives his life by them regardless. Maybe there's something more impressive in never having thought them through. In just living this way by sheer necessity — as though it were the only way to live. It's impossible, though. Charlie's like the waiters at the restaurants he works, playing out their parts too perfectly to be real.

And these restaurants, they're all over town. I'm sitting on the stall reading a *Playboy* Charlie had in his car, and listening to him talk. The sound of nostalgia and then a faucet and then thank-yous from everyone. Thank you for listening. Thank you for caring. Thank you for supporting the Charlie Brickell Foundation. The old Republican walks out, back to his life.

"Charlie?" I say.

"What?"

"How much have you made?" Our voices have the echo of a bathroom.

"A hundred fifty-five."

"Shit, that's awesome."

"It's good," he says.

"For two and a half hours of work?"

"These people are pissing me off. Let's go."

I walk out of the stall and yawn. "Where do you want to go?" I ask.

"Wherever."

"What's wrong?"

He gives me a dismissive glance and says, "What?" He stuffs his money into his pocket.

"I don't know," I say. "You're being very . . . terse?"

"Don't be such a girl."

"Oh, fuck you."

He laughs. "Come on."

Charlie also does this credit card fraud-type scam. He tells me a little about it on the way back from Ender's on Monday night. It's pretty complicated, and I'm not sure if I exactly understand it myself.

Wednesday after school, he decides to show me. I grab some pills from the pantry and swallow them. Got to keep to the schedule. Then he picks me up. We go to the mall and park toward the entrance of one of the big department stores. He tells me that making money is easy. The trick, he says, is going through with it.

On the way in, he flicks a cigarette onto the pavement and says, "There are a million things you could come up with off the top of your head if you actually sit down and try to figure it out. Fast, easy ways to make money."

"Illegally, though."

"Illegally, sure, but you're not really hurting anyone. And if you are, fuck 'em. Teach people to be more careful with their shit. It's providing a service in a way."

"That's one way to look at it."

"Yeah, that's the spirit," he says, moving his sunglasses from his eyes to his collar.

It's early, and the store is mostly empty. Dresses hang from racks, hovering dead above the ground. Mannequins stand decapitated, stiff with rigor mortis. Whose decision was it to give them nipples? The store is cold and vacant, a mausoleum at noon. Standing at the door, Charlie tells me to make conversation with the saleslady. This is some kind of diversionary tactic to take the attention off of him while he's doing whatever it is that he's doing. The woman's skin is tanned and wrinkled, like mud and newsprint paper. I'm on the spot and trying to think quickly. I ask her where the men's room is.

Charlie, who is searching for something in the garbage can next to the counter, glares at me.

She points down an aisle and tells me to turn left at the end.

Okay. Bad stalling technique.

Out of her line of vision, Charlie gestures at me to keep going.

I ask her which aisle, and she points down what is pretty much the only aisle. Then I just sort of stand there for a while, and after that I smile a little. She doesn't know what to do, so she smiles a little, too.

Charlie is still digging in the trash can.

The lady then repeats her instructions on how to reach the restroom, when Charlie finally nods his head at me and begins walking out. I thank the woman and debate whether to follow Charlie or walk to the restroom. I find myself walking about a quarter of the way to the restroom and then abruptly stopping to follow Charlie.

When we leave, I ask Charlie, "Are you sure this is a good idea?"

And he says, "Of course I'm sure. I need to buy something. What do you expect me to do?"

"What if you get caught?" I ask him.

"I'm not going to get caught."

"But what if you do?"

"I won't," he says. "Calm down."

"I am calm." The sun is hot above our heads, casting a blinding white in the glass of the cars in the parking lot. The asphalt glistens, looks like it would melt your hand at the touch. I ask him if it's big. The thing he's buying.

And he asks me, "Physically?"

"Yeah," I say. "Physically."

He shrugs and says, "Yeah, sort of."

We get into his car and drive back to my house.

Charlie's on the phone talking to a real-estate agent.

On the car ride home, he tells me how credit card fraud is done. Pretty complicated, which is clearly a big part of the allure for him. Something with the receipt and the merchant number and the authorization number, the account number, lots of numbers. With this new buffet of digits you make a couple phone calls to get the last few bits of information that give you full access to the account. Then all you have to do is order your product and have it shipped.

Now, into the phone, he says, "Yeah, that's perfect. Fantastic." I look up at him from the TV screen. The phone is wedged between his shoulder and ear. "All right," he says. "Thanks so much."

He hangs up and tells me he's heading out.

I ask him where he's going and he tells me, "Out."

I frown. "Don't worry," he says, "I'll be seeing you soon."

He leaves and I can't think of anything else to do. There's homework, I know. Studying. I sit idly for a few minutes.

My mom comes in and says, "School's just started and you already have a C in chemistry. At this rate, you're going to ruin your chances of getting into a good college. And *last* year, you had three C's as final grades."

"I had an A in history."

"Colleges aren't going to want to take someone with three C's as final grades."

"So whatever, Mom, I won't go to college."

"You're grounded," she says, and leaves.

Yeah, yeah, yeah. Who's going to notice?

I go on the computer and waste some time. I have the five-move-checkmate conversation with a couple people. Or, really, five-move-stalemate.

hey

hey

wats up

nm u

nm

And that's about all anyone has to say to anyone.

Later, my mom comes into my room again and looks at me. She studies my face as a mother might. "You have so much potential, Henry."

"Okay."

"You're not even trying."

"Yes, I am. If I weren't trying I would have all F's."

"You could be getting straight A's."

"So could anyone."

"That's not true."

"Sure it is, if you just convince yourself that school is the most important thing in your life."

"Enough. I want to start seeing improvements in your grades, or there are going to be consequences."

"Fine, whatever."

"It's important."

"Yeah, it's because you love me."

"It is."

"I really don't understand how you can be so adamant about something so obviously pointless."

"It's not pointless, Henry."

"Okay, then how often do you use trigonometric functions when you're dealing with clients in New York or L.A. or wherever?" She recoils at the mention of her job. Either guilt or stress or both.

She says, "Well, obviously every single lesson isn't going to apply directly to your life."

"Okay, well how often do you sit down with your business associates and start discussing the religious imagery prevalent in *Frankenstein* or Shakespeare's use of unrhymed iambic pentameter?"

"Not often — but see how smart it makes you sound?"

"You can't give me a straight answer because you know it's totally pointless." I think about Charlie's defense of decent middle school education. "I mean, I'm not saying there should be no school. I definitely acknowledge that it's important to read and write, and to know fractions and decimals and so forth. And I *remember* those things, because I use them in my actual life."

"Well, you never know where your life is going to take you. I had no idea what I was going to do when I was in high school. You may end up using trigonometry every day — who knows?"

"I hope not, because there's no way I'm going to remember any of it."

"Henry, listen to me. I went through high school. Dad went through high school. Everyone you know over the age of eighteen went through high school. It's something you have to do. It's a rite of passage."

"What does that mean, rite of passage?"

"It's a —"

"Yeah, yeah, I know what it *means*, but it's just a nice name to put on meaningless tribal crap."

"Henry, it's not all meaningless! I use math in my job every day."

"Oh, yeah, adding and subtracting the hours it will take to get from the house to the airport, from the airport to the hotel."

She stands, quiet, breathing, fuming. She says, "You think it's fun for me, Henry? You think I want to be away all the time? I don't, but it's my job."

"Okay, I'm sorry . . ."

"And school is your job. If I treated mine the way you treat yours, I wouldn't have it anymore. You sit around all day doing nothing, going out with your friends — this is *paradise*, Henry. Stop feeling sorry for yourself."

I grab my math book from the floor and open it to the middle.

"Do you know how to solve for a derivative?"

She leaves the room.

"Do you have the periodic table memorized?" I look at the empty hall from my chair.

"You're missing the point, Henry," she says from outside.

"*You're* missing the point. I just said the classes I'm taking are a waste of time, and you turned it into something else."

She's back in my room. "Well, *you* brought my job into this."

"Okay, and you turned the tables to make me feel guilty when it has nothing to do with what I'm talking about."

"But it does. It has everything to do with it. You can question everything your whole life — sure, what's the great philosophical value of doing the business I'm doing, what's the point of anything? You can question everything and avoid ever doing anything. But it's counterproductive. No matter who you are, who you know, no matter what — I mean, Henry . . . you have to find somewhere to fit into the world."

Somewhere to fit into the world? Some job in some city, surrounded by the same idiots. Or probably right here. Right here in the Magic City where I'm going to die. And a job? The options, God, what is there? I guess it's just a matter of accepting to live a completely pointless life, lest we should become counterproductive. I stay on the computer for a while and eventually find my way into bed.

10

FRIDAY, I SEE BILL BEFORE SCHOOL, and he's telling me about how he had this whole long conversation with Rachel Flagler the other day. And, oh, how she's just the sweetest girl ever. But she wants for them just to be friends. He understood, though.

I hear him saying, "She didn't want to ruin the friendship."

"Oh."

"That's understandable, right?"

"Perfectly."

"What?"

I yawn and scratch the back of my neck. "Nothing."

"Don't say nothing if it's something."

"It's nothing."

I walk the halls thinking of Rachel and wondering how Bill can be so oblivious.

I get to first period and everyone's talking loudly, standing up, running around. I'm exhausted. I rest my head on my sweater and close my eyes against the bright morning lights and plastic black chairs. Mr. Englewood comes in, and I watch him watch the class for about forty seconds. He and I are the only still, silent forces in the room. He's wearing a blazer and holding a thermos for coffee. Eventually, everyone settles down a little, taking notice of him. Then, he explodes.

"I cannot believe you people!" he says. "I should *not* have to come into my own classroom and find . . ." and he keeps talking, but my eyes flutter open and closed and I can't make out his words. Everything has the hum of a distant lawn mower. I wonder what day it is. I look at my watch.

"It is completely outrageous," he says. "I try to assume you people can be mature, and look! I walk in to find *this*. It's disgusting. I've been standing here for five minutes! You all have an F for the day."

People put their heads down. Solemn, somber. We're sorry.

Just to show us how pissed off he really is at our behavior, he gives us a pop quiz. He even says the words *pissed off* to *really* show us how pissed off he is, and a couple kids smile with shock and delight. He seems pleased by this effect. The quiz itself is typed, and it makes me wonder whether he was planning on giving it to us anyway or if he just had one already typed up for such an occasion. At the top it says *Your Welcome*, and I wonder what qualifications you need to become an English teacher.

I don't know anything on the pop quiz, so I just bubble whatever looks right and then try to go to sleep again.

I think about Becca. It was just about a week ago. She's keeping to her normal hallway paths because she doesn't want this decision to be affecting her life that way, and I keep to *my* paths because I still really want to see her and, moreover, I still really want her to see me.

I see her on the way to math. She looks bad. Not ugly, but bad. Her skin is like old paper and her eyes are like bruises. Her face looks narrower than usual, the skin stretching tighter around her cheekbones and chin.

I can only hope that I am in some way responsible. Whether she made an effort to look good for me before or whether she is depressed now at my absence or whatever it may be. If I can't have power over her decision-making process, at least I can have power over her physical being.

Last night, I told Charlie that Becca and I had broken up. We were drunk. I said, "It was about a week ago." I hadn't wanted to tell him before. I knew he would just tell me I had done the right thing, when I knew that it was the wrong thing.

"No shit? Good for you."

"It's not good for me. I really want to be with her."

We were sitting on the floor of my kitchen; the refrigerator light kept us up. My mom was in Atlanta and my dad was in New York.

"It was so good," I said. "I fucked it up."

"Don't be a fucking idiot. It was just some bullshit you were clinging to. Just some stupid security blanket." He looked at the bottle of beer in his hand and finished it. "Cheers."

"Cheers yourself," I said, and felt like crying.

"Don't fucking cry," he said.

"I'm not."

When school ends, I start walking toward the back gate where the student parking lot is. Becca's standing there looking off into the distance in that way she does. The bottoms of her pants go over her shoes, so she floats around like a ghost, dead but stuck here with the living, bored and vaguely annoyed.

Broken from her trance, she looks directly at me and almost stares me down, with a strange, thoughtful look in her eyes. Then she wrinkles a brow and turns away, hovering briskly through the crowd of humans.

My daily path brings me to Bill, and he asks me, "What's up?"

"Nothing."

"Cool," he says. "Do you want to hang out later? Drive around or something?"

"I can't. I'm doing something with Charlie." It occurs to me I could invite him, but I don't.

"Oh," he says. "All right."

"Yeah," I tell him. "Maybe tomorrow, though." I know this is a shitty way to treat your best friend, but what can you do?

I walk to Charlie's house from school.

(where do you live?

i can't tell you that

if you told me you'd have to kill me?

i hate people who say that

sorry

it's okay

why can't you tell me?

just can't

so how do you expect me to come over?

i don't know

just tell me you douche

okay

why didn't you want to?

couple reasons

why?

i'll tell you sometime

okay)

The walk reminds me of Miami, just mud and broken beer bottles and dead grass and dying trees and gray skies and hot and humid and grimy and far. I walk past a girl smoking a cigarette, standing against a fence. I recognize her face from the halls. She's sort of pretty, but with acne and fake blond hair. She takes a long drag and extends her jaw to blow smoke up in the air from her bottom lip. I rarely see girls smoking by themselves outside like this and I decide I kind of like it.

I realize how tired I am. The sky beats down, thick and damp, and it drains me of everything. It's like a vampire, staying alive on our energy. I swing my bag in front of me and take out a plastic bag from my pill compartment. I open the top and put the three pills in my hands. The three o'clocks. I take out a water bottle, down them, and assume everything is okay.

When I get to Charlie's house, he's sitting out front in a plastic lawn chair, wearing black and no shoes, with a beer bottle in one hand and a cigarette clamped between his index and middle fingers. He has on a pair of large, dark sunglasses.

There's a big FOR SALE sign hanging out in front of his house, featuring some real estate agent with horns, teeth blacked out, and a mustache drawn on. Leaving town? I wouldn't put it past him — blowing into my life like this and out just as quickly.

"You moving?" I ask.

"No. My uncle always leaves the sign up so he can figure out how much the house is worth if anyone ever stops by," he says. I can't tell if he's being sarcastic or not.

I ask him if he wants to go inside, and he swallows the rest of the bottle, tosses it onto the sidewalk with a shatter, and takes a long, pensive look to the left. He jumps up and looks around as if I just woke him, then says, "What's up?"

"Not much, really."

"Come on," he says. "Let's go do something."

"What do you want to do?" I wonder what Charlie does all day.

"I don't give a shit," he says. "Just something. I'm bored as hell."

So we go driving around, emitting carbon monoxide gas and depleting the ozone layer, and I see all the Miami images blurring past. In Miami, there are two sections: condos and areas that are not condos yet. Every time a building or shopping center or recreational park for children with terminal illnesses is knocked down, a new complex goes up.

I look outside the car window and I picture South Florida in twenty-five years. With the Jurassic Park of cranes and bulldozers forever propelling the hideous tropical skyline higher, the sun will be nearly invisible from the streets below. Only those powerful enough to own the penthouses will be fit to view the pure light of day. All others will have to create huts from broken-down palm trees, or be forced out of the area into Central Florida, working as characters in Disney World.

I look back into the car and ask Charlie where we're going, and he says, "I don't know. Do you want to go to that party tonight?"

"What party?"

"Some party at Keith's house. Everyone's invited." Charlie's car is a 1965 Buick Skylark. Candy apple red, with a white roof and red interior. It's beat-up as hell. The left taillight doesn't work. The back window on the right is cracked by what looks like a bullet hole.

"It's an open party?" I ask him.

"No, it's just that he invited everyone."

"Oh."

"Yeah, so are you going?"

"I wasn't invited."

"So?"

"So, you said it's not an open party."

"When?"

"Just five seconds ago."

"Well, anyway, are you going to come?"

"Yeah, whatever."

Charlie smiles. Whenever I'm in a pissed-off mood, he gets all smiley like this.

He says tonight I will meet a girl who will be better than Becca ever was.

I say okay. I'm vaguely aware of my posture, slumped over with my arms crossed. I stare out the window.

We drive in silence for a few minutes. Charlie looks over and says, "What are you crying about now?"

"I'm not crying."

"Well, what's the matter?"

"Nothing."

He looks at the road for a minute. "Let me tell you, Henry," he says and points out my window. "You see all these houses?"

"Yes." The houses glide past his finger.

"You go inside any one of those houses. There is a girl with a pussy and tits."

I laugh, despite myself.

He nods at me, "So what the fuck are you crying about, huh?"

"I'm not crying."

"Could Becca shoot sparks out of her ass?"

"What?"

"Could Becca, on command, send sparks flying out of her ass?"

"No."

"Did her tits tell jokes?"

"No."

"So what's so special?" he says, then cracks his neck.

"I don't know. I know she doesn't have magic sex organs, but I guess there are just other things about Becca that I'm foolishly clinging to."

"Well, at least you acknowledge your stupidity. That's step one."

"You're an asshole."

Charlie shrugs and smiles.

When we get to the party, there's loud punk music playing. I've never heard the song.

Will I wake up tomorrow?

Will it be another replay of today?

By the time we get there, everyone has had one or two drinks, which means they're acting ragingly drunk. Keith comes to the door to greet us, slurring words and laughing at random.

"What song is this?"

He throws his hands up in the air. "Not my CD." He puts

the beer up to his mouth and winks at us. Charlie motions me to follow him.

There are so many people and the music is loud. The bass is turned up and my heart ticks to the fast snare beat.

A girl wearing sunglasses is bobbing her head. Charlie goes up to her while I get something to drink.

I grab a red cup and fill it up with some beer from the mini-keg. Then I watch Charlie talking to this girl. After a few seconds, she tells him to fuck off and he smiles, tips his hat, and leaves. She sees me looking at her and walks off and, when she does, I see the girl with orange hair who'd been behind her. It's Rachel Flagler. We make eye contact by accident and she looks away. I look away and she walks away. I can't do this. I see her and I think:

Rain.

Thunder.

Lightning.

Wind.

Destruction.

Solitude.

Death.

You know.

I see her, and she's beautiful. I see storm clouds rolling in and I'm short of breath and I'm thinking in sound effects. In crashes and whooshes and great explosions of shattering glass. It comes into my chest like my heart has forgotten itself and my lungs are two tiny plastic bags.

So I should avoid her, pretend she's not here, have a good night. Or find Charlie. Find Charlie and leave and get the fuck out of here. Whatever, just, just, just not by any means go up to her and talk to her.

I cut through people drinking and talking, touch her shoulder, and say, "Rachel?"

Her mouth opens an inch. Her eyes open. Her eyebrows raise. She is trying to let it in, opening every part of her. She tries not to act like anything. It makes me feel good, this power. "Henry?" she says.

"Rachel."

She steals back control of herself and lets a small smile spread across her lips. "Wow, how've you been?"

"I've been okay. And you?"

"Fine," she says. She's short. Her hair is a sharp strawberry blond. She looks good.

Neither of us says anything. There's nothing to say.

The music plays. She bites her bottom lip.

"I'm sorry," I say.

"For what?"

"I don't know."

She nods to the ground. "How are things with you and Becca?" She makes eye contact with me for the word *are*.

"Bad."

The Philosophy of Martyrdom, by Henry Fuller

1. Try to conceal your sadness.

"I'm sorry. Why bad?"

"Oh, God. I don't know. It's fine. It's" [sigh for effect] "it's all over with."

2. Take responsibility.

"I had no idea. You guys broke up?"

"Yeah. I don't know. It was awful. It was probably my fault anyway."

3. But not *too* much responsibility.

"What happened?"

"It was brutal. She said she was sick of me. She never even gave a shit about me in the first place. I should have known. I don't know what I was thinking."

"I'm so sorry," she says . . . and she means it. I kind of wish she didn't mean it. Then again, just because she's a decent human being doesn't automatically mean she won't want me.

I tell her that it's okay. I've been getting over it. "It's tough," I say. "It was just really perfect for a really long time, and then it kind of fell apart. The way this stuff always happens to me, you'd think I'd be used to it by now."

She scrunches her lips up and moves them into her cheek, squinting her eyes with understanding.

The thing about Rachel Flagler is, she has a better body than Becca. Maybe she's even prettier in general. Certainly in a conventional way, she is. Becca can be a bitch, just a total fucking bitch. But, oh, God, thinking about Becca's bitchiness makes me forget all about Rachel. I can hardly breathe. But Rachel is so, so good. She is so good.

Rachel and I are talking, I can tell, but what's going on in my head is a sort of mental competition between Rachel and Becca.

RACHEL FLAGLER: Good body (1 point)
Decent human being (1 point)

REBECCA TUTTLE: Lips (2 points)
Bitchiness (1 point)

RACHEL FLAGLER: Kind of boring (-1 point)
Nice, maybe to a fault (-1 point)

". . . And so obviously after my mom said *that*, I figured I had lost my chance for good. I guess she didn't realize . . ."
"Right, right."

REBECCA TUTTLE: Depressed/Depressing (-1 point)

RACHEL FLAGLER: Freckles (1 point)

REBECCA TUTTLE: Hot eye makeup (1 point)

RACHEL FLAGLER: Very nervous (-1 point)

REBECCA TUTTLE: Smarter than me (-1 point)

RACHEL FLAGLER: Impressed by me (1 point)

". . . and then I tried out for the tennis team . . ."

REBECCA TUTTLE: Broke up with me (-10 points)

BILL SCHNEIDER: Nice haircut (1 point)

CHARLIE BRICKELL: Leather jacket (3 points)

MOM AND DAD: Parents (1 point)

KEITH: Threw party (1 point)

RACHEL FLAGLER: Saved my life (4 points)

Eventually, red cup in hand, Rachel says, "I kinda gotta pee."
"Go for it."
I find a spot on a couch and sink into it. The music pours in
through the stereo, chainsaw punk rock guitars and loud tight
machine-gun drumheads. A kid next to me rocks out, shredded
black Converse All-Stars bobbing to the rhythm. And through a
raspy, fucked-up, cigarette voice, I hear:

*Don't talk to me about boredom, don't talk to me about
    pride.*
I sucked it all up. I swallowed it down. It's fine.

I turn to the kid. "Who is this?" I say. He turns to me, a metal
spike beneath his lip.
"Who?" he says. "The music?" He is tall and awkward with
a bony face and a shaved head.
"Yeah."
"The Lawrence Arms," he says. "I think it's, uh, a mix actu-
ally. Of their stuff."
"It's really good."
"Yeah," he says. "It's pretty poppy Fat Wreck shit. This song's,
uh, '3 A.M. QVC blah blah blah Shopping Spree something.'

I'm not sure what it's called. It's on their record, uh, *Apathy and Exhaustion*. It's not bad. You might like it. It's, like, poppy and whatever."

"Cool."

"Yeah, I guess."

This kid's a douche. But maybe I will pick it up. I stand to go grab some more beer. And, somehow, there she is. Because I have not been fucked with enough tonight. Becca. There: eyelids drawn, neck forward, white plastic rim to her red, red lips. I feel myself stepping back, away. *Becca* at a *party*? Oh, no. My heart's doing that *thing* again. My chest caves, twists. I should bolt. I should never have come here. My shoes are cemented to the tile, although my feet and the rest of me are doing their best to break off. Then it's too late.

She looks up at me and says, "Hey."

"Hey."

"How've you been?"

Find a tone. I need to find a voice. Calm, deep, casual. "Fine."

"Good."

I look at her and she looks at me. "You don't go to parties," I say.

"Neither do you."

"Touché."

She tilts her head and pushes her eyebrows together. Her eyes grow sober and she says, "I kind of want to talk sometime."

"About what?"

"I don't know. Just things." Her voice is frustrated with her words. She speaks like something inside has been stretched to its end.

"Now?" I say. Would I ditch Rachel for Becca? Yeah. Oh, yeah.

Becca inflates her cheeks and blows the air back through. "No. Sometime though. Maybe. I don't know. I guess I kind of don't . . . I don't know."

I smile. I wonder whether I feel the beer. Becca tightens her lips and says, "I think I'm just going to go, actually." I wonder if I've missed something important.

"You sure?" I say.

"Yeah." And she turns and starts walking off, waving vague good-byes at me and looking gone. I don't move after her, but I say, "Is it that you want to get back together?"

She turns slowly, carefully. "No," she says. I move my shoulders and walk off before I even see her walk out the door. Whatever. I'm glad she's gone. Home. Good. Nothing changes. I fill up some more beer.

Eventually, I see Rachel again, walking aimlessly. I take down the rest of my drink. I am feeling it. In my limbs, I feel my movement, I feel the path of my body through space.

I find myself following her around the house, talking. My mind can no longer focus into mental point-system charts. Rachel wins. She's with me, which is worth an infinite number.

And I must be doing a good job acting interested, because Rachel and I are in someone's room with a couple drinks.

She seems nervous. This is nothing new from her. But I'm nervous, too.

For a long time, we're both sitting on top of the bed, listening to the music flooding through the open crack in the door. Finally, we look at each other. If movies have taught us anything, it's that this is when I'm supposed to make out with her.

So I do. I lean in and say, "Rachel . . ." Her eyes tell me I don't need to say anything else. They are open and vulnerable. I am, too, maybe.

My lips press against hers and I try to be soft at first, but I can't — it's been so long. I touch her face and her neck and her teeth are soft against my lips. We are entwined and I feel violence in my chest, the intensity, and I can't take it. It's too much. I have to pull away. She looks sad, but not because of that.

"What's wrong?" I ask her.

"Nothing," she says. She scrunches her lips into her cheek. She looks off the side of the bed at the door. Her dimples stand out, and I decide I'll give her a point for that when I can think straight.

"Are you sure?" I ask her.

"Uh-huh," she says, and smiles a little.

I'm trying to decide whether I really care if she's sad or not. I guess I do, a little. I sure as hell am acting like I do.

I put on this really charming smile and tell her that everything's going to be okay. I don't even know what I'm referring to; it just seems like the thing to say.

Finally, she looks up at me and smiles and kisses me on the cheek. It's kind of funny that she kisses me on the cheek after we just made out. This whole night's been all out of order.

Out of nowhere I say, "I could have died."

i could have died i could have died i could have

"What?" she says.

"I don't know."

We both sit for a second. The phrase hangs in my mind, in slow, quiet repetition. For a moment, I'm in a room, looking out a window at green, green grass.

"Do you want me to walk you home?" I ask her.

"Okay," she says. Another unfamiliar song hammers out of the stereo as we leave the party.

Walking to her house is impossible. I see flickers of the rain. I need pills. We're at her door and I need to run, need to get home, into bed.

"This was nice, Henry."

"Yeah."

"I . . . are you okay?"

"Ah, yeah. Just, I just am feeling a little sick or something, all of a sudden."

"Oh. Do you want me to get you —"

"No." I smile. "No, I'm fine, really. This was really nice, Rachel."

She smiles.

I try to keep my balance.

"So, I guess if you want, give me a call sometime."

I smile again, glad to be able to get out. "I definitely will."

"Well, 'bye," she says.

She closes the door and I walk quickly in the direction of my house. Slowly, my body calms. I was so close to being normal. At the party, it was barely even there, like nothing ever happened.

And so much is being left unsaid. So much has been taken away by the current and we tried so hard to forget.

11

THE SHOE BOX IN MY CLOSET, the one I haven't looked at in something like a year, all that's in there is the torn rag of a sweater.

After the party, I walk back home and I don't look in the box.

I undress, take a shower, and don't look in the box.

I brush my teeth, wash my face, and don't look in the box.

I go to bed and don't look in the box.

This is the sort of pattern I've developed over the last year.

People used to think you could only get post-traumatic stress disorder from war and battle. Shell shock, they called it. Then they made a nice, four-word medical explanation to account for the experience, for people standing up in restaurants, flashing back, having episodes. Post-traumatic stress disorder, PTSD — the veterans had an excuse, and it was fine. Then they found out it could also come from rape or domestic abuse or a sudden unexpected death or a natural disaster.

You can find all this information somewhere in my brain,

somewhere cut off by the chemical reaction the pills cause. The idea is you're not supposed to think about it. That's the whole problem. I don't see Rachel Flagler too often these days. The therapists said — they don't usually advise this, *but* — to avoid her if I could. The idea, they said, wasn't to form a support group. This wasn't one of those things. The idea was that this was ancient history. Let it die.

It started with Becca calling me on the phone. It was a year ago, so we'd been going out maybe two months. At the beginning of that summer. Everything still felt good. We never fought. Not ever. I was, what, fifteen.

The phone rang and it was hurricane season and the skies were electric. I picked it up and looked out the window. The wind made the glass shake. From behind the houses across the street, I saw the sky illuminate from the ground up, and lightning spread out against the black like the naked branches of a tree. Becca said, "What are you doing?"

I was reading a magazine.

"Nothing," I said.

"Are you looking outside?"

"Yeah."

"Me, too."

I heard myself breathing over the phone. Thunder crashed and I jumped a little.

"Shit," she said.

"Yeah."

"What's the matter?"

"Nothing, really. I just have shit to do for school."

"Are you reading something?"

"No," I said, closing the magazine. "I'm hungry."

It was about nine o'clock. "Did you have dinner?" she asked.

"No."

"How come?"

"My parents are out of town and I didn't feel like making anything."

"Really, your parents are out of town?"

"Yeah, you know they've been out of town all the time lately. Just this year."

"Yeah, but still, during this storm. Do you want to come here or something? I'm sure my mom wouldn't mind."

I smiled and said, "I'm sure I'll be fine."

"All right."

"Anyway, it's not supposed to be so bad. I checked the weather online, it's just supposed to be a little tropical storm."

"M-hm."

I laughed. "Look, I'll give you a call if I get hungry."

"You lost your chance," she said. Then we hung up and I turned on the TV.

Nothing happened for a few minutes. Things ticked or hummed. Air-conditioning noise.

Then, a bellowing splinter, and the roof opened up and the TV flung itself into the coffee table, exploding into a million tiny pieces of glass and plastic, shards of table and screen getting lost in one another, and the windows blew in, tore themselves from the wall and flew into the house, the kitchen, the dining room, the foyer. I was in the middle of all this and I thought about all the shit in my room that would be gone forever. The TV and the computer. The sound is what I remember most, beating down, slamming everything, the way you think the sound of thunder comes from lightning, the sound seemed to have a sort of responsibility for everything — it was a torrent. Everywhere was wet and torn and broken.

I remember I ran to the door. It was almost funny struggling with the lock to open it, knowing that every other orifice in the house was gaping open, everything rushing in and out. The whole universe came down around me like daggers of ice. I remember feeling my heart and hearing my breath in my head. I thought about the hurricane shutters sitting in the laundry room. I thought about Noah's ark and being left behind.

Everything felt permanent.

I ran down the block. I slipped and fell and cut my knee open, blood pouring with the water down my leg. The sound was hard and steady; some angry static turned up all the way.

I ran past the trees and fences and stop signs and cars with their shattered windows. A gutter built into the sidewalk on the other side of the street looked and sounded like a waterfall. As the lightning electrocuted the sky to a halt, I ran. I saw a girl, screaming, running. I saw her illuminate white and turn white with the wet street when the lightning flashed. The rain hid everything, every sound, like outer space. It gave every sound its own, and a tree destroying a car had only a faint thump. I heard Rachel Flagler screaming, though.

I ran to her. She was hysterical. Her eyes were bright red and she wouldn't stop screaming. I grabbed her arms and she settled down and we stood there, hearts beating in time to the rain-drops on the pavement. We didn't know where to go. The rain pummeled us, took everything from us, and it was only Rachel, me, and the rain — a constant — never leaving, never. The water fell like shells, like it was a war. I saw a dog walk past in the rain and she ran after it. It was tiny and white. It must have been scared. Rachel called something at it, and it scrambled around and fell into the gutter. I saw her plunge herself face-first and I ran over. Her arm was shoulder deep in the gutter and, if the rest of her had fit, she probably would have been in it herself. She screamed, "No," and I tried to pull her out, but she would not move.

Her nose was bleeding and the tears and rain and blood mixed on her face and she yelled, "No," over and over like she would never stop. She threw her arm in again, trying to reach for the dog, and the skies flashed. I passed out; I don't remember it. Everything went black.

When I woke up, it felt like the sun would rise any minute. I was in a room, on a couch, my head facing a long window. The rain was dripping silently outside. I felt my knee and then looked at it. It was wrapped in drenched purple fabric, a sweater. It hurt like hell.

I thought that I must be in Rachel's house. I stood, my knee and my skull pulsing. My eyes felt tired and soft. I drifted into the hall. I wanted to see Rachel. I quietly opened the first door. It was a small bathroom. I kept gliding down the hall. I turned the knob of the next door, opening it slowly. I put my head up to the crack and saw Rachel in a big white bed. I looked behind me, down the cold hall.

I walked into the room, Rachel's face soft and sideways against a pillow. I touched her shoulder and her eyelids slowly floated apart. "Hey," she whispered.

"Hey."

"Did you drag me in here?"

She sat up against the headboard, a big T-shirt settling on her body. "Yeah. Sort of. My parents helped."

I sat down on the edge of her bed. The rain began pouring in my head and I shivered. Rachel pulled the fold of the blanket and asked if I was cold. I got under the covers, sitting against the headboard, and looked at her. "I could have died," I said.

She looked at me, silent and serious. I touched her hand under the blanket, the nerves of my fingertips magnified.

"Do you want to call your parents?" she said.

"They're not home."

"Do you —"

"I'm going to kiss you now."

"Okay."

I took her face in my hands and kissed her lips, soft and smooth. We sunk beneath the sheets, our mouths together, our bodies entangled. We were one unit, one entity, and it felt like I didn't have to fight anything alone ever again.

i could have died.

I pulled away and looked at her. She was beautiful. She had gone to school with me for five years. I didn't know her very well. This was the first time she had ever been beautiful.

She bit her bottom lip. Did she know about Becca? I brought her face to mine again. We lay there on her bed, kissing, as the sun rose quietly through her windowpanes.

I left before her parents woke up. I told her to thank them very much for me. Outside, I glanced at the gutter and thought about the dog. It lay there at the bottom, somewhere down there, floating the way dead things do. It was just a dog. I wondered why Rachel had gone after it.

I didn't recognize my house. The debris had spilled onto the neighbors' lawns. I threw up on the sidewalk. Then the pills and the therapy and the numbing and everything else began.

12

I WAKE UP THE DAY AFTER Keith's party and it's hot outside. It's late September and Charlie and I are going to the beach.

I brush my teeth and shave and put on a white T-shirt and board shorts. My eyes look lost in the mirror, two brown orbs just hovering in space. I didn't sleep well last night and I try to chew the taste out of my mouth. I think about Rachel.

In my room, the digital clock says it's nine-thirty. There's a picture of Becca on the end table that I've been pretending not to notice. I put it in a drawer. The beach has not been an easy thing for me. *Beach* makes my brain think of water and flooding and ultimately being abandoned and alone and dead. I bring two extra pills in a Ziploc bag in my pocket.

Charlie gets to my house around ten. He honks, and I say good-bye to no one and lock the door.

We get to South Miami and park somewhere around the beach. I feel myself sweating through my shirt.

Up ahead, I see a homeless guy with an old baseball hat, sitting against a building. I feel the change inside my pocket. He's holding a souvenir cup in his hand, and I drop the change inside as we pass.

"God bless," he says.

"You're a good kid, Henry," Charlie says.

"What? You have something against homeless people now, too?"

"Certainly not. Not any more than I do against anybody else."

"So what then?"

He smiles and shrugs.

"Don't be a douche. Tell me," I say.

"All right. I'm trying to figure out why we give money to the homeless," he says. "Any thoughts?"

"I don't know. It's good to help out other people."

"Why?"

"I don't know. Are you going to say it's because society tells us to do this, so we do?"

"No."

"Well, the truth is a couple dollars one way or the other isn't really going to make a difference in my life, but if it means that this guy can eat lunch today, then I don't see a problem with it."

"I didn't say there was a problem with it. I'm just trying to figure out why we do it."

"It's just the right thing to do."

"As determined by?"

"Well, society, I guess. But then again, I feel like it's the right thing. So is that just some societal programming?"

"Maybe. Regardless, there had to be some reason you decided to do it."

"Well, I told you. It might make a difference in this person's life and it doesn't really effect me negatively."

"Right." He presses the WALK button on a pole so we can cross the street. "But entertain this notion."

"What?"

"Well, it seems to me every human action must be made for self-interest, you know?"

"Sure. To a degree," I say, and we start crossing.

"No, no degree. I'm saying that every, solitary action you make as a human being is done purely and exclusively for personal benefit."

"Maybe."

"Well, think about it."

I bob my head side to side with uncertainty. "You're going to say that I did the homeless thing because it makes me feel good about myself."

"Right."

"So what about, you know, philanthropists, organizations, all those . . ."

"I'm saying philanthropy is bullshit. Altruism is a lie. It's all a big crock."

"You think? I mean, there are people who dedicate their lives to these things."

"There are people who dedicate their lives to all kinds of bullshit. What else can we do really? Religious clerics or stamp collectors or whatever the fuck you do, everyone's just dedicating their lives to shit that doesn't matter."

"Well, what *does* matter?"

"Come on, you know this. Just us. Our existence as individual human beings. What we do for ourselves, how happy we are."

I don't say anything for a few seconds. "Well, even if it's true that we only give charity because it makes us feel good about ourselves, why should it?" I say. "Why should doing it make us happy?"

"Well, on one hand, there *is* the society aspect, but I think there's more to it than that, because there's a reason why these things pop up in society. We didn't arbitrarily decide that charity is good."

"Is it like religion, you think?"

"Not really. Religion says plenty of things that we don't do as a society. Abstain from premarital sex. Honor thy father and thy mother. All these things."

"So why do we do it?"

"Why do we do anything?" he says. "It all comes back to the same thing, and I'm tempted to believe that this is pretty much the only true human emotion. When you strip everything else away, I think it comes down to a desire for power and control. Just like anything."

"So . . ."

"So by giving money to homeless people, we're exerting our power over them. We have something they don't. And the whole idea of 'a few dollars here and there doesn't make a difference to us' is all the more reason. We control their happiness and sadness just on our whim. On something that barely affects us. And *that's* what makes us feel good. Knowing we have that power over another human being."

"That's a little depressing."

"Why should it be?"

"It just is."

"Why? When it comes down to it you still *are* doing something good for another person. What difference does it make if it's to make you feel good or to make them feel good? It helps them either way."

Charlie's sunglasses are bright with the sun. He scratches his whiskers and cracks his neck.

"But it's not in my best interest to lose the money I spend on a homeless guy," I say. "If it were just for power, it would be irrational."

"Ah, but you make the mistake of assuming human beings are rational."

"Is that a mistake?"

"Yes," he says as we get to the beach. The sun is high above us and bright. I squint.

"Why?"

"Well, if what we naturally desire as human beings is power, but what matters to us as human beings is happiness, we run into a rift. We can't possibly do what's best for us all the time, because we have no choice but to put power before happiness."

"But doesn't power make us happy?"

"No, power makes us powerful," he says.

"Does power even matter?"

"It matters because it puts you in control of your own life. The only thing that matters really is you and your personal experience and existence. Fuck everything else. For all you know, everything else is an illusion. God and Santa Claus and what you see in the news — you can't know anything about any of it."

"Yeah, well you need to have a little faith in some things, I guess."

"Bullshit. Fuck faith."

"Well, you can only say fuck everything to a point. Otherwise what is there?"

"There's you. And your existence. And that's what matters."

I stop. I can't think of anything to say. I watch Charlie watch a couple kids build a castle from sand.

"Little men with their little worlds. Everyone wants to be God."

A breeze comes up from the water. The sky is only blue and clear, and it reflects bright blue on the surface of the ocean. The sea turtles are dying. Condos go up and they cast deep purple shadows against the shallow of the water. The turtles hatch from their tiny eggs and try to survive in a world that wasn't meant for them, but they're left cold and frozen and dead on the beach before they even get a chance. Cold and dead, the way we all go. I tell Charlie.

"Who gives a shit, they're fucking sea turtles."

He looks at me and I laugh a little. It was much more thoughtful in my head.

"What about science?" I say. "You have to have some faith in science."

"Fuck science, too," he says. "Science is just another religion."

"I don't know about that," I say.

"All right," he says, and looks at me. "What does a religion do?"

I think before I say anything, but I can't think of anything to disprove him. "To give people some kind of sense of purpose. To explain things."

"So how can you say science doesn't have the same goal?"

"Well, I don't see how it gives people a sense of purpose necessarily."

"It's the exact same fucking thing," he says. "Science says, 'This is how the world works and you're a part of it.' That's your purpose. And undoubtedly science does attempt to explain things just like religion. Adam and Eve or evolution or whatever, we're just trying to explain the world we inhabit."

"Yeah, but scientific facts are proven with tests and studies. They're facts."

"Facts? Fuck facts. Ask any of these religious zealots whether Adam and Eve is a fact. Creationists. They think all those things are facts. Facts are just what we all agree upon as a society to be true. If science proves anything, it proves its own falsehood. Science proves itself wrong over and over and over again. The only thing science has going for it is that it allows itself to be proven wrong."

"I don't know if that's the only thing. All the progress we've made as a society has come from science."

"Progress? Come on. What the fuck's so different? We're still killing one another, still hurting one another. Fucking, laughing, eating, breathing, dying. How much has changed? We're still fighting the same stupid fucking war with our stupid little tribes. And over what? Power, control. No different than our relationships on individual levels. Everything's a fucking microcosm. But, shit, now we have automatic staplers. Digital maps in our cars. Caller ID. Now we know the chemical breakdown of an atom and we can heat up food really, really fast. That's progress!"

Charlie takes off his sunglasses and he says, "It's all a bunch of bullshit. It's about money and it's about power. If you control the facts, you control the whole world."

"What about —"

"What about nothing," he says. "What? Cures for disease? Great. Now we can stretch out our lives into long, safe, boring carousels, everything in us trickling away one drop of blood at a time. Fantastic."

The sun shines against the sand.

Charlie says, "I say let's live our fucking lives. Go out and do things. Fuck safety and fuck regrets. Let's just live, man, and let's not worry about everything else."

Two girls on towels in bikinis are looking over at us. They're ahead to our left. I wonder about which one I'm going to get. The less attractive one probably, but I can deal with that.

"You with me?" he says.

"Sure."

"Good."

Charlie makes eye contact with the girls.

"But I mean, you can't say you know. You can't know God didn't create the world," I say.

He stands up and I don't know whether to stand. I start and stop. As he walks away, he keeps his head turned toward me. "You think God created the world?" he asks me. "Bullshit. Any kind of benevolent and righteous being would never create a fucking world like this. It's impossible. God didn't fucking create the world."

Before he walks away completely, he turns back to me one final time, pointing his finger at me. Some people on the beach look over.

"Henry," he says, "the Devil created the world when God wasn't looking."

He kicks down the little kids' sand castle and goes somewhere with the girls.

I sit on the beach by myself for a long time and think about Becca's lips.

I picture them hovering against black, like the lips from the beginning of that movie all those pretentious kids watch.

I think about taking off my shirt and getting a tan. The ocean, I try not to let it make me think of, you know . . . WATER which leads to RAIN which leads to FLOODING which leads to DEATH. DEATH and PERMANENCE and DEATH.

I try not to think about PTSD. I try. And I'm thinking about Becca.

I'm thinking about getting a tan, and how, every time I see a relative from out of town or meet someone new it's always: "Well, you're from Miami. Shouldn't you have a tan?"

I leave my shirt on.

What's the Deal with Power?

Problem Statement: Do we, as humans, desire power/control/domination above all else?

Hypothesis: Because of our evolutionary survival instincts, we will be prone to act in accordance with that which will yield the greatest personal benefit to us individually in terms of power.

Data:

Shit, it seems accurate historically.

See: Slavery.
See: Genocide.
See: Sexism, Capitalism, Feudalism, Racism.
See: Your relationship with Bill.

But.

But.

But what about Becca?

Conclusion: Uncertain.

So, yes. There's also Rachel. There's Rachel and I should be so happy about Rachel. She saved me.

And I remember Becca's lips when I said to her that I would love her forever, and I think, *Stupid. Stupid. Stupid.*

And there's Rachel, who has long orange hair and who smiles quietly to herself. Rachel who is so good.

And Becca, and the time once when my parents were out of town and Becca lied to her parents about where she was and stayed at my house all night.

We sat outside on the grass of my backyard and watched the sun rise.

And I said something about forever. How this should last forever. How I want it to last forever.

And she looked at me and then looked at the sun, and I wanted her to say, "Yes, Henry, yes, I want this to last forever, too." But she didn't say anything. And that gave her everything. I still loved her. I probably loved her more. Why did she always look so sad?

Rachel Flagler, who I used, to make Becca jealous. To win some power back and some control. It was always intentional. Everything is.

So I'm never going to get emotionally attached to anything ever again. Everyone can be my old blanket.

Here on the beach, right now, all the people and their lives. Interesting thing about the beach in Miami — people don't really make a day of it. They come, stop by for five minutes to talk on their cell phones, eat a sandwich, leave.

I exhale. I close my eyelids. The whole surface of each eye tingles from sleep.

The white tide rushes onto the sand and out, and the little kids rebuild their castle. The tide comes in and takes away a little. One kid says they should move it somewhere else maybe.

I decide Charlie is not coming back, at least not for a while, so I stand up. As I do, everything falls into perspective, and I can see the little kids really are little.

I look at them and then pan my eyes across the beach. It's like watching someone's life. The little kids are going to turn into the assholes and bitchy girls, who are then going to get married and turn into the obnoxious parents, who are then going to turn into the old people, and then they're going to die. The end.

I take a walk around the beach and try to look confident.

The sand is soft against my flip-flops. I stand facing the horizon and look ninety degrees to my left until all I can see is condos, then scan across the water a hundred eighty degrees until all I can see is condos again.

I finally get off of the beach and into the city. It still has that whole art deco look, which is nice for a painting, but a little excessively thematic for a city. It's like living in a huge amusement park without the rides.

I wonder where Charlie is right now. Or where Rachel is, or Becca.

I walk around the city for about an hour and nothing interesting happens. Eventually, it starts to rain. I head back to the beach to find Charlie. I feel the extra pills in my pocket. It occurs to me that he could have left already, and I'd be stuck here. I try to keep calm. I could end up in the middle of the street collapsing into fits and spasms. I recite the alphabet in my head so I won't think about it.

A. B. C. D. E. F. G. I walk faster. My stomach begins to hurt. H. I. J. K. L. M. N. O. P. Then I start to feel dizzy. Q. R. S. T. U. V. I run. I'm fine. But you can never be too careful with rain. W. X. Y. Z.

When I get to the beach, Charlie's hitting golf balls into the ocean. It's kind of dark from the clouds and the rain, almost like night.

He's the only one there.

He looks at me and says, "Ready to go?"

. . . H I J K . . .

"Sure."

He throws the golf club back over his shoulder and heads in my direction.

I'm freezing cold and I can't stop Q R S T U V can't stop thinking about the hurricane.

Every time I think I'm over it, I'm not. I laugh to myself. This is what your mind does to you. You say, "No, I don't want to think about this," and it says, "Well, ha-ha-ha."

Remember when you were a little kid in your room sitting up and saying, "Okay. Don't think of monsters. Don't think of monsters." And then that's all you could think about.

Well, this is like that, except one time at your house a bunch of monsters came and almost killed you when your parents were gone.

Your mind has a way of becoming your enemy.

I find myself in the backseat of Charlie's car.

I wake up screaming.

Charlie looks back and smiles. It's still raining. He has his windshield wipers on all the way.

Charlie says that he fucking hates the beach. He goes all the time. I think he just likes to be angry.

He asks me what the fuck I'm screaming about.

"I don't know," I say. "Why do you go to the beach so much?"

"I don't know. What the fuck's the difference?"

"You say you hate the beach, but you go a lot."

"So?"

"I think I'm going to throw up," I say, and there is rain sloshing all around, on the windows and all around me.

Then I say, "At least sometimes at the beach at night, you can see the stars and stuff."

"You can't see the stars until you tie a rocket ship to your ass and get the fuck out of here."

"Charlie, what the fuck are you talking about?"

"What?" he says.

"I think I'm going to throw up."

The car is a rocket ship.

"Don't do it, man."

I can see stars.

"I have to."

I feel the pills in my pocket and take them out. My hands won't stay still. The bag shakes and the pills shake inside. I can see them and I take one out and put it on my tongue. I can't swallow it. I put the other one on my tongue, but I can't swallow it, either. I spit them out.

I fall in and out of sleep a couple times in the backseat of Charlie's car, and nothing makes sense.

The last time I wake up, I'm crouched over on my front steps. I vaguely remember Charlie carrying me out there in the rain. He said something, but it's all hazy and I can't make it out in my head.

It's drizzling. A shiver runs up my spine, and I have a spasm at the neck.

I clumsily stand upright and dig around in my pockets for my keys. I fumble around trying to connect them with the lock, and then I stumble inside.

13

THE NEXT DAY, CHARLIE'S LEANING OVER a spa counter and saying, concerned and quiet, "Did anyone turn in a room key from the Fontainebleau Hotel? I think it fell out of my pocket while I was on one of the machines."

"Let me look," the man says, and unlocks a drawer beneath the counter.

Charlie nods at me. This spa is cosmetically different from the gym, full of old men in fancy workout suits. But it's all the same really. A pissing contest either way. Whether it's about who can lift more or who makes more money, who has more facial hair or who has their nails manicured into masculine semicircles — the people my age at the gym or these old men at the spa, you compete and you compete until you die.

This morning, Charlie called and my voice tasted like hell. I said, "Hello?"

"What are you doing?" he said.

"I'm in bed."

"Get up, I'm outside."

"Go away."

I heard a loud honk from the phone and from outside.

"Come on," he said. "Get your ass out here."

"I'm not dressed."

"Get dressed."

"This better be good."

"Of course it's good."

I grabbed my wallet, phone, and keys from the end table and pulled on a pair of shorts.

In the car, I asked Charlie where we're going, and he told me to some fancy-shmancy spa. I said, "Goddamn it, you said this was going to be good."

"It will be."

"What's so good about a *spa*?"

"Well, where do you want to go?"

"I don't know, but still."

"I just thought it would be fun. Break into a spa, have some nice swanky lunch, be home before two. Where's your sense of adventure?"

"Damn you and your adventures."

He laughed and said, "Goddamn it, don't be such a weasel."

"You're a weasel."

We got onto Collins Avenue and parked in some master meter lot.

Charlie said, "So, we're gonna walk around to the public beach, then hop over to the spa/resort beach area, then slip into the indoor spa."

"We won't get caught?"

"No. But say we get caught, then what? They throw us out and we go home."

I nodded.

Now, inside the spa, Charlie stands at the counter and the man produces a white plastic card that says Fontainebleau Hilton and has an arrow.

"Thanks very much," Charlie says. The man nods and goes back to a fitness magazine.

Earlier I had seen some decent person turn in the card to the man at the desk. The guy said he'd found it on the floor. I noticed it was a room key for the Fontainebleau Hilton Hotel. I told Charlie and said, "Man, it would be really easy to . . ." and already Charlie was up at the desk, asking about it.

With the key to some room in the Fontainebleau, we walk into a sauna and Charlie tells me that these people, they're the ones tipping him at the restaurants. The ones who are so old and so rich that they can do whatever they want. There's a simple equation for this too, he says:

If the amount of money they have - the number of dollars that can be spent per year $\bullet$ (the years they have left to live) is $\geq$ zero, they can do whatever they want.

We sit there in towels. "This is stupid," I say after a while, and we leave.

In the car, I ask Charlie what we're going to do at the Fontainebleau Hotel.

"I don't know," he says. "We'll see what's going on when we get there."

"I have homework and shit to do."

"Stop crying."

"I'm not," I say, and I look out the window. Palm trees and

you can see the heat hanging in the air. People walk up the streets in bathing suits.

"So what happened yesterday?" he asks me.

This is why you don't make close friends when you have PTSD.

"It's this disorder that I have."

"What is it?" he says.

"Uh, post-traumatic stress disorder."

"Huh. What happened?"

And the recitation:

About a year ago, my parents were out of town and this hurricane blew away my house when I was home alone, and I developed this phobia toward rain and other situations that remind me of the disaster, but I'm doing much better now because of my medication, although every now and then the disorder acts up again.

Charlie says, "That's what you're always popping pills about."

"Uh-huh."

He shrugs and puts on sunglasses.

On the left side of the road, the hotel rises into view. It doesn't have a name written anywhere or a sign. Charlie turns the car in and pulls up to the valet. We get out and close the doors.

Inside the hotel, it's like walking into the Miami Beach of the 1950s. Some kind of other world, some Las Vegas, where time doesn't matter, or even exist really. Everything's bars and ballrooms and vaudeville and laughing.

Charlie walks to the front desk and I follow. I hear my phone ring in my pocket. It's Rachel. I turn it off.

At the desk, Charlie holds the room key in his hands.

"Good afternoon, sir."

"Good afternoon."

"What can I do for you?"

"Ah." Charlie looks down at his key. "This is going to sound really stupid, but I actually . . . I actually just completely *forgot* my room number. I can't believe it, I was just up there a second ago. I have my key and everything, do you think you could just swipe it or anything like that?"

"Sure. Do you have identification with you?"

Charlie smiles bashfully and shrugs. "It's actually in the room with my wallet and luggage and everything."

The man smiles and says, "Of course, may I?" He takes the key from Charlie. "There you go, Mr. Anderson," he says, and tells us the room number.

We have lunch at the hotel. Everything is all ritz. I have a crab cake sandwich, and Charlie has whatever's the most expensive thing on the menu.

"Some place," I say, putting my napkin on my lap.

"Yeah, man," he says. He puts his napkin in his collar and winks at me. This is ridiculous.

The waiter comes and brings us water in champagne glasses with lemons, and leaves. We both take the lemons out.

"It still tastes like lemons," I say.

"The world is a cruel place sometimes." He slides his sunglasses down the bridge of his nose and back into place. Bright light comes in through the windows.

"So what's the plan?" I say.

"I won't know until it happens," he says. "But I'm expecting good things."

"This is ridiculous."

Charlie smiles and moves his shoulders, looking off somewhere else.

When we finish eating, we get the tab and the waiter says, "Thank you very much, sir," and hands us the bill. We will, of course, be charging it with the room key.

Charlie signs *Anderson* in big extravagant letters and says, "Come on, let's check out our room."

We get into the elevator and take it up.

Watching the numbers rise to our floor, I say, "What if they're in there?"

"If they're in there, we get in and say, 'Holy shit, looks like the desk gave out two of the same keys, those bastards,' and we all have a good laugh."

"That works."

We walk to the room and Charlie slides in the key. He turns the handle, leans slowly into the door, and slips in. I follow. I see a rectangle of dim light from behind the closed blinds and the room is blue with darkness. Charlie locks the door and slides the latch and chain. I flip on the lights. The place is pretty snazzy.

Charlie stomps over to the suitcase in the center of the room and begins throwing clothes out of the bag. Then he lifts two hangers — a dress and a tuxedo.

"You can be *Mrs.* Anderson," he says.

"You just want me to play house with you."

He winks and drops the dress, then takes the tux into the bathroom and closes the door behind him.

"What are you doing?"

"Most restaurants in this town are onto me by now," he says

through the door. "I figure tips at the dining room here are going to be pretty solid."

I go over and sit on the bed and bounce slowly at the foot. In a minute or two, Charlie comes out with his suit pants on and his button-down shirt half tucked in, tie hanging limply through the collar. "Can I get a hand?" he asks. He holds out his arms, and I button up the cuff links at the end of the sleeves. He then ties his tie and puts the jacket on.

"So what should I do?" I say.

"Whatever you want, man, have a good time." He picks a bathing suit from the floor and tosses it on my lap. "Take a dip if you'd like. I'm sure they have a beautiful pool. Maybe you'll meet some people."

"Yeah, maybe."

"Or are you still in mourning over Becca?"

"I don't know. She's been on my mind I guess. I don't know, I'm over her."

"Christ," he says, tightening his tie.

"Whatever, man. I'm over her."

"Right." He grabs a wallet off the dresser.

"I am. I even hooked up with this girl Rachel at the party the other night. Becca's not even anything. I don't know what I was saying."

"Yeah." He pockets the money and puts the wallet back. "And I'm Mr. Anderson."

"What does that mean?"

"Hooking up with some girl at a party doesn't make you over Becca any more than stealing his key makes me this Anderson guy. We're both playing dress-up now, but only one of us is acknowledging it."

"Whatever, go to your fucking bathroom —" I say, cut off by a violent noise. I turn my head. The door opens, clunks, stops, blocked by the chain.

"What the hell?" a man's voice says from the hall. Then banging. He tries to look in through the crack of the door.

Charlie and I look at each other, eyes wide.

"Do we just pretend we're not *in* here?" I whisper.

Charlie bites his bottom lip, smiling, and slowly creeps to the door.

"Dude," I say.

He smiles at me and then turns to the door. "One moment, sir."

"What the hell's going on in there?"

Charlie quickly motions me up and I head to the door. He undoes the latch and we both glide into the hall, Charlie bringing the door abruptly shut behind us. We're head to head with this angry, middle-aged couple: the Andersons.

"Mr. Anderson, my name is Charles Brickell, I'm head of the keys and locks department here at the Fontainebleau. This is my assistant, Shelby." I try to keep a straight face and I wave. We are never going to get away with this.

"There seems to be a small problem with your keys," Charlie says.

"I know, I know, I already got new keys. What, did they find the old ones?" Mr. Anderson says.

"Mr. Anderson, we have reason to believe —" Charlie begins.

"Listen, kid, I don't have time for this. I have an important function downstairs in an hour. I already lost enough goddamn time trying to get a new set of keys from the assholes downstairs, so how about getting out of my way." He takes his key to the door.

Charlie snatches the plastic card from Anderson's hand and says, "Sir! As the head of the keys and locks department of the Fontainebleau Hotel I cannot, with a clear conscience, permit a man of such abhorrent manner and repugnant language to enter my hotel room with one of my keys." Between two fingers, he snaps the card in half. "Now get out of my sight, fiend!"

Anderson's face turns red to purple. Veins spring up in his neck and on his forehead. "Why you fucking little —"

"I will not stand here and be insulted," Charlie says. "Shove off, Anderson."

The man looks at his wife and says, "Anita, go get the elevator." She walks nervously away. Charlie's nose and Mr. Anderson's index finger almost touch as Mr. Anderson says, "I'm reporting you to the management!" He turns away.

"I *am* the management!" Charlie yells back. Then he grabs a stack of plates off the floor of the hallway, where they had been left for room service to take away, and hurls them one by one at the couple, as they scurry toward the elevator.

"Yeah, go on! Get out of here, you lowlifes!" Charlie calls after them, still throwing dishes. "The Fontainebleau Hotel doesn't need your type around here!"

The couple quickly gets into the elevator and the door closes behind them, just in time for a final plate to crash and shatter against it.

For a second, we stand there, grinning, facing the elevator, blood pumping, looking around at the smashed ceramics and letting the scene replay in our heads. We look at each other.

I cross my arms. "This is why we can't have nice things, Charlie," I say. Charlie adjusts his bow tie. I look back at the steel doors.

"We'd better get the fuck out of here," he says.

"Would it be wise to take the elevator that the Andersons just went down in?"

"Good call, let's do the stairs."

We trudge down the stairs, Charlie's fingers sliding along the rails, his tuxedo slightly baggy. I get an urge to call Becca. At the bottom of the stairway, Charlie says he's going to the dining room, but that's his hiding place. I have to find somewhere else.

"Seriously," he says, "be inconspicuous."

I get to the lobby, avoiding the desk. I turn on my cell phone to call Becca but there's no reception. I find the pay phones and put in thirty-five cents. The thirty-five cents that used to be twenty-five cents and will soon be fifty cents and then a dollar.

I call Becca and it rings a bunch of times and I get her answering machine. "Hi, this is Becca. Leave a message."

I hang up.

I dial again, and again I get her voice mail.

There are a lot of people walking around the lobby. Couples, families with children, old people. Carts being wheeled around with people's luggage. The noise the wheels make on the tile of the lobby, and the reflections on the waxed floor.

I call Rachel. It rings and she picks up.

"Hello?" I hear her voice. It sounds high-pitched and quiet on the phone. Even more than in person, like she's talking out of a tin can.

I don't say anything.

"Hello," she says again.

I drop my voice a couple octaves and mumble, "Hi, I think I have the wrong number. 'Bye," and I hang up.

I picture the confused look on Rachel's face. I feel bad, so I call her back.

"Hello?" she says.

"Hi, Rachel, it's Henry."

"Hey, Henry, um, did you just call a second ago?"

"Yeah. I mean no. Well, I mean, I tried to call, but it was, um, busy or something."

"Oh, because — hah, well never mind."

"Sure."

"So, what's up?" she asks. "I tried calling you yesterday, but you weren't home."

"Oh, yeah," I say, "you know. I was kind of sick."

"Oh," she says, "I see."

"Yeah, you know."

"Yeah."

Facing away from the wall, I open my mouth, raise a brow, and inhale. Mr. Anderson walks by and I quickly turn around to face the phone.

He catches my glance and walks over to me angrily.

"Hey!" he says, "you're the goddamn punk kid who was in my room!"

"Excuse me?" I say.

"What?" Rachel says.

"What?" I ask Rachel.

"You! You were with that kid!" Mr. Anderson begins trying to grapple the phone out my hands, but I pull it back up to my ear.

"Leave me alone," I say, "get out of here."

"What?" Rachel says.

"Not you," I say to her.

"You goddamn kid!" The man's tugging at my arm. "Get off that phone!"

"Listen, sir, I don't know what you're talking about," I say.

"Henry, what's going on?" Rachel says.

"What's your name, kid?" he asks.

"What's the difference what my name is?" I ask.

"Henry?" Rachel asks.

"Rachel," I say, "I'll call you back."

"Okay?" she says, the way girls do with that looming question mark, hanging over your head. I hang up the phone and it goes down like a guillotine.

"Goddamn it, kid, get off that goddamn phone!"

"I am off," I say. I point at the phone, which is hung up.

"You're coming with me!" he says and tries to grab me. I bolt — hearing distant cries for security — through the lobby, out the sliding glass doors, and off the premises.

14

THAT'S IT. IT WAS FUN, but that's it. I'm sitting outside a little ice cream parlor at a café table. I clean my face with a napkin. I think about Charlie throwing dishes in the hall. Somewhere I hate him for that, for being able to do that. It *was* fun, though. I'm just glad no girls saw. Then he'd be this amazing rebellious stallion and I'd be the sidekick, the *friend*, Shelby. (*Shelby?*) Regardless, I am ready to go home.

A table next to me is crowded with people. It's three girls in their usual composition and a couple guys, collars popped, long hair all around. Not that I'm listening, but I've gathered that they're in from out of town.

"I cannot *believe* they didn't have a Nordstrom at the mall."

"I know. I was surprised they even had a Burberry."

"Ugh, those outfits are so tacky anyway."

"No, come on, they're cute."

"I thought you said you liked that hat."

"Well, it looked cute on you."

"I cannot believe how much we spent today."

"I know, my parents are going to execute me."

"Ugh, same."

"Sorry we dragged you guys there all day."

"No, I don't mind shopping."

"Aw, they were good sports."

"Yeah, Paul's a metrosexual."

And there's an uproar of laughter.

"No, but really," one says, commanding the attention of the group. "I think it's so ridiculous that people would spend so much money on a Rolex watch. I mean, hello, if it tells the time, it tells the time, you don't need to spend, like, thousands of dollars on it."

"No, that's a really good point actually."

"Yeah, that's so true. I never thought of it that way."

"Yeah."

Maybe Charlie would say something. Maybe he would say, "Yeah, well, if that's so fucking true, why don't you just buy your clothing from Fruit of the Loom?"

They would fall in love with him. If he said it.

The phone rings from my pocket and I say, "Hello."

"Yo. Where are you?"

"At some ice cream parlor. I got chased out of the hotel. Pick me up."

"I could do that."

"Do it."

"I *could* do that. But I was thinking —"

"No."

"— seeing as I'm already *wearing* a tux —"

"Dude, no. Whatever it is, no. You said we'd be home before two, and it's, like, three-thirty."

"Fine."

"What?"

"Fine, we'll go home."

"Yeah?"

"Yeah, sure, are you close by?"

"A couple blocks over."

"Okay, cool. Well, start heading over here, I'm just gonna get my car from the valet guys —"

"I'm not going back into that hotel."

"Jesus, man, you don't have to, chill. I'm not trying to lure you back into the Fontainebleau."

"Good."

"Check it out: If you're that opposed to coming back here, I'll pick you up at the Whitebook Hotel. You know where it is? It's like three hotels over."

"Yeah, I know it."

"Okay, just meet me there. Start heading over."

"All right, cool."

I get to the Whitebook. Charlie's car isn't there. I wait outside for a few minutes in the afternoon sun. Rachel calls and I stare at the phone, debating whether to get it.

"Hey."

Rachel's small, wavering voice: "Hey, is everything all right?"

"Oh, yeah. Everything's fine. This guy just really wanted to use the pay phone."

"Oh."

"Yeah, I think he was probably drunk or something."

"Where are you?"

"I'm on like fortysomething street."

Charlie's buzzing on the other line.

"Oh, cool, what are you —"

The noise again, and I can't hear Rachel over the call-waiting.

"Listen, Rachel, my other line's clicking in. I'll give you a call later, okay?"

"Uh, sure, okay —"

"Okay, well, talk to you then. 'Bye."

"'Bye."

"Hey, where the hell are you?" I say, now to Charlie.

"Where are you?"

"Outside. You told me to meet you here."

"Yeah, but I didn't see you, and I couldn't just stay parked in the middle of the road, so I went inside."

"All right, well, let's go."

"Sure, just come meet me in here. I'm in the Drucker Room having a coffee."

"Okay." I go up, around the driveway, and head in.

At the desk I ask, "Hey. How do I get to the Drucker Room?"

"The Drucker Ballroom?"

"Yeah, I guess."

"Just head that way and you'll find it on your left-hand side."

"Great, thanks a lot." I walk down the echoing hall. I open the door, but this can't be right. People stand at the entrance, talking, laughing. Everyone is wearing a tuxedo. The women wear black dresses. I shuffle in, trying not to be noticed. I think, maybe it *wasn't* the Drucker Ballroom I was going to after all. Maybe it was —

"Henry!"

I look over and see Charlie standing with a circle of men, some in their twenties and thirties and some older, all with drinks in their hands, laughing.

"Henry," he says again, gesturing me over. "A little under-dressed, huh?"

"What?"

"He's the retarded cousin," Charlie says to them, and winks. They all laugh. He takes off his jacket and hands it to me. I put it on.

He says to me, "They're on *Laura's* side."

"Oh."

"Yeah, go get yourself a drink," he says.

"I'll get one later."

"Do what you like." He turns to them. "Anyway, good to meet you. Got to go make the rounds, you know." They all nod and laugh, and we walk away.

"Dude, I look like an idiot," I say.

"You're dashing."

"I'm wearing shorts."

"No."

"Yes, I am. What the fuck are we doing here — you said we were leaving."

"We *are* leaving."

"All right, good, let's go."

"*After* the wedding."

"Now we're crashing weddings, too?"

Charlie puts his hand on my back and whispers, "Yo, keep it down." Then he straightens up. "Come on. We'll hang here for a couple hours, maybe meet some girls, free dinner, then we go home. You got something better to do?"

"I have homework and shit."

"So, what, are you going to Harvard or something? Don't be such a killjoy, come on."

He's smiling hopefully and I can't help laughing. I mean, who says killjoy?

"There we go! That's the Henry I know, huh? C'mon. It's John and Laura's wedding. We gotta celebrate their union. By the way, if anyone asks, we're on John's side."

"Who would ask?"

"That's all they do here. They ask what side."

"Fine, but we are lying *low*, dude. No more close calls."

"Of course, you think I'm an idiot? We'll lie low."

Then we eat a lot of food. In my head, I'm thinking that it's funny to be here. It's a good story. I wonder if that's why we're doing it — if these things are just for the sake of being able to tell people later. Like: Look how cool my life is, I crashed weddings when I was in high school. But that's not the reason we're supposed to say. We're supposed to say, *Yeah, we came for the free food*, as if it were just that. The cocktail hour ends at four and everyone herds into the main ballroom. We stay behind. When the room clears out, Charlie walks to a table for place cards, and he takes one that says *Richard and Sylvia Blanc*.

"No-shows," he says.

"You sure?"

"We'll find out." He shrugs. "Come, Sylvia."

"I always have to be the girl."

We get to the table with Laura's friends. Everyone is talking and laughing. There are six men and three women and Charlie and me. They talk about grad school and their careers and money.

One looks over at us. "Hey," Charlie says.

"Hey there," the guy says, drunk. "I hope I'm not supposed to remember you from high school."

They all laugh.

"Not us," Charlie says.

"Phew. I'm Todd, I went to UM with Laura."

"I'm Abbey," one of the women says.

"I'm surprised Richard and Sylvia didn't show up," the woman beside Abbey tells her.

"You get married, and that's what happens," someone else says.

"I'm Charlie. This is my brother, Henry."

"Nice to meet you."

"And you're on . . . ?"

"John's side," I say.

"We're John's cousins," Charlie says. "Henry was really more like a little brother to John though. He had trouble in school up in the city, so Mom thought it would be a good idea to send him to live out in the country with John and his family."

"Oh," a few say.

"But, oh man, does Henry have some stories," Charlie says. They're drunk enough to be interested.

"No, not really," I say.

"Oh, come on, don't be modest, Henry. They're great. Tell them the one about the tractor and the pigpen."

"The pigpen?" A few laugh. "I didn't know John lived on a farm." The room is sleek and black.

"Oh, yes. He was all farm," Charlie says, nodding. "Come on, tell it."

"I really couldn't," I say. "You tell it."

"Oh, if you insist. You can tell me if I'm messing it up."

"I'll let you know."

"So Henry, since he was a little kid, he was always obsessed with, you know, pigs. He'd been living on the farm with our cousins for about four years, so he was, I guess, twelve. John was probably sixteen or so, and they were doing chores around the barn, only Henry couldn't do any chores because he has very delicate hands, see. Meanwhile, John accidentally left the keys inside the tractor. So Henry's out there alone in the barn and whatever, and they always told him, 'Henry, do not open the gate of the pigpen,' because one time there had been an incident and all the pigs had gotten out. So Henry says, yeah, yeah, that he won't open the pigpen, but they all know he really wants to. But he says, no, no, I won't open the gate. So he doesn't. Instead he gets on the tractor, revs it up, and slams through the fence. You know, of the pen. I don't know why, the kid's crazy you know, so all the pigs start squealing and freaking out and shitting all over themselves, and Henry gets out of the car and it sort of lurches forward into the mud and shit and pigs, and he jumps out and jumps into the mud with the pigs, I don't know, to save them or whatever, compassionate kid that he is. He dives into the mud, you know, and looks up and this big, fat white pig shits all into his face, exploding because the pig's scared and all. So Henry takes off his shirt, you know, to wipe off his face and everything, and then John comes out. Sees the tractor in the mud, the fence broken, pigs dancing all around, frolicking into the rest of the barn, shitting everywhere, and sees Henry, face covered with shit, shirt off, surrounded by frightened pigs."

Everyone is laughing. This is definitely *not* lying low.

"So that day," he says, "my mom gets a phone call from Tennessee that Henry here's molesting all the pigs. My mom gets him on the phone and says, 'Damn it, Henry. I will not have any son of mine molesting pigs!' you know, and so Henry, as punishment, has to clean the pig shit for the next two years as his chore, delicate hands or not."

"Oh, my God," one says, wiping her eyes.

"Yeah," Charlie says. "This kid's crazy."

"But you and John were close?" someone asks me.

"Um . . ."

"Oh, yeah," Charlie says. "I'm telling you they were like brothers." He looks at me and bites his lip. "Sometimes I wish *we* could have had that relationship."

"I'm going to grab a drink," someone says and winks at me. A couple people get up with their glasses.

"Do you have any more stories?" someone asks me.

"Oh, yeah," Charlie says. "Tell them about the time you and John got lost for a week in the woods when you guys were at sleepaway camp together. With the bear."

"Um . . ."

"Or do you want me to tell it?"

"No. One time, uh, me and John were at sleepaway camp and we got lost in the woods and there was a bear."

Everyone stares.

"Yeah? And then what happened?" one of the girls says.

"Nothing, it was a stupid story."

"*Henry*," Charlie says. He looks at them. "Henry's so shy. Tell them about the bear. How it stole all your clothes and you tried to take the clothes back and you developed a psychosomatic reaction and lost all your hair and John had to take you back to the camp buck naked and with all your hair gone."

Everyone's eyes open and laughter surrounds me. What a stupid noise, laughter.

"Oh, my *God*, is that true?"

"I wish we still had the pictures," Charlie says. "*Someone* threw them in the fireplace one day after a little tantrum." He points at me with his thumb.

"That is so funny."

"The kid's nuts, I'm telling you," he says.

"Perhaps I *will* get a drink," I say.

"I'll get you one," a girl says, "I'm about to get one myself. You are so funny." She smiles at me and shakes her head.

The people who got up to get drinks sit back down.

"Did we miss anything?"

"John and Henry got lost together in sleepaway camp," someone says. "Henry lost all his hair and clothing and almost got eaten by a bear!"

"Really?" someone says to me.

I inhale and throw up my hands. "I guess so."

"That is *so* weird."

"Yeah, you're telling me."

"But you did get your hair back?" someone says.

I look at Charlie. "Yeah," I say. "Ultimately." They nod in relief.

"But you have to tell them about the time when you and John won the International Junior Karaoke Award in Tokyo," Charlie says.

"Oh, my God," someone says.

"That's amazing."

"I didn't know John could sing."

"Oh, yeah," Charlie says. "International champs, these guys."

"What song?" they ask me.

"What was it, Henry?" Charlie says.

"I don't know."

"You must remember."

I shrug. "Okay." I can't think of anything. "It was . . . 'I'll Stand by You.'"

"Right, right," he says.

"By the Pretenders?" someone says.

"Yeah," I say. "'I'll Stand by You,' by the Pretenders. International Tokyo Karaoke. Yeah. Crazy times."

"And you guys were close."

"Yeah," I say. "Like brothers."

The girl brings my drink and I pour it down my throat.

What happens after is bad. The toasts begin. The best man. The father of the bride. The how much we love you. The jokes. And then something ridiculous happens.

Charlie looks to me and says loudly, "Henry, why don't you go up and toast John. He's practically your brother."

"Yeah!" someone says. "Say a few things for your brother."

"Yeah, Henry. Tell the pig story."

Hands are on my shoulders.

They're saying, Yeah.

Henry.

Yeah.

The pig story.

Tell it.

Everyone's touching me and saying, "Go up."

They put a champagne glass in my hand.

"No," I say, and I laugh. Ha-ha. No thanks. I really couldn't. "Do it!"

"Really, I'm not much of a speaker."

Then a few other tables catch on. They point.

"Henry!" they say. "Yeah, do it."

And pretty soon half the place is chanting my name.

So it's either . . .

Sit here. And have everyone chant my name. Until I go up.

Or go up.

I stumble onto the stage. Someone hands me a microphone. It whistles.

In their seats, people mutter, "It's John's brother."

It's John's cousin.

It's John's long-lost twin separated at birth.

I look at the bride and groom in their seats, John and Laura. Laura, smiling. John, confused.

The champagne glass is in my left hand and the microphone is in my right and I say, "John."

I'm sweating. The room is dark. The lights are on me.

"John. What can I say?"

He looks at Laura. She's looking at me.

"John," I say. "What can I say about a guy like you, John?"

I draw a blank. All I can think about are the gruesome ways in which I'm going to kill Charlie. I have nothing. I don't know any of these people. Hell, I don't know John's last name. The seconds drag, terribly and painfully. I don't want to do this. There are certain lines that it's not cool to cross. There are certain things . . . I mean it's someone's actual wedding. And I don't know if it's some sort of social contract, if it's something inherent that I have and Charlie doesn't, something about making other people feel uncomfortable — I don't know what it is. My throat tightens and I feel the absurdity in my stomach. But the seconds hang in the air, piling up, one at a time, and I have to say something, anything.

So I tell the pig story.

The whole thing, long and terrible, and all completely false. Ridiculous and impossible. No one could believe it. But they laugh. They laugh the whole time. Maybe they think I'm a drunk friend. Maybe they think it's true. Maybe John really did live on a farm. I don't know. Everyone's cracking up on one another's shoulders.

This is the stupidest thing ever, and to stand there the whole time and see the confused look on John's face and Charlie smiling and me up there sweating. Fucking Charlie. The fucking bastard.

"Cheers," I say, and I hold up the champagne, and everyone holds up their glasses. "Cheers," says everyone.

"Thank you," I say, and hand the microphone to whoever's around and I'm going to be fine — maybe I'll even let Charlie live. It wasn't horrible; everyone had a good laugh. It was ridiculous, but I'm going to be fine, and then Charlie stands up and puts his hands around his mouth and says it.

He fucking says it and everyone cheers and hollers.

He doesn't know when to stop.

And he says, "Sing 'I'll Stand by You'!"

"No!" I say.

Everyone protests. "Sing it! Sing it! Sing it!"

"No, hah. Really. I really couldn't. Really."

What the fuck is this?

Sing it, and they bang on the tables and the silverware rattles and someone gives me the microphone back and winks.

I raise an eyebrow, desperate.

The keyboard starts.

"No, I seriously can't do this."

Charlie nods at me. He winks. His smile is all teeth.

"No. Really. I really can't."

"Henry! Henry! Henry! Henry!"

The keyboard player on stage starts with the opening chords.

I hold the microphone down. I can't believe this is happening.

"Get Charlie up here," I say to the table.

So that's how it happens. That's how it happens that Charlie and I are front and center stage in the middle of a wedding for two people we don't know, me in shorts and a tuxedo jacket, Charlie in a bow tie and slacks, here in the lobby of the Whitebook Hotel, arms over each other's shoulders, singing "I'll Stand by You."

And we belt it out with everything we have.

The sun is down, the wedding is over. We walk along the dark lighted sidewalks of Collins Avenue, drunk. Everything swims in and out of my consciousness.

Charlie says, "Yeah. Things are good."

I ask him how his parents died, and he laughs and laughs.

On a beach, Charlie tells me that there are three kinds of people in the world.

Rachel called at some point after the wedding. Saying, "Henry? Are you okay, Henry? Are you drunk?"

Charlie tells me to name anyone. Anyone I know can fit perfectly into one of these three groups.

Rachel said, listen, maybe she should just call me later. Or I could call her. I said, okay, Rachel, yeah, that sounds fine.

And thinking about Rachel made me think about Becca,

and oh, God, how I wanted to call Becca. Call Becca, drunk, and blame it on that later. But I didn't.

I tell Charlie I miss Becca and he says, oh, yeah, brother. Me, too.

And Charlie talks about religion. If we were all raised to believe that the color blue was really called green, wouldn't we all believe it?

Well, sure, but that's different.

He acknowledges that, yeah, that's different, because if we all believed the color blue to be green then it would be. Since green is just a creation of man.

But then isn't God just a creation of man?

Well, yeah, but blue is also a creation of man.

So, therefore, if blue were something objective and true to the universe, we would be lying to ourselves for calling it green.

And maybe blue really is green. Or vice versa.

But we make it all how we want, so what's so bad about doing what's comfortable?

What's comfortable isn't what's true.

Well, yeah, but we don't know if what's uncomfortable is true, either.

Well, we don't know anything.

No.

"So, are we so much better?" I say. The moon hovers above us and the sky and the sea are inky blue and the sand is white and cold.

"Than?"

"I don't know. Today I was sitting at this ice cream parlor and I heard all these kids talking. Really, really rich, you know.

Talking about how much money they spent today and stores and clothes and just all this complete bullshit, you know?"

He smiles and nods. "That's people for you."

"I know, but are we really so much better? Sitting around, asking ourselves these questions, with answers — no matter how hard we try or how much we want to pretend — we can never *really* know? I mean, are we?"

He looks up and shakes his head a bit. "I think so," he says.

"Why?"

"I just think those things are important, and clothes and credit cards and shit like that aren't."

"But why?"

"It's important to question things. It's important not to accept everything we're told. Yeah, those kids with their credit cards and vacation homes aren't hurting anybody, fine, but do you think any of them have ever put a decent, genuine thought into anything in their lives? Anything that matters?"

"Well, what *does* matter?"

"I know what doesn't matter and it's fucking Diesel shoes and aviator sunglasses and malls. That's what doesn't matter."

I think about it. "I agree. But I'm not going to sit and say I'm superior to them as a human being."

"Whatever makes you feel noble," he says.

But while Charlie's telling me about losers, assholes, and cool people, and being a pawn, and religion, and the government, the only thing I'm really thinking about is Becca.

When Charlie asks me if I want to go back inside, I think about Becca.

And I look out into the ocean, and remember how Becca and I used to go sit at the park and talk. And about all the stupid bullshit. The way everything deteriorated and the way I just let it happen.

And it's painful and terrible and it rips me apart.

But it's still kind of amazing, somehow.

So I tell Charlie, just hang on. I'm trying to enjoy this.

And he says, all right, and smiles.

He stands up.

I sit there for a long time. I don't know how long. The sand is cold and soft and smooth. The tide washes up on the shore and floats back into itself. Charlie walks up and down the beach, where the sand meets the water, hands stuffed in his pockets. The ocean splashes on his feet and ankles. He looks up at the sky every so often and laughs.

Finally, I tell him I'm ready, and we silently, comfortably, walk back to the hotel and take the elevator up to the roof.

There's the low hum, always maintaining the imperfection of silence. The midnight refrigerator noise. That buzz.

Somewhere right now, the angry Mr. Anderson is sleeping. Somewhere my parents are sleeping. Maybe together, maybe in different states. Becca is sleeping somewhere, in that way she does, curled up in a ball beneath her covers. Rachel sleeps in her room, and maybe she wonders what Friday night meant to me. Bill is asleep, probably in his living room, with cards in neat stacks on the floor.

15

SOMETHING LIKE COLONIAL RESISTANCE to the Sugar Act generated debate between Parliament and the colonists about the definition of blank. A, B, C, D, or E?

C. Mercantilism. It could be anything.

Back to reality. That's the way it goes.

So now it's Monday, and I have
A. An American History test.
B. A headache.
C. Two and a half hours of sleep under my belt.
D. All of the above.

And it is
A. Seven forty-five in the morning.
B. Becoming obvious that this Becca thing is a problem.
C. A problem.
D. I have a problem.

Because, you know, I am being

   A. Irrational.
   B. Irrational.
   C. Irrational.
   D. Irrational.
   E. Irrational, I know, I know. It's the same thing as
   F. Post-traumatic stress disorder.

The effects of a traumatic experience are similar to the aftermath of a bad breakup. Explain.

Because of the irrationality and stupidity of the colonists, they are unwilling — nay, physically unable — to recognize their own flaws. To recognize that they must

   They must . . .
   They must, you know.
   Move on with their lives. Or whatever.

You are at school Monday. After the unusual events of Sunday evening, why the fuck did you do this? You moron.

   I don't know. Bad idea. Charlie offered to take me.

And where is he?

   At home.

But here you are. At school.

   I know.

Sitting at a cold desk, taking a test on American History.

   Fuck off.

So now it's Tuesday. Becca passes you in the hall and you are unable to look away. You discover you still feel as strongly for Becca as you ever have, despite your reluctant acknowledgment of the irrationality of said attraction.

A. True.

B. False.

Rachel calls you Wednesday. You don't pick up. You realize you still feel a strong sense of attachment to Rachel — a manifestation, perhaps, of your attachment to the hurricane, yet you push her away, arguably in a feeble attempt to push away your past, although you realize, with however small moral responsibility one can muster, that it is probably — certainly — unfair to give her the identity of an event that was obviously no fault of her own.

A. True.

B. False.

But if you think about it, how much have you done to prevent yourself from becoming involved with her, really? It's easy to avoid her. You have no classes together. The one time you see her again, you hook up, unsure of how you even feel about her or the idea of being with her, and then give her no further thought. You feel

A. Guilty.

B. Like you should feel guilty.

C. Like you should feel that you should feel guilty, and then rebel against this guilt through the denial of responsibility, thrusting yourself into an undeniable, although not altogether unpleasant, nihilistic hedonism that leaves you with no answers, but no real questions either.

D. Sick.

E. Like you should probably feel sick about this lack of morality, but that you don't really quite feel sick, but that, maybe if you did, you would have morality, and then no further reason to feel sick.

On the beach Sunday night, Charlie Brickell, wearing a rumpled tuxedo vest and looking into the infinity of the ocean, said there were only

A. Losers.

B. Assholes.

C. Cool people.

D. And that's it.

But don't we all manifest these traits at different times, among different people, in different moods? It's all subjective. Everything is. I think that's the idea.

End Time.

Thursday: English. Vocabulary. Analogies. I see Bill in the hall and he asks, "Where have you been lately, dude?"

Bill is to Henry as loser is to blank.
    Asshole.

Henry : Charlie :: loser : _____.
    Asshole.

Henry : Charlie :: Bill : Henry.

But that's just logic. End Time. That's math.

If Henry = x, and Charlie = y, and Bill = z.
And loser = a, asshole = b, and cool people = c. Then if

$z/x = a/b$

and

$x/y = a/b$

it must be so that

$z/x = x/y$

So we have an extreme on each end. With Bill, Charlie, and me, it's loser, asshole, and cool person.

$x = 2$
$y = 3$
$z = 1$

Find the mean. Two plus three plus one, over three, equals two. If $x = 2$ and Henry = x and x = the average, then Henry, by some property of equality, maybe transitive, equals average. Henry = average. Loser, assholes, cool people. Find the mean.

Vocab. Crack open that thesaurus.

Function: *adjective.*
Synonyms: medium, fair, fairish, indifferent, mediocre, middling, moderate, so-so.

Mediocre? Fuck you, Merriam-Webster. Ah, but it's true,
isn't it? Oh, well, probably so. I take it back. You'd know better
than I.

But while we're at it, just for a small kick.
1. function: *verb*
   Etymology: akin to Dutch *fokken* to breed (cattle), Swedish
   dialect *fokka* to copulate.
1. intransitive senses
2. meaningless intensive
3. transitive senses
usually obscene

Obscene? There's nothing special about the arrangement of
letters. We give everything the value we decide upon.

End Time. Turn in what you have. I wish I knew. School goes
on and on, Thursday dripping lazily into Friday. What can I do
to make things right? Would I even know it if they were? The
halls are wall to wall with corpses, packed together economically,
Japanese. We're all breathing and moving, destination to destination, the cycle goes on. Take a pill, float to class, sit back
down and repeat until the bell. Then go back home and dread
tomorrow until the next morning and repeat.

16

BECCA CALLS TONIGHT. Friday night.

I pick up the phone. My lungs aren't big enough. I try to take in the air and I'm like a dying fish tangled up in phone cords.

When I hear her voice, it sends me into a thousand déjà vus. Every time she ever said,

"Henry," she says softly now.

"Becca."

"I cut myself with a razor."

I don't say anything.

"Henry?"

"Is your mom home?"

"No."

"Do you want me to come over?"

"Are you busy?"

"No."

She doesn't say anything. She won't ask. Everything is about power maybe, but I let her win. I want to see her so badly.

"I'll be there in two seconds."

I hang up the phone and grab the keys and leave. I open the car and jab at the ignition until it goes. Becca's house is close. My hands shake on the wheel and my foot at the pedal. I park, jagged. The car door closes loudly and metallically.

I run up to the door and it's locked. I pound at it over and over. No one's getting it. Obviously. And I can just see Becca huddled into a dark corner somewhere, dying, and me, standing out here.

"Becca?" I say loudly. There's no answer.

"Becca?" I say again.

I run around to the side of the house and try to find an open window or something. I jump the fence to her backyard, and there's nothing. It's invigorating to know you're still capable of exerting some kind of energy.

I search around and find an open window, protected by a screen. I unearth my house key from my pocket and poke a hole through the cross-hatching. I'm pretty frenzied. I keep poking holes until I get them all to connect. I slide myself into the room, feetfirst, and I'm in the house.

I'm in a bathroom.

I run out of the room and decide if I ever kill myself it's absolutely not going to be pills. It would be too fitting.

The hallway leads me to the living room and I see the couch. I stagger backward for a second and breathe hard. I freeze, confused. I remember why I'm here, and my feet take me to Becca's room. All the lights in the house are off.

I find her lying there on the floor like a dying animal.

She looks up at me. Her head is lowered, so her eyes just sort of roll up in her head until they meet mine.

She has on red lipstick. She's wearing all black.

For a second, this makes me think about necrophilia.

"Did you find the key under the mat?" she asks.

"Um, yeah," I say.

"Okay, good."

We stare at each other and that's all. I look at her left wrist, bleeding quietly.

"Why did you do this?"

She shrugs gently and looks at a corner of the room.

"Do you have bandages?"

"In the kitchen pantry." She leans back on the wall. She's biting her lower lip and seems about to cry. I leave the room.

In the pantry, all I see are chips and snacks. I try to imagine the thoughts going through Becca's brain. I look in the cabinet above the pantry, and the reek of every spice drawer I've ever smelled overcomes my nostrils and eyes. I quickly shut the cabinet and look at the one to its left. Bottles of pills. Aspirin, Tylenol, Nyquil. All that junk. For lightweights. I shuffle through all of it. I find a first-aid kit in the back of the cabinet, cloaked behind the curtain of bottles.

I grab it and walk back to Becca's room. She's on the floor, bleeding. Her teeth touch at the tips and her lips are open around them. Her eyes are dim beneath half-closed lids.

"I'm sorry," she says to the wall, throaty, airy.

"It's okay," I say, and I wrap the bandages around her forearm, and the blood spreads into a small red-brown inkblot. She looks up at me. Her eyes are the reversed white and black of the moon against night. Her eyebrows bend in a tragic arc, broken by the bridge of her nose. Her straight, dark brown hair hangs dead and limp.

In my head, the red scratch is still there, not deep enough.

"Why did you do this?"

"It's stupid."

"I'm sure it isn't."

"You'll think it's stupid."

"Try me."

"No." Her lower lip quivers. Her eyes are wet.

"Do you want water or something?"

"Yes, Henry, what I need is water."

"Well, what the fuck, I don't know what to do! What do you want?"

She sits up and props up her knees, resting her bandaged forearms flat against them, laying her head down sideways.

"Come sit here and hold me," she says. Her mouth is closed small and her eyes look into mine.

"Okay," I say. I sit next to her. I put my arm around her back and wrap it around her body. She starts crying. I feel myself breathe. Small drops of dark blood stain the carpet. It's on Becca's hands. Her lips are trembling so you can just make out her bottom teeth and gums.

She cries softly and I feel the warmth on my chest. Slowly, she stops and her body feels asleep.

I stare at her white wall and the open crack in the door to her room.

I want to say something perfect. I could rub her back and whisper that it will be okay, or I could tell her that she has every reason to live. I could. My eyes crawl up and down the room, and I see the razor sitting in blood against the wall. Becca walked into the bathroom and took a razor out of a drawer and walked back to her room and thought whatever she thought and pressed the small, cold blades against her soft, white arm until blood came up. Trickling down her forearm. I wonder what she thought when she saw it. I wonder if she'd ever done it before. Was there a last straw?

The cut was shallow, pink, a slit. Would Becca do this for attention? For my attention? If so, she went a little overboard with the theatrics. She could have called to tell me she stubbed her toe and needed some companionship, and I'd have been here with an ice pack.

The blood clots quickly against the white cloth like the drying stains on the carpet. Becca breathes drowsily on my chest. I look at my watch and then down at her hair.

And I can't help but feel a little guilty.

Her parents get divorced, she comes to me. She cuts herself, she comes to me. It's going to start looking suspicious.

I rub her back and she looks up at me, her hand resting on my chest.

She says, "I can feel your heart beat."

When she says it, I can almost feel it myself, pulsing, dictating my breathing. I say, "Do you want to go get a burger?"

"I'm a vegetarian."

"I know that."

"Right."

"A salad then?"

She doesn't say anything.

"If you just want to go to bed, I understand."

"I'll go," she says. "I'm just going to change into long sleeves."

"Okay."

I walk outside her room. The house is even darker now. She closes the door and emerges seconds later in a gray shirt, sleeves hanging limp past her knuckles.

"Okay, let's go," she says.

We walk outside. I take the keys from my pocket and click the doors open. Jake's Diner is over the expressway and we sit in the car. I can't stop glancing at Becca. She won't look at me. When we get there, I park and we get out. The diner is a big silver trailer. We get in and I tell the hostess, "Two," and she walks us to a booth. The lighting inside is strange.

We sit down across from each other, the table feeling too big, the space between us too far.

"Were you trying to kill yourself?"

"No, I was trying to draw a portrait."

"I just meant you were maybe, I don't know. Maybe you just wanted to feel that or something."

"I know. I'm sorry. It was that a little bit."

"Well, what is it?"

Her hands move in speaking gestures and her mouth opens to talk. She breathes uncomfortably.

"Nothing. I'm fine. Let's just talk about something else."

"How can you expect me to?"

"I don't know. I'm sorry. Please."

"Okay."

"Okay, thank you. What's good here?"

"The wraps are good."

I watch her eyes scan slowly down the menu and then scroll quickly reading the description. I can't look away from her. She looks up at me a few times. She bites her lips and puts her head down on her arms against the table. Her eyes pan up to mine. She breathes out.

"I don't know what to tell you, Henry."

"Don't worry. Everything's going to be okay now."

She smiles and shakes her head and turns away from me.

"What?" I say.

She opens her mouth crooked to say something. "I don't know."

"Tell me."

"What do you want to know?"

"Why did you do this?"

"Fuck, can't you fucking just let it die?" Our eyes lock. "So to speak," she adds. She smiles, I don't.

I put my hands on the table. "I can't. I care about you and I want to know what happened."

She enunciates every word and says, "If you care about me, you'll leave it alone because it hurts me to think about right now. Okay?"

I mumble, "Okay."

"Fantastic."

She runs her fingers through her hair. A waiter walks to us. He looks at me and down at his pad. "I'm not getting anything," I say.

Becca gives me an annoyed look. He looks at her. "Whatever, I'm not getting anything, either," she says to me.

The waiter looks at us. "I mean, one of you has to get something."

"I don't know, then, whatever, do you want anything?" I ask him.

"Sorry?"

"I don't know. Forget it. Whatever. Get me a cheeseburger and a Coke."

"All right. Can I start you off with an appetizer?"

"No."

"All right, and today's specials are —"

"That's all, thanks."

"Um, just give me a second. The specials are the Cuban sandwich, which comes with —"

"Thanks, we don't want any."

"Well. We have to read the specials."

"But we don't want it."

"Uh. You may be surprised. We have the Cuban sandwich, which comes with —"

"Please."

"Which comes with, uh, black beans and rice. And we also have a seafood platter special, which has fried shrimp, calamari, and conch fritters. And the soup of the day is lobster bisque. And, um, clam chowder also."

"Okay."

"Can I get you any of those?"

"No."

"Okay."

"Thanks."

"All right."

"I'll have the vegetable soup," Becca says.

"The lobster bisque?"

"No, um. Just the vegetable."

"Oh," he says. He looks sad as he walks away.

Becca shrugs.

"People are ridiculous."

"Yeah," she says, and smiles like someone who never really learned how.

"I missed you," I say.

She nods slowly and looks at my forehead and then my eyes. "I missed you, too."

"It's hard. After so long."

"Yeah. It's . . . hard to adjust sometimes."

I nod. "It's just really tough getting used to everything. When you're used to always being able to, I don't know . . ."

"It's hard not to have someone to call when you wake up in the middle of the night."

I breathe out. "Yeah."

"But look," she says. "Here we are."

"I took it pretty bad."

"It wasn't easy for either of us."

"I don't know. I think I took it worse than you somehow."

She smiles a half smile and holds up her wrist, her sleeve up to the end of her thumb and says, "Do you think so?"

I let out a laugh and look at my silverware. "Maybe not."

"No," she says, and nods and smiles to herself, eyes on the floor. "Maybe not."

The waiter comes with my Coke, a big, curvy diner glass with crushed ice and a straw. "So that's what all this was about?" I ask.

"What?" she says.

"The cutting? Was about our breakup?"

"Oh, God. I bet you'd like that."

"What the fuck's that supposed to mean?"

"Oh, calm down."

"Two seconds ago, you just said that the cutting was about —"

She puts her hand up and dismisses me: "I know, I know what I said."

"Well, what then?"

"What, are you just trying to figure out all the techniques you can use to get it out of me?"

"See, you don't even care about telling me or not, you just want to know something I don't."

"Yeah, that's right, Henry, this is all to spite you."

"That's not what I'm saying."

"Well, what *are* you saying?"

"I just meant it was difficult to deal with things alone."

"I said I missed you. I'm sorry that I didn't miss you enough to cut my wrists."

"I wasn't saying you did."

She tilts her head. "Well, what are you saying?"

"Whatever."

"I just felt alone — like completely alone. That's all."

"You could have called me anytime."

She throws her hands up. "Yeah, I guess I could have."

"What? What now?"

"No, you're right, I should have called."

"Fuck, Becca, I'm only trying to help." I feel the soft of my fist go down against the table and we both jump.

"I appreciate the offer, but calling you wouldn't have solved anything."

"Well, I'm not saying I know the answers to all your problems, but it can't hurt to have someone to talk to."

"It's different, though. I mean, yeah, the problem was that I felt alone, but I'd put myself there —"

"Well —"

"Just listen. Shit. The second I try to tell you you're already cutting me off."

"I'm sorry."

"It's fine. What was I saying?"

I open my mouth and look at my Coke.

"Okay," she says. "I put myself there — alone — for a reason. I didn't want to have to always rely on you for everything. I didn't want to be a — I was too dependent on you. It was like I needed you to be able to be happy. I didn't want to need someone that much."

She looks at me thoughtfully. "I don't know," she goes on. "I felt like I was useless somehow. I wanted to know that I could be okay on my own."

"Becca," I say, "you're one of the strongest, smartest, most independent people I know. You're not useless. But you should know that I want to help."

"Yeah, yeah, yeah," she says, "thanks, but that's not what I need. I didn't break up with you to make sure I needed you. I broke up with you because I don't need you."

I don't say anything. Then I say, "Oh."

"Oh, come on. I don't mean it that way. You don't need me, either. None of us needs anyone else. We're human beings. Clinging to each other is absurd, and it's not any fucking kind of way to live. I'm not even seventeen years old. I don't want to acquire any bad habits. I don't want to be married now."

And cue the automatic brain signals —

Other guys, other guys, other guys, other guys

"Well, were there other guys or something on your mind?"

"Not at all, actually. It was pretty much the opposite. I didn't want other guys. I didn't want *any* guys. I just wanted some time to myself. Except, I wasn't really *finding* anything. And I started getting really depressed. That's the only time the idea of doing something with other guys crossed my mind. I thought maybe it would make me feel better about myself. I mean, you and I were both single for the first time in a year — it's not such a huge coincidence we were both at that party that night. Of course, being there just made me feel worse." She stops, looking across for a long time, twisting something quietly in her head. "But the whole idea of other guys . . . it was only, if there *were* other guys I didn't want to have to worry at every turn and watch my words and dance around subjects in conversation."

"Oh, come on."

"Oh, come on, what?"

"That's bullshit. You'd love to watch my reaction to whatever guy story you have that *accidentally* slips out."

She nods, and then she smiles. She really looks at me now. "We're all bad people in different ways," she says. "Don't assume I want the same rise out of you that you want out of me."

"Why did you call me?"

"I don't know. What is it that you're looking for? That it was a cry for help? Fine, maybe it was. Big deal. It didn't solve anything."

"Do you still want to die?"

"It's not that I wanted to *die*. I didn't even think of it in terms of that. I just wanted . . . I wanted control, I guess? God, it sounds so stupid now — any way I describe it sounds like one of those teen magazine true stories. But . . . no. I don't want to die."

"Well, what *do* you want?"

She stops, wrinkles her eyebrows together, and opens her mouth to breathe in.

The waiter comes with the food. Becca smiles politely at him to break her eye contact with me. He places the bowl down in front of her, with a spoon hanging off the edge of the saucer. She puts the spoon in the soup and moves it around a little, looking through the bowl.

"Becca?" I say.

She's frustrated and she says, "I don't know, Henry."

"Are we going to get back together?"

"I don't know. Is that really such a good idea?"

"Well, then why did you bring me here?"

"Can't we interact on the same plane of existence without needing to be boyfriend and girlfriend? Is that what you thought this was? Some intricate scheme? My big, showy way of asking you back out?"

"Oh, please," I say.

"Well, isn't that what you're saying? That I went through all of this because I was too nervous to ask you back out? That I cut myself so I could throw myself back at you, back into a dependent, needy role, the insecure girlfriend, and you the dashing hero, come to save things, to whisper sweet nothings in my ear and save the day?"

"No." Okay, maybe yes. It crossed my mind.

"Look. I don't know what I want. But a boyfriend's not what it is. I still need to find myself and figure things out on my own."

"What do you mean you need to figure things out on your own?" I ask. "What's so terrible about your life? Didn't what we had mean anything to you?"

"That has nothing to do with this."

"Well, wasn't it good?"

"Sometimes."

"Weren't you okay then?"

"Yeah, I guess. I don't know."

"You were. You were great. Up until the very last days, everything was great. It was perfect. What we had was just a slump. Nothing. Something we could have gotten over and emerged from better and stronger. It's like you were just trying to find a way out. Like you wanted it to come crashing down to an end. If everything's okay, why does it have to end?"

Her eyes penetrate me, and she seems so sad and so angry, so unsure. "Because, Henry! Because how can I *know* that this is okay? And what if I'm not content with okay? What if I want my life to be something more valuable than a long series of things that were okay?"

"You're twisting my words," I say.

"I can't twist your words unless they were flexible to begin with."

"Fine, let's just go," I say.

"Whatever," she says. She frowns and looks at her hands. "Before we go, though, I just want you to know that I still want us to be friends. I don't want us to mean nothing to each other just because we aren't going out or whatever."

"Yeah, yeah, yeah."

"I mean it, Henry."

"Well, before we go, while we're on the subject, I want to finish my cheeseburger," I say.

"We should probably get the check, too," she says.

I take a bite of my burger and chew.

I lean back against the booth.

We both exhale.

17

THE BIG TRIGGER WAS WHEN I PASSED OUT and no one could get me up. That was the catalyst into the world of pills and PTSD.

After the hurricane, I told my parents what happened. They saw the house — shingles and concrete. I think they felt responsible. They said that they were so sorry, that they would stop being away so much.

"What's important," they said, "is that you're okay."

I thought about it. I tried to think of examples of things that were okay. Dogs. Dogs were okay. I was not a dog, though. Cherry Coke was okay. Football was okay.

4. Connecticut
5. Chalk
6. Nail clippers
7. Comedy Central

All these things were okay, but I was not any of them.

After the hurricane everyone wanted to know if I was these two letters.

"Yes," I said.

That's all you have to say. If you're not going to go out of your way for attention, people aren't just going to give it to you for free.

Becca was sitting on her bed with her legs beneath her. It was after the storm, and she said, "Henry, what's wrong?"

I said, "Nothing." I didn't smile, I just said it. I was wondering whether I was trying to get sympathy. Whether I would have just smiled if I wasn't. Smiling is pretty easy to fake. It was possible that this was for attention. I felt horrible enough, though. I was sitting on a chair. She got up from the bed and took me by the hand onto the bed with her. I smiled a little then, but the smile was sad and fake-looking I knew.

"Look at me," she said. She took my face in her hands. "I want to know what this is."

The day before, we had been making out. Then I heard tapping on the glass of her window and that was it. The rain sounded like pebbles against the side of the house. I saw everything all at once, closing in around me, my throat tightening, the air, Rachel Flagler, the wind all around me. I was on my knees in Becca's room trying to breathe. She was jumping around. My vision was flying back and forth between Becca and the hurricane. After a little while, I got myself together. That was the first of it. Of what the doctors called "re-experiencing."

I told her I'd better get home and I left. I was thinking, Fuck fuck fuck fuck fuck fuck fuck fuck thunder death lightning rachel flagler rain responsibility becca fuck abandonment destruction rubble trees water dog gutter shit alone completely utterly completely I walked home in the rain and fuck fuck I had no idea what to do I had no idea what was happening to me.

And I was thinking, Okay okay okay I am crazy absolutely I am insane what the fuck what the fuck has happened to me what the fuck why why the fuck did this happen to me why the fuck did my parents fucking do this why the fuck don't they fucking care don't they care do they care do they even care at all no of course of course they don't fucking bastards fucking children fucking selfish bastards.

I wondered if it would happen again. If I would have these breakdowns now, if this was my new life. Walking home in the rain, the entire time my gut in my neck, feeling that with the slightest touch I'd puke up every organ in my body. I got home for dinner and everyone was on their best behavior, being super-extra-post-hurricane nice to me.

Oh, hi! You were at *Becca's*? How *is* that old girl?

And all I could think of was myself, pathetic, disgusting, sub-human, on my knees in Becca's room.

And out the window, behind my parents' smiling plastic faces, was the rain, pouring, laughing. The food in front of me, all around me, the smell. Coke and water. Forks, silverware. I felt my mouth, open, unmoving. The rain shushed on and on.

I knew I was going to throw up. I stalked over to the sink and let myself empty whatever I could. I threw up, and then everything was gone until my eyes focused slowly on the painted white hospital ceiling.

At the hospital, they heard the whole story. "So take this medicine," they said.

And this.

"And this."

And these.

"And these."

The day after I blacked out, they let me go back home. Becca held my head in her hands and said, "Is this about the hurricane?" I didn't tell her I had been at the hospital.

"I don't know."

She slanted her mouth. Those red lips, if lips could break your heart, they would look like Becca's did.

I was terrified of kissing her. I was afraid I would freak out in the middle, throw up in her face or something. I didn't know. And the more you tell your mind not to think about something, the more it does.

So, you tell yourself, when you're kissing Becca, don't think about THE HURRICANE. Under no circumstances should you think about THE HORRIBLE STORM THAT DESTROYED YOUR HOUSE WHEN YOUR PARENTS WERE GONE GONE GONE GONE GONE GONE GONE. Don't think about THE RAIN. Just don't think about it. Think about something nice.

Ha-ha-ha.

Okay.

That afternoon, I left Becca's to go see Rachel. I told her about the pills. She didn't pry. We sat talking in her den for a long time. I knew that soon Rachel would be out of my life. She had to be. It made things easy.

The episodes didn't stop after that first day in the hospital. As soon as I got home, it was happening again. Re-experiencing. I thought, couldn't it just be that one time at Becca's? Wasn't that enough for whoever wanted to punish me?

In the middle ages after the plague killed everyone, those spared wondered what it meant. What was God trying to say? What was He trying to tell the world? Some abused themselves. Others went insane. Why had this happened to them? They felt lost and confused and alone.

I wonder what those not spared felt. I don't know what it feels like when the infection of blood leads to subcutaneous hemorrhaging, causing painful black splotches on the skin and swollen lymph nodes, accompanied by fever, delirium, and death. But I know what it's like to wonder why. It's crap, let me tell you.

And they dragged me back to the hospital every few days, and the doctors said, "And how long have you been experiencing these episodes?"

"And why didn't you mention that before?"

They moved me to a special wing or ward or whatever it was.

"They just left you at home by yourself?"

"Weren't there storm warnings days before?"

"How did that make you feel?"

"How does this make you feel?"

"And how do you feel about that?"

I don't know. Bad?

In Becca's room with the lights out, after I told her what had been going on, she kept asking me to talk to her about it. I didn't see how she could help. And she never did help, really.

"I just think it would be good for you to have someone to talk to."

"I know."

"So why won't you let me?"

"There's nothing to help. This is ridiculous anyway. This whole thing, I feel completely ridiculous."

"Don't."

"Well, I do."

"Well, you shouldn't."

"Okay, fine, I don't anymore."

"Whatever, Henry. Nothing I say is going to do any good. Maybe you should just go."

"Yeah, yeah, fine." So I left.

And I went to Rachel's house, where it was all so simple, so fleeting.

"And these are visions you're having, or just memories?"

Yes, visions. Or maybe just memories. I don't know.

"And does it have any physical manifestation?"

I throw up sometimes. I lose reality.

"And do these episodes occur frequently?"

What do you mean, frequently?

"Does this happen often?"

More often than it happens to most people, I would think.

Then they write a lot on their pads. They didn't give me one therapist. I had a revolving door. They were all on varying levels of pompous, talking to me like a deaf foreigner. Slowly, loudly, enunciating. With calm, smarmy *Uh-huhs* and *Mm-hms*.

Within a couple weeks, they had all the pills for me. We decided to see how effective they were as we went along.

I stopped seeing Rachel. I stopped taking her calls. She didn't understand. And the more I pushed her away, the more she persisted. She was getting too attached, too clingy. I shut her out. She stopped calling.

And I remember one time specifically, I remember standing with Becca at the front of her house with a big, broad mirror on the wall. She was facing the mirror, getting something in her purse from the counter at the entrance. I was behind her, looking off, looking sad. I remember working up just the right face of hopelessness and desperation, so when she would accidentally glance at me in the mirror, she would find my reflection, just the utter countenance of despair.

And it worked, too. She said, "What's wrong?" And if you just try not to think about it, you can pretend you're being genuine. Especially when you really do feel that way.

But it didn't matter. All of my inner turmoil was seconds from disappearing — because now I had pills. And with the pills everything would change. Science and medicine and psychology and history were on my side. Logic. Because things made sense. And things could be reduced to models.

Everything was going to be A-okay.

The night Becca cuts herself, I can't sleep. In the car, my head is screaming, bloodcurdling shrieks, raging, an angry black sea. Becca is on my right, looking out the window. It's raining a little, but my body suppresses everything now. I think about

Becca, about the stupid attention-cuts in her arm. I know what she's doing. She dragged me here because she couldn't bear for me to be over her. She needed to call me, to remind me how much I want her, just so she could tell me that I'm not "what she needs right now" because she's too busy finding her inner-Buddha or whatever.

Fuck.

The highway lights float past us and I think, Okay: Let us be rational about this. On a conscious level, no way is Becca thinking she's trying to do this to me. So what is she *thinking*? What *was* she thinking? Was I on her mind at the same time as the blade? Too many questions and I have nothing.

Okay, so maybe she's thinking that she cut herself

A. To kill herself. No. She said herself that wasn't it. And I don't believe she'd really kill herself anyway.

B. To *feel* (?) something. But what does that even mean exactly? She wanted to know she was still alive? I don't know — you always know you're alive. Why is pain more indicative of life than boredom, or anything else for that matter?

C. To get attention. This is a big possibility in any/every situation — the inevitability of living with other human beings.

D. For control. But even still — control? What, like control of her body or something? For that she could braid her hair.

Having debunked any other possible explanation for Becca's self-mutilation, only one conclusion holds:

Becca wants me — desperately — and needed to get me to notice her.

Okay, okay, I understand that that's not true — but why not? I mean, she came to me for comfort. She wasn't going to bleed to death. She just wanted me to see. *Look! Look what I've done! I am such an interesting individual! I am so twisted and deep and troubled!* Without me to hold witness, she wouldn't be the Becca Tuttle Character, she would just be a girl with shallow cuts in her wrist.

But if it was just a matter of getting me to notice her, why doesn't she want us to be together now? I gave her what she wanted, now where's the payoff?

In some great leap of asceticism, has Becca created a dichotomy of what has always been a unified phenomenon for me? Is it *What Becca Wants* vs. *What Becca Needs*?

And she thinks — okay, I *want* to be with Henry, but I *need* some time on my own with Buddha, et al.

Is she purposely depriving herself of what is comfortable and convenient in order to work toward the possible greater good of self-fulfillment? She is!

Wow.

What a bunch of total bullshit.

Becca looks at me now. Her eyes are almost desperate.

"What?" I say. I don't look up from the road.

"Nothing." She wants to tell me. I want her to tell me. But then someone would have to stoop to the foulness of actually caring, which concedes the loss of all power.

It's not going to be me.

"Henry. Can we be mature for one second?"

I smile. "One," I say. She looks at me, smiling, and I look at her.

"Thanks, that's exactly what I meant." My eyes are back on the road. She says, "I do care about you, you know. Despite what you may think."

I nod, but it doesn't mean anything to me.

"I do," she says. "Don't nod just to humor me — I'm serious."

"Okay, well I guess I just don't understand this whole thing, this whole cutting yourself and needing to be alone. I mean, what — you want to find yourself or whatever?"

"Oh, please, don't reduce me to a cliché."

"Isn't that what it is?"

She looks back out the window. "Yeah, I guess so," she says. "Just more senseless teen angst crap."

I nod. "Yeah, pretty much."

She looks at me, slowly shaking her head. "You judge me so much."

"Becca, please —"

"You do. You judge everything so much. That's why I could never be with you when I'm feeling like this, when I'm questioning things. I mean it when I say I care about you, but you are such a narrow-minded judgmental asshole."

"Oh, and you're just this tolerant, broad-minded saint."

"Well, look how you're treating me! Need I remind you of your *own* little psychological quirks? And what did I do? I tried to *help* and *be there for you*. You pushed me away, of course, because you were ashamed. But I'm not ashamed. I don't know everything about why or even how I feel right now, but I'm trying to understand. I'm not trying to run away." We pull into her driveway.

"We're here," I say to the steering wheel.

"Do you understand what I'm saying?"

"Sure."

"Henry, look at me."

I look. "What?"

"Do you understand why I'm doing this?"

"I don't know. I might be too blinded by my own sense of shame and fear."

"Whatever," she says, and shuts the door.

Yeah, yeah. Go kill yourself.

I drive home, park, and stumble into bed. My dad is in the living room watching TV. He calls my name. I say, "What?" into the pillow.

"Hey, come in here."

I roll onto the carpet and drag myself into the room.

"What's up?"

"Nothing."

"What are you doing?"

"Sleeping."

"Come watch this thing with me."

"What is it?"

"Look." I glance at the screen. It's some program about the Rock and Roll Hall of Fame. Some retrospective. Green Day is on, playing Ramones' songs.

"I like these guys," he says.

"Yeah, they're good."

The lights are dimmed and I lean my head against the couch.

"Where's Mom?" I ask.

"She's getting home tomorrow." He doesn't look up from the screen.

"Where is she, though?"

"Seattle?"

"Hard to keep track."

He laughs. "Yeah."

I keep watching the show.

"Hey, listen, I thought maybe I'd take you to a Dolphins game sometime, or maybe we'd go play golf or something sometime."

"Okay."

"I mean it, you know."

"I know."

"You sound skeptical."

"What reason have I to be skeptical?"

"Just wait." He points his finger at me. He's a good guy, I think. It's too bad.

Lying in bed that night, I think I could have handled the Becca situation better. I wonder if it's true, though — if Becca just wants to be some movie character. I guess everyone does. I smile and realize that I sort of liked it when she called me a narrow-minded judgmental bastard. It meant I had *traits*, that I was a real person. That she thought about me enough to determine I had a nature.

It means I don't have to float around trying to figure out who the hell I am. (and, for the record,

narrow-minded: *resolute*

judgmental: *judicious*

bastard: . . . well, at least I'm not a nice guy.)

I think about Charlie, how a night like this would never happen with Charlie. There are no ex-girlfriends or aloof parents in Charlie's world. Just sing-along weddings and funny, angry, stupid TV protesters. With Charlie, there aren't moral dilemmas. There's not even a future — just *now* and what feels good *now*.

I think about it being eleventh grade and how I can't believe it. How I'm going to be at college soon. Good. I'll be the fuck out of here. If I can get in anywhere, that is. And if I can't get in anywhere, I'll just leave. One way or the other, after high school, this fucking city is going to be behind me forever. Maybe my relationship with my parents will improve after that. Or maybe they'll just look back, wistfully, wondering what happened to their son. Oh, well, they had plenty of chances. I don't care anymore. Anyway, I wonder about what the fuck I'm going to do with myself. How I'm going to make any money so I can live. Certainly there's nothing I really want to do. There are things I *could* do, but it's just meaningless, just to make ends meet. So great. I'll get out of high school and not get accepted to college anywhere — or get accepted to college, either way — and end up with some lousy, shitty job because I don't like anything enough or I'm not talented or motivated enough to do anything decent. Fine, great.

And what's Becca going to do? Same as me. Same as everyone. We're all in this together, besides Charlie.

Is that what you have to do then? Steal and cheat and be obnoxious and loud? Yeah, probably. And the thing is, I really like Charlie a lot. That's the worst part. And why? What the fuck is so attractive about Charlie? Why the fuck is *he* invincible?

Because he doesn't have any vulnerability? None at all? It's impossible. There's something. There's something there, something that would get to him. He's a human being like anyone. Smarter, maybe, fine. But still. Fucking Charlie.

I don't care anyway. It's no use, it doesn't make any difference. This is life and it's going to continue to be. With Becca or without her. Regardless of any twisted ninth grader's wet dream I may have had, of course I'm not *marrying* her. Even saying that, I don't completely believe myself. There's a part of me saying: "Hey, you know, it could happen. When she's done with her spiritual quest. You never know, eh?"

Yeah, yeah, yeah, except when you do. Optimism is such crap, I swear. It's funny, me lying around trying to substantiate these stupid bourgeois fantasies, these dreams of marriage and suburban bliss — me, hung up over the things I claim to hate, the things that probably ruined my parents' lives.

So what I should do is be an actor. That would be fantastic. Or just a celebrity. Just someone attractive and rich, worshipped, loved and hated, someone in the eye of the public, to be seen. And oh, God, how I loathe actors, too. The whole idea of putting yourself out there for everyone to see, it's so pretentious, so exhibitionist. It's such a shitty thing to do. To live for the sake of others. Isn't that what it is? Putting on a show. Not just in the movies or in TV, but when you're on magazine covers and giving interviews, you're not living the way everyone else lives. You're living to be seen. You're just being an actor your whole life. And how can you not? How can you just be yourself with that kind of audience? Or with any kind of audience? Even with just one other human being to view your actions? Even in your own presence, how can you know whether you're being yourself or just putting on some show, acting out the role of the movie hero you've created for yourself?

So:

Is that what Charlie's doing?

It seems like the answer has to be yes, but if so, he's doing a good fucking job about it. And if the job is that good, if it's that real, does that just make it his real personality? If he believes it, doesn't that make it so?

I wonder what Charlie's doing right now. Lying in bed at his uncle's house? I can hardly picture it. I can only imagine him somewhere, fucking some girl or doing some crazy shit, actually living his life as a human rather than some gear, some component in this giant appliance that is the world. And how does he get away with it? I have to go to school. I have to do my homework and get grades. Why can't I just drop it all? I'm only doing a half-assed job anyway. Why not just go all the way with it? Yeah, that's what I'll do. Yeah, Henry. That's what you're going to do.

Then — the next day — I get an urge to call Bill. But why? Why not Charlie? Now, when I've barely seen, let alone really spoken to, Bill in (how long?) weeks, maybe — now I want to call Bill. I feel guilty. What is on Bill's mind, even? Last time we talked, he was all wanting to court Rachel Flagler and be her steady guy and give her his school pin or whatever. That was before the first time I even hung out with Charlie. And I wonder what it is. But then it's sort of obvious. If I told Charlie what's been going on with Becca, he'd say . . . *Oh, ha-ha, she wants attention, ha-ha.* Which I guess I agree with, but it's somehow more significant than just that. I don't know.

I don't want to make it more dramatic than it really is but —
whatever — I call Bill.

"Yo," he says.

"Hey, Becca tried to kill herself or something."

"Fuck, are you serious?"

"Yes."

"Shit!"

"Yeah. It was pretty nuts."

"Holy shit, is she in the hospital?"

"No. At least, I don't think so."

"Well, what happened?"

"She cut her wrist."

"A lot?"

"Not too too much."

"*Why?*"

"You know how she is."

"Jesus."

"Yeah. It was pretty fucked up."

"Yeah."

"Anyway, do you want to hang out or something?"

"Sure, what time is it?"

"Like, eleven thirty. Want to grab some lunch or something?"

"Okay."

"Good, come over. I'll order a pizza."

"All right."

I hang up and then order a pizza. An extra-large pepperoni.
I would have asked Bill what he wanted, but he would have said
he didn't care. That used to annoy me. Not really anymore. Or
at least, not right now.

Then Bill's there and we're playing video games. And no one's saying anything about *what have you been up to, we haven't hung out in a long time, what have you been doing, why did you ditch me for Charlie?* and so on.

We're sitting in front of the TV, on the couch and on the floor, drinking Cokes.

"So," he says, "I heard you hooked up with Rachel Flagler."

My chest jumps a little. Someone knocks at the door. We look at each other. He pauses the game. The doorbell rings.

I make some expression and go to the door and pay for the pizza. I bring it to the kitchen and open the box on the table. I grab two paper plates.

We sit down.

"Did you hook up with Rachel Flagler?"

Shit. Just get it over with. "Yeah."

He nods.

"I'm sorry."

"You should have told me."

"I know."

"Well, whatever, it doesn't matter."

I grab a slice of pizza. "I didn't know you still liked her."

"Oh." He takes a slice and bites into it. His eyes are fed up with me.

"What?"

"Nothing."

"No, what is it?"

He puts down the pizza. "Look. Hook up with Rachel Flagler all you want. But don't tell me you didn't know I still *liked* her."

I think about it and I guess that line was just a justification, a sort of self-pardoning *by the way*. The truth is Bill never even entered my mind as far as Rachel went. Rachel was about the hurricane, not about Bill. So did I know he still liked her? What was the difference?

"I mean. I wasn't sure if you did," I say.

"Whatever." He starts eating again.

"Come on, Bill. I'm sorry."

"I know, just forget it."

"No, I really am. Listen." And all this time I never, ever mentioned what happened with Rachel and me to Bill. He knew not to ask me anything about the storm. But it makes a pretty good excuse now. And it's true. "Rachel and I have kind of a history."

He looks up. "You do?"

"Yeah. We do."

"Before Becca?"

"Not exactly."

"Jesus Christ, Henry. During?"

"Let me explain."

"You don't have to explain. Why didn't you tell me?"

"Well, that's what I'm getting into."

"*I* would have told *you*."

"It was during the hurricane."

He takes a sip of soda. "Oh."

We watch TV. Charlie calls later. Bill's in the living room and I go answer my phone in the kitchen. Charlie asks what's going on. With Bill there, I don't know what to tell him.

Charlie says he's bored. "Let's go somewhere," he says. He's eating an apple or something similar.

"Bill's over."

"So? I know Bill."

"You do?"

"Yeah, from poker. Bill can come. It's all good, let's just get the fuck out of here."

"Loser, asshole, cool person?" I say.

"Bill? Loser. I'll be the asshole."

"I'm not sure if this is a good idea."

"What are you talking about?"

"I don't know."

"Okay."

"Okay what?"

"You're worried that Bill and I aren't going to get along, or I'm going to get into some kind of argument with him, or that I'm going to think he's lame and think less of you because you hang out with someone like Bill."

"I don't know. No."

"Come on. You know that could never happen."

"What do you mean?"

"I could never think any less of you. It's physically impossible."

"Oh, go fuck yourself," I say. He laughs. He's happy, the bastard.

"So come. I won't be mean to your stupid boyfriend, come on."

"All right, all right, when do you want to go?"

"Now."

"Let me just shower first."

"Why, you got a hot date? Let's get out of here."

"Fine, fine. Let me at least ask Bill."

I ask him. He tries to think of an excuse not to go, but he can't come up with anything good.

"It will be fun. We'll see a movie or something."

"All right," Bill says, like I'm dragging him to the gallows, like I think this is some fantastic idea.

18

THERE ARE A COUPLE FORMULAS to make movies.

The Retarded AIDS Cry Fest
This one stars a bunch of A-list celebrities who play characters who are either retarded or diseased or dying or have someone close to them who's doing one or more of those things. This is for the Academy Awards. The protagonist — or everyone around him — dies at the end, so we can all learn the difficult truth of life and everything, but only if we realize that life is only difficult and truthful because of how beautiful the beauty of everything is and how wonderful and beautiful we all are deep inside, and how even people with terminal illnesses and cancer and AIDS and mental retardation are beautiful in their own beautiful, retarded ways.

The Feel-Good Teen-Sex Comedy "Romp"
This one stars a bunch of twenty-five- to thirty-year-olds playing high school students or college students, with a lot of talk

about penises and masturbation and a couple shots of breasts. This is really for my demographic. They make pacts a lot and decide they're going to get laid or turn the nerdy girl into prom queen or play tricks on teachers, until eventually Act Two ends and they realize the Big Message — that they really do love the girl, or that they can't let their parents run their lives, or that there is more to life than beer and parties, etc. Then the last scene is back to the funny rompyness so we won't think they're waxing sentimental or anything.

The Creepy Little Kid Supernatural "Chiller"

This is when there are some supernatural forces haunting a house or a hotel or a town or a video, and no adults realize what's going on because of their jaded ways, leaving only a creepy, weird little kid, often with some sort of supernatural powers of his/her own, to figure it out and be tormented by it. Eventually, one or two adults catch on, and are subsequently laughed off by the rational other adults and aided by some "crazy old" superstitious man or woman who speaks slowly and carefully, with phrases like "Sure, every couple years, someone comes here to ask about the old abandoned McGilligan place." Eventually the creepy little kid and his adult helper kill off the evil forces — leaving, of course, enough room for possible resurrection of said forces should a franchise option arise. The little girls also like to sing nursery rhymes a lot, really quietly.

"Then there's the Bruckheimer," I say, "which involves a great deal of explosion and fire, and which stars this invincible hero with some haunting past that has rendered him an incredible badass, who learns to let the sensitive-yet-bad-assed-big-breasted feminist who spews wise cracking remarks into his life. (That's Hollywood's interpretation of feminism: being bitchy and really hot.) About two-thirds in, he, as a result of the explosions and fires and car chases, becomes temporarily disillusioned and questions his own invincibility, but then, thanks, in part, to the inspiring speech of his big-breasted feminist friend, realizes that badasses do *not* question their invincibility, and so, returns to his state of invincible badassedness and does the chick many times."

Bill and Charlie laugh. When I am bitching, I am in top form. Eloquent and casual, words rolling off my tongue like caramel, drizzled. We are in the food court. The lighting is strange. Bright but far away, like the sun from past the asteroid belt.

"What time does the movie start?"

"Twenty minutes," Bill says. He sits uncomfortably.

"Okay, we're fine then."

"Will it be sold out?"

"No."

Charlie doesn't talk. He wears his sunglasses inside like an asshole.

Twilight sun comes in through the skylights. Bill and Charlie have strange orange faces. It's a stop sign lit by headlights reflecting onto a face on a street corner. It's a mall, and everything serves as an artificial substitute for reality. Or something like that.

"You look like an asshole wearing your sunglasses inside."

"Yeah, well," Charlie says, "while this may be the case, I take comfort in knowing I'm not an angsty, dumb-assed, crybaby weiner who bitches about school and life and girls and doesn't do anything to stop it or solve it or make it better, other than piss and moan for sympathy and attention, and scorn others for their lack of authenticity and their hypocrisy — vaguely, happily unaware of my own laundry list of shortcomings."

Bill smiles and looks at me. Charlie shrugs.

"Go fuck yourself, the both of you."

Bill laughs. "I didn't say it."

Charlie drapes an arm behind his chair and tips his hat.

"Your hat's stupid, too."

"You already know where I stand on the issue of your criticism," he says.

"That's not true anyway. I'm aware of my shortcomings."

"Oh?"

"I am." I really am. Charlie doesn't believe me, maybe. Bill doesn't, either. Oh, whatever. Like they're so righteous.

I look at Bill and he stares off somewhere, conscious of it, conscious of his breathing, of the position of his eyebrows, of his hands and feet. He's wondering what Charlie thinks of him. I'm sure he never thought twice about it when we all played poker together — but now Charlie's role has changed. Because of me.

"You done?" Charlie says. I look down at my tray where there's half a pizza and a couple fries.

"Yeah, whatever, let's go get seats."

He grabs the pizza off the plate as I'm about to clear it into the garbage and swallows it. Bill dumps his tray.

We walk through the sludge of bodies. "So where does this movie fall on the Henrometer?" Charlie says.

"Oh, this is the Dick-Tits-Fart Sex Comedy. The stupid older brother of the Feel-Good Teen-Sex Comedy Romp."

"What's the difference?"

"This one doesn't have any delusions about its importance, but it's probably a worse movie all around."

"At least it's not TV," Bill says.

"Amen."

INT. ERIC'S HOUSE - DAY

ERIC, JOHN, and CHRIS are sitting on a couch drinking BEER with ALCOHOL so we can identify with them.

                    CHRIS

    Jesus Christ, John, you sure get your dick stuck in a lot of things.

                    JOHN

    I know it.

Chris takes a swig from the bottle. Then John does. Then Eric. Then John. Then Eric. Then Chris.

                    CHRIS

    I am so drunk. We should go smoke some weed now.

JOHN

Yeah. I smoke weed so often. Smoke, smoke, smoke. That's me. It's because I'm a stoner-slacker, yo.

ERIC

Being a stoner-slacker is mad cool.

CHRIS

I'm going to go get the bong. John don't get your dick stuck in anything while I'm gone.

ERIC

Dildo.

Eric farts. Chris jumps up from his seat and goes into a closet. Eric and John make armpit farts to keep the AUDIENCE'S attention while the plot thickens as Chris rummages in the closet. Chris emerges with the bong.

JOHN

Yo, Chris just came out of the closet.

Eric and John laugh for several minutes.

                    ERIC

   That was a mad good double-entendre, yo.

                    JOHN

   Yeah, dude. I'm an eloquent motherfucker.

                    ERIC

   Someone say balls.

                    CHRIS

   Balls.

                                        CUT TO:

INT. MOVIE THEATER - NIGHT

The audience is roaring with laughter. BILL,
CHARLIE, and I sit slumped over. My feet are up
against the chair in front of me, Bill has his
head resting on his hand, and Charlie is passed
out.

                    ME

   This is ridiculous.

                    BILL

  Yeah, this is horrible.

Charlie snores loudly. A booming profanity
reverberates around the room from the speakers,
and the crowd doubles over, eyes tearing with
mirth.

                              CUT TO:
INT. NICOLE'S HOUSE — EVENING

Chris sits with NICOLE, an attractive twenty-
five-year-old college freshman with enormous
breasts. They are drinking wine.

                  NICOLE

  Oh, Chris. You're such a good friend. I'm
so glad that we don't have to confuse this
with sex.

                  CHRIS

  But Nicole, sex doesn't have to confuse
things.

                  NICOLE

  Yes, it does.

Chris stands up to pour more wine into his glass
and accidentally spills the red liquid all over
Nicole's blouse.

                    NICOLE

   Oh, no! I better take this off.

                    CHRIS

   Uh.

Nicole quickly unbottons her shirt and casts it
aside on the floor.

                    NICOLE

   Oh, no, it's all over my bra, too!

                                        CUT TO:

INT. MOVIE THEATER - NIGHT

It is dark, and the lights from the projector dance on the
heads in front of us. I punch Charlie in the arm to wake him.
"What, what, what the fuck do you want?" he says.
"Come on," I say. "Let's get the fuck out of here."
"All right, all right."
I look over at Bill. "We're leaving?" he asks.
"Yeah," I say, "did you want to stay?"

"No," he says, "this movie is terrible."

"I know."

"Can we still get our money back?"

"I don't know," I say. "We can check."

Charlie scratches his head beneath his hat and looks up. "There are tits on the screen," he says.

Bill nods at him.

We stand up and shuffle to the exit. Everyone's in stitches.

The halls between the theaters are empty. "That was about to become a Feel-Good Sex comedy anyway," I say. We walk through the angled labyrinth. Mega-ultraplex. Screens like vast skies, projecting the images of gods. To be praised. To be worshipped and emulated.

"How?" Bill says.

"With that guy and the girl. The writers were using him as the sensitive guy to make it deal with popularity and sex and being the nice guy and so forth. Very philosophical."

"Yeah, that movie was chock full of social commentary," Charlie says, hands in his pockets.

"The comment was male genitals are funny to make jokes about and breasts are fun to look at," I say.

"Yeah. The comment was never underestimate human stupidity."

"Fucking movies are destroying the world," I say.

"Eh . . ."

"What?"

"You can't blame the movies for providing something society will pay to see. If millions of dollars weren't to be made on dick and fart jokes, no one would invest in them. But the fact is, society hasn't grown up past a fifth-grade human growth and development class. Don't blame movies for the destruction of society; blame society for destruction of the movies."

I stop. "If the film industry provided something better, people would go see that. Good movies would do well."

"Bad movies would do better."

"Yeah, well. Maybe there's a level of responsibility . . ."

"Fuck responsibility."

"Yeah, yeah."

"The film industry doesn't make money based on how responsible they are."

"And making money is the most important thing?"

"To whom? A corporation? No. Family, friends and recreation are the most important thing."

"What about integrity?"

"What about it?" he says.

We get to the box office desk on the interior of the theater. I look past the counter at the restaurants across the hall. In front of us are an older man and woman getting refunds for our movie. The man behind the desk hands them their money and they glide out.

"Can I *help* you?" the guy says, nearly rolling his eyes.

Charlie holds his ticket out and says, "We want to refund these tickets."

The guy grabs the ticket from Charlie's hand and begins studying it. Charlie smiles at me.

"No," he says. I look up.

"What do you mean, no?" Charlie says.

"I can't refund your tickets."

"Well, that's not true."

"Why can't you refund our tickets?" I say.

"Be*cause* you can only refund tickets within the first forty-five minutes of the movie. *Your* movie started fifty minutes ago."

"That's ridiculous," I say.

"Not only is that ridiculous," Charlie says, "it's false. Our movie didn't start until thirty minutes ago at earliest. I didn't pay nine dollars to watch military ads and antipiracy PSAs and listen to Xbox and the Gatorade company brainwash me into buying their shit."

"That's nice, but I still can't let you refund the tickets. Tough break. Enjoy the mall."

My God, I hate this self-satisfaction. I hate that this guy thinks he's smarter than us. "Come on," I say. "Does it really make a difference?"

"Yes, it does make a difference. There's a *difference* between forty-five and fifty, in case you haven't reached that level in math yet."

"Jesus Christ," Charlie says, "we just saw you give those two people a refund for the same movie."

"They weren't giving me this kind of attitude."

"So, what then? You're punishing us for giving you attitude? I thought this was about policy, I didn't realize it was about low-income workers power-tripping on easy targets. And regardless, we didn't give you any kind of attitude until you refused to give us our money."

"It's not *your* money anymore. It's the theater's. You gave it to us. If you don't like the policy, you don't have to come back."

"And I won't, but I'm not leaving until you give us our money back."

"No, you're leaving now. Good-bye." The guy looks a little nervous now. Making him feel this uncomfortable is making me a little uncomfortable. I'm ready to leave. Bill watches, his eyes on the desk.

"Fucking hell, just give us the money. Do they pay you a fucking commission on every customer you're an asshole to? It has no effect on you, other than whatever sense of superiority you derive from playing gatekeeper with a couple teenagers, just give it back to us."

"No."

This is nine dollars we're talking about. But I know Charlie isn't going to leave now.

"Listen," I say, "can we please just have the money? We'll go away. We won't bother you anymore."

"You guys are not going to bully me into breaking the rules. I'm calling security."

"Security?" Charlie says. "You're telling on us to your big brothers? Who's bullying who?"

The clerk picks up the phone and starts dialing slowly, staring at us.

"Holy fucking hell," Charlie says. He grabs a pair of scissors off the desk and cuts the phone cord in half in a single motion, sheathing the office supply in his pocket. He grabs the phone by its broken cord from beneath the man's ear and lobs it across the desk of the box office and into the corridor of the mall. He jumps over the desk and puts his arm around the clerk.

"Can we please just have our money back, please. We're customers, just like anyone else. You played a bad movie, and we want our money back. Is that really so much to ask?"

A couple people walk by.

Charlie smiles and winks at them. "It's okay, we're friends," he says.

The guy is trembling. He's afraid of the scissors. Charlie takes a step back from him and puts a comforting hand on his shoulder.

"Look: I don't have a problem with you; you don't have a problem with me. I'd like to think we could be friends. I didn't want to make a mess. I'm sorry about it. It's just that I see you giving those two people back there their money, and then you say no to us, and it's just not reasonable, you know?"

I look at Bill. He looks at me and shrugs, speechless, eyes open. We're the audience.

"Now come on. Let's start with a clean slate. My name's Charlie, what's yours?"

"Karl."

"Karl," Charlie says. "Fantastic. Can we please have our money back, Karl."

Karl gets twenty-seven dollars out of the register and gives it to Charlie. Charlie looks at it for a few seconds and then makes a sour face.

"No, Karl, I can't take this from you. I want you to have it. But I don't want you to put it in that damn machine there. That goddamn machine is evil. I want you to really have it. It's yours. Put it in your wallet, get a haircut, buy a shirt." Charlie smiles. "Hell, Karl, you can shred it and decorate your apartment with the pieces for all I care. I just want you to know there are no hard feelings and we're all friends. Is that okay with you, Karl?"

"It's okay," Karl says. And he actually looks kind of happy somehow. He seems to feel that everything's okay.

Karl and Charlie shake hands. "You're a good man, Karl. Don't let anyone tell you otherwise."

We leave the theater, and I am so shocked that it takes me about forty seconds of walking before I start laughing.

Even Bill laughs.

What the fuck just happened here?

I'm not sure, but Charlie doesn't say a word. He just keeps on walking, hands in his pockets. He stops for a second and looks down at the cold mall tile. He picks up the phone receiver, a few inches of cord still attached, and puts it in his pocket. A trophy, I guess. Something to remember his new friend by.

We keep walking.

Bill walks next to him, laughing.

"Who the fuck *are* you?" Bill says.

Charlie looks over at me and smiles, then back at Bill.

He tips his hat.

"Charlie Brickell," he says. It's over the top. He knows this.

The escalator carries us down the empty skeleton of plaster. It feels late around my eyes. Gliding down, I ask, "What now?"

Charlie shrugs. "There's some party over in —"

"No, no more parties," I say, thinking of Becca, of Rachel. "Bill?"

"I don't care."

"You guys can come over if you want," I say. "We could hang out there until we figure out something to do."

The mall is empty, closed, stores locked away in their prison cells. Every footstep echoes and rings on the slick tile. We talk and laugh as we leave, through the automatic sliding doors and across the exterior of cafés and into the parking lot.

In front of my house is one palm tree and across from the tree, on the other side of the street, is a lamppost. Bill and I park in my driveway. I twist the key and turn off the car. Charlie parks behind us and gets out. We get out to meet him.

"Why am I wearing this hat?" he says.

"What do you mean?"

"Just what I said."

"I don't know, to keep your head warm."

"Wrong."

"Because it looks cool?"

"Why should I be concerned with looking cool?"

"Because you want to be cool?"

"Can't I be cool without a stupid hat?"

"I guess not," I say. "What's the point of this?"

"Nothing, here." He puts the hat on my head.

I am Charlie Brickell. How does it feel — this hat atop my head? Am I Charlie Brickell if I think I am?

?Do any of us know who we are

!Of course

?How can we

!We simply do, we wake up each morning in our same skin and grow slowly accustomed to our person

?Is this truly knowledge of the self

!Yes, what more knowledge do you desire

?Something more abstract

!Abstractions cloud what can be seen clearly in a bathroom mirror

?So what about the acts and the charades and the parading around

!Acknowledging them is impressive, but possibly counter-productive

?Counterproductive

!We use these acts to achieve our ends, making people feel guilty or think we are cool or feel whatever emotion we theatrically instill in them — if we acknowledge all acts . . .

?We are reduced to nothing

!Exactly

?Because

!Because it is all an act, really . . . when we cease acting we are left with gray, unavoidable immobility

?So to act is to

!To act is to exist . . . consciousness of this action will simply undermine us and drive us insane

?But how can one avoid consciousness

!One cannot

?Can't one

!No

?Therefore

!Therefore the more conscious we become, the further removed we become from our existence

?Which is bad

!Which is very bad

"Let's get a coconut," Charlie says.

"From where?" I say.

"From your tree."

I look up at the towering palm. I had never noticed the coconuts.

Bill stands looking up with his hands on his hips.

"How are we supposed to get it?" I say.

Charlie surveys the tree, its lack of crooks or branches. He puts his arms around it and shakes it from the base. Nothing happens. We stand aside. He picks a rock up from the ground and chucks it at the coconut. It bounces off, back onto the ground.

He looks at us. "Give me a boost," he says. Charlie takes off his shoes and throws them aside on the grass. Bill and I knit our fingers, and Charlie steps into my hands and then into Bill's. Charlie is in the air and he reaches above his head. "Just a little higher." We push him up.

"I think I got it," he says. "Just a little . . . more . . ."

We push higher, his feet pressing against our hands and our chests, and the strain is so much, and his legs push back against us, and he says something and we all fall.

"Goddamn it," he says. "I had it. One more time."

Bill and I groan and Charlie smiles and jumps back into our hands. "Have you ever even had a coconut?" I ask.

"No," he says from above us. "How are they?"

"They suck ass."

"Oh, well, just a little higher." He is on his toes, leaning forward against the tree and struggling to reach it. I hear a cracking, tearing noise and Charlie screams out, "Ha!" and falls backward onto the ground with the coconut in his arms.

"Now how do you open this fucking thing?" he asks.

I stand in the middle of the street and look both ways. "Over here," I say, and open my hands. Charlie tosses the coconut at me and walks to the middle of the street. It's heavy and grimy in my hands. I look up at the brim of Charlie's hat on my head.

"Do you hide yourself on purpose?" I say.

Charlie smiles. "Over here." I toss the coconut underhand. He catches it.

"Do you know what I mean?"

"Of course I do."

Bill walks into the street and Charlie tosses the coconut at him.

"Some other time," Charlie says to me.

"God, that movie was bad," Bill says. He tosses the coconut at me. "Who writes shit like that?"

"And the acting," I say.

"It was better than real life," Charlie says.

"Maybe so," Bill says.

The coconut means you can talk. The conch. And I wonder if Bill knows what Charlie's talking about. I wonder if I do.

that real life is an act and that these actors are doing just as good a job as the idiots acting out their lives day to day

Charlie understands exactly, I think.

Eventually, someone drops the coconut and it cracks a little bit. Charlie holds it above his head, his mouth ajar, silhouetted black against the light of the lamppost. Nothing comes out.

"Isn't there supposed to be juice or milk or some shit."

"Yeah."

"Why isn't it coming out?"

"You have to crack it more."

Charlie takes the scissors out of his pocket and stabs at the husk. Bill and I watch. He puts his mouth on the dirty wooden globe.

I look at Bill. "What are you thinking?"

"All this stuff about acting and everything."

"Really?"

"Yeah." My, how profound we have all become.

"Fuck," Charlie says, and slams the coconut on the ground. He takes the phone receiver from his pocket, with its dangling plastic curlicue, and smashes the coconut until it is all in pieces.

It's silly, but Charlie can't look silly. It's our fault that he can't. It would be so good to laugh at him and call him ridiculous and reduce him to nothing, but it's too fundamentally perverse. The broken coconut sits on the ground, a victim of rape and murder, of something catastrophic and antiestablishment and morally repulsive — not like a piece of damaged tropical fruit, but like a landmark in historical rejection and futility.

"Tomorrow I have a surprise for you."

"What is it?"

"You'll see."

When Charlie is in the car taking Bill home, I hang on to the side, my arms in Charlie's window, holding on with everything, and he drives faster and faster down my street, looking at me, until my feet hit the ground and roll under the car and I flail off and skin my knee open, bloody and filled with dirt and pus. Charlie's hat rolls off my head. When my body hits the ground like a sack of basketballs, Charlie stops short and looks back at me. His head cranes out of the window and he says, "Are you okay?"

I wave and look at the blood and the dirt and the palms of my hands. "Yeah," I say.

He drives off with Bill. I think about Bill and Charlie alone in the car. I am not jealous, exactly, but I am something. I pick up Charlie's hat. I wonder what they're talking about as I limp back home and shut the door behind me.

19

I HATE MYSELF FOR DOING THE WORK I'm doing, but I guess I have to go to college. I try to pretend the ends justify the means or something like that.

The college admissions rubric is based on the hours of your life you are willing to waste in their name. The more meaningless after-school shit, community service, clubs, the time you spend studying — the more shit you do that makes you miserable, the reward is they'll take you. It's not such a bad estimate of who will be successful in life, I think, if that's what they're looking for. The more of your existence you'll give up for the sake of other people's ideals, the more successful you'll be. When the ideals become your own, you are officially a mature and sensible human being. An adult.

Doing calculus makes me want to break walls. I open the pill pantry and hold a clear orange bottle between two fingers. All this medicine — I feel ridiculous, pathetic. How much longer will this go on?

Charlie calls and says his order came in.

I say, "What?"

"Do you believe in God?"

"What?"

"Do you?"

"No."

"Good."

"Why?"

"Do you believe you're free?"

"What do you mean?"

"I'm not exactly sure."

"Pick me up."

"Fuck off."

"What do you mean your order came in?"

"I'll be there in a little bit."

I hang up and the phone rings.

"Charlie?"

"It's Rachel."

"Oh."

"Don't sound too excited," she says.

"Oh, no, it's not that, I'm just doing some math. I'm kind of out of it, I guess."

"Sounds fun."

"Yeah, it's a blast, let me tell you." It's funny, this small talk. It's almost as if I didn't hook up with her after the hurricane that changed my life and then abandon her because I was in the middle of a relationship and then not talk to her for almost a year and then hook up with her at a party over a week ago and avoid her since then. Almost.

She laughs a little. "I was wondering if you wanted to hang out or something later."

"Oh. I can't. I have plans."

"Oh, all right."

"Sorry."

"No big deal."

"Maybe some other time, though," I say.

"Okay — how about tomorrow after school," she says.

"Um . . . I'm really not sure Rachel, I might be —"

"Okay, it's fine. Forget it."

Oh, no. I'm being too cruel. I guess I should —

"'Bye," she says, and hangs up. I cringe, hitting the END button.

At around twelve, Charlie picks me up.

The car ride is smooth, like driving over clouds. The windows are rolled down, and the breeze feels good on my face. The air is cool. It's a nice day.

Charlie sits with early afternoon light growing around him and one hand on the wheel, biologically smug. I ask, "Where are we off to?"

"The Garden of Eden," he says.

"Where?"

"You'll see," he says. "Enough with the questions."

I decide to leave it alone and enjoy the ride. Charlie is wearing his leather jacket. His sideburns have curled farther down his jaw, and it looks like he hasn't shaved in a week. I look at my knee, pink and exposed from last night.

We don't take the highway, but rather a bunch of unfamiliar winding roads, free from much traffic or sound. The feeling is welcome. The surrounding area is changing back and forth, from trees to small residential neighborhoods to major commercial areas. Some of it looks dilapidated, brown in the sun, which rises slowly as we drive, like a city carved of wood and mud. Trees line the streets of the neighborhoods, palm trees and oak trees, outlined against the sky.

The small houses make me think of everyone in the world as individuals. The small stores. What are the people in there thinking at this very instant?

And Charlie's asking me, "Do you want to get some lunch?"

I say, "Okay."

We stop at some breakfast place. Some pancake chain. The seats squeak and the table is slick, an ice rink. It reminds me of diners and Becca.

"So, God?" I say.

"What about him?"

"You tell me."

"You denied his existence. You're going to hell."

"Ha ha ha," I say.

And I think his or His? His or Her? O spelled without an h . . . h for heresy and heathen and hell. O Lord. Lordy, lordy, lordy.

"Do you believe in fate?" he says.   *No.*

"No."

"Love at first sight?"   *Rachel?*

"I don't think so."

"Love?"   *Becca?*

"I don't know."

"Do you believe in predestination?"   *Um . . .*

"Isn't that the same as fate?"

"I guess. They're all just words."   *But still . . .*

"I don't," I say. "You don't, do you?"

"I didn't think so, but now it seems   *He can't.*
obvious."

"Obvious that it's true?"

"Sure. That it's the same fate for everyone."   *Ohh . . .*

"You mean we're all going to die?"

"Right."

The waitress comes. "Can I get you fellas something to drink?"

"Coke."

"Water, please."

"What?" he says at my expression.

"I'm not sure if that constitutes fate."

"Doesn't it? It's our ultimate fate. When everything is said and done, the conclusion was already written."

"I feel like fate is something that takes away from your freedom, though. Like something that makes you feel helpless or whatever."

"But death doesn't do that for you?"

"I think of fate as, like, I don't know, a way out of responsibility or whatever. Something to blame the path of your life on."

"Something that makes effort futile?"

"Right."

"So isn't it the same with death?"

"Is it?"

"Sure. You work your ass off for fifty years, or you sit around doing nothing, and you end up dead and underground. Or, better yet, if you devote your life to helping the poor and teaching children to read you end up in the same six-foot hole as serial rapists and murderers."

"That's why you asked if I believed in God?"

"Right. Because if you did, you could say, 'Well, that's why God puts the good guys in heaven and the bad guys in hell.'"

"It would be nice to think that."

"So why don't you?"

"I don't know." I pick up a pink packet of sweetener and shake it between my fingers. "It sounds like a cop-out or something to keep everyone under control. What's that thing Karl Marx said?"

"'Religion is the opiate of the masses.'"

"Right. Yeah. I guess I just think that, first of all, I can't believe in something without evidence. Otherwise it's just arbitrary. Like, why believe in God and not in whatever, Greek gods or whatever, other than that I was raised in that type of society?"

"Are your parents religious?"

"I don't think so."

"And what do you mean 'without evidence'?" he says and smiles, sliding his silverware from the napkin. "It was in a book! A really, really old book."

I nod. The waitress sets down our drinks.

"Ready to order?"

I glance at a menu. "Yeah, I'll have a cheeseburger."

"All righty, and for you?"

"Bacon cheeseburger."

"And can I start you off with some appetizers?"

"No thanks," Charlie says, "you?"

"No, thank you." I take a sip of water. "I still think, what you said about fate I mean, I don't think death is quite the same."

"Because it's a truism."

"Well, yeah, partly. I mean, to live is to die or whatever, but it just seems —"

"Memory," he says, "is the only gauge through which to measure our lives. Without our own memory, it's like we never existed. So after we die, after our memory leaves us forever, it all may as well not have happened. The happiness, the sadness, everything becomes nothing. And what we'd like to think is that making a mark on the world, leaving our name for the history books to read and for the world to learn into infinity, we'd like to believe in our legacy, and that if we just work our asses off or we do something really special and wonderful — even something notorious, we can achieve immortality."

The way Charlie talks, I look for a teleprompter.

"But scientists and inventors and presidents," I say. "People we're forced to learn about and remember, people who society *makes* us remember, do achieve immortality."

"No they don't. They're dead. For all they know, the day after they died, the entire world deemed them buffoons, laughingstocks, or forgot about them altogether."

"Well, I think they can pretty well assume . . ."

"You can't assume anything. I think you lose most of your faculties for assumption when you die anyway."

"So what then, what? We should just roll over and do nothing because we're going to die anyway and it's all useless?"

"I mean, that's up to the individual. Once you acknowledge that, yes, it is useless, and, yes, it is short, and, yes, it is brutal and harsh — that the universe is indifferent to you and will go chugging along after you die whether or not you choose to grace it with your insignificant and entirely unnecessary presence. Once you acknowledge all that, and at least you're being honest with yourself, do whatever the hell you want is my feeling. Just, I don't know, don't harbor any delusions of immortality or importance or whatever."

"Is it so bad? Harboring delusions and thinking you're important?"

"Even when you're not?"

"Even when you're not."

"I mean, I guess it's different for everyone. But yes. I think it's bad to lie to yourself."

"Why?"

He takes a sip of his Coke through the clear, plastic straw. He shrugs. "If you lie to yourself about your own being, about your own nature and importance, you go through existence as . . ."

"As your own audience."

"Yeah," he says. "Exactly."

The car ambles forward through the home stretch. I still don't know where we're going. There's a lull in the conversation, and I say something dumb. I don't spend enough time thinking about it, about the context. But it's on my mind, and some contrary voice inside of me says, "Becca tried to kill herself."

He looks over at me and smiles. "What the fuck does that mean?"

"She cut herself in the wrist."

"Christ. How do you botch that?"

"I don't know."

He shakes his head. "That's such a load of bullshit."

"Why?"

"If you want to kill yourself, you kill yourself. Anything else and you just weren't willing to go far enough to get attention."

He looks back at me. My poker face is on.

"I mean, there are plenty of condos around here to jump off. Or she could just walk into the ocean with some sandbags, that's pretty romantic."

"She wasn't actually trying to kill herself. It was just, y'know, a cut."

"Wow, so she didn't even *bother* with the whole suicide pretense? She was just pretty much admitting, like, yeah, I want attention."

"All right, enough. I shouldn't have said anything."

"I didn't mean to hurt your feelings, baby." He rubs my shoulder with his hand.

"Oh, fuck off," I say and push off his hand. "You're just being an asshole for the sake of being one." I don't want to think about Becca and Charlie in the same notion. Because all that can bring me to is how Becca would want him.

He looks back at the road. "So, tell me about this Becca girl. What's her deal?"

"What do you mean 'what's her deal?'"

"I don't know, is she hot?"

"She's good-looking."

"What is she, your grandma or something?"

"What?"

"You feel weird talking about her like this."

"No. I don't care."

"Did you fuck her?"

"Go fuck yourself."

"Negatory, huh?"

"Whatever, go fucking die."

Charlie smiles. "Did she have good tits? I feel like tits are being overlooked these days."

"They were fine."

"Too bad about the no-fucking thing, though. Especially if she had good tits."

"Go kill yourself."

"Don't joke about stuff like that," he says and looks very happy.

"You pretty happy with yourself, fuckface?"

"I am, now that you mention it."

"I'll bet you are."

"I am."

A development rises through the trees. It's a community of FOR SALE signs. The grass is crew-cut short, flowers, landscaping, and no cars in the driveways. Not one. Stakes dug into the front lawns, crucifixes dangling plastic cards of

HELLO!

I COST ONE MILLION DOLLARS!

I AM PERFECT, WITH HIGH CEILINGS

&

A POOL

&

A WATERSLIDE

&

STUFF!

MARBLE TABLETOPS!

SEVERAL BATHROOMS!

WITH BIDETS!
TO WASH YOUR GENITALS!
&
ANUS!

Charlie rolls by slowly, eyes skimming past the addresses, and then pulls us into a driveway. We get out and look around, out at the great white sky. We stand, Charlie and I, two tiny specks against the vast acres of geometric perfection. We stand awkward, ugly, human.

Charlie walks a little farther, into the center of the street, which stretches on for miles, back and forth, in perfect ninety-degree angles and then in Grecian curves — not just curves, but precise chunks of cosine functions or fractions of pi. The houses are identical, if not in structure then in essence.

Here is your reason for taking high school math. Real-life applications for mathematical principals. Because where would I be if I were not able to correctly identify these concepts in architecture? Lost. Confused.

"What the fuck is this?" Charlie says.

I don't say anything. I think about all the everglades that must have been here. All the dead, little, homeless alligators. I think about Becca and her teen angst sigh against the marsh playing dress-up, the cultivated swamp. *This is what it would be like to die*, she said, *if no one actually wanted to go through the trouble.* God, I wish I could just open Becca back up again. I wish we could talk — without the power struggle, without the superiority — just like two human beings on the same team. God. How *normal*. I miss nice things.

I follow Charlie past his car and behind the house, over cobbled stepping-stones and into the backyard.

There is a large pool and luxurious patio furniture.

"Who furnishes empty houses?" I say.

"The developers."

He leans down. At his feet is a large, cardboard package. He picks it up and holds it in his hands. He shakes it instinctively.

"What is it?"

"I'll show you later."

We go back around to the front of the house and put the package in the backseat of his car.

We stand on the sidewalk, two tiny machines of skin and muscle, blood and chemicals, looking up in the afternoon air. Two small shapes on a long strip of perfection. Charlie and I look at each other.

"Well, this beautiful little hub of perfection is a few months away from being the same hell as everywhere else." He squints and scratches the back of his head.

My eyes trek down the street. "Good," I say.

"It will just be a show. Tricking itself into believing that all these pounds of plaster and concrete represent the truth for the little animals who live inside of them. So fuck it," he says. "Fuck perfection, because it doesn't exist."

I nod. "Not outside of little mathematical equations."

"Well, fuck mathematical equations," he says, eyes gliding past every window, every mailbox, every doorknob and topiary.

"I feel like I'm going to vomit or something. There's something — I don't know, too confident. It's patronizing," I say.

"It's like patting us on the head and telling us everything will be okay."

Charlie looks at me for the first time. "Open up the trunk," he says. "There are two baseball bats and about a dozen cans of spray paint."

The sun moves slowly across the warm afternoon sky to the hushed sounds of hissing and shattering.

We sit in my backyard, looking at the sky. The destruction is still fresh in my mind, and my hands feel strong. I feel human. I try not to think too much about it. I try not to analyze it.

What Charlie did was, he had the package delivered to some vacant house. He called up the delivery service and told them he wouldn't be in, but to leave it out back in the patio. I guess this is something they do. No one has to sign for anything.

It's dark. Charlie finally shows me what's inside the box. He lets me open it.

When I hold it in my hands, the box is lighter than I'd imagined. What could it contain? The human soul? The meaning of life on a small sheet of paper? It seems like it has to be.

Something profound and dangerous, invincible, something I could never fully comprehend.

And it's a case of Frankenberries. The discontinued Frankenstein cereal, part of the original General Mills "Monster Cereal" campaign.

Charlie tells me, mouth full of marshmallows, lips stained pink, that in the 1980s, General Mills came out with three new kinds of cereal: Frankenberries, Count Chocula, and Boo Berries. Strawberry-frosted marshmallow bits, chocolate-frosted marshmallow bits, and blueberry-frosted marshmallow bits, respectively.

"Of course," he says, "the chocolate cereal was the only one that survived."

I look down at my bowl. The milk is pink, and I'm about halfway done. It's my third bowl.

I shovel a spoonful into my mouth, and while chewing, I say, "So. You stole someone's identity so you could buy sixteen boxes of cereal?"

The cereal squashes up and down between his teeth. Through sloshing, crunching noises, he says, "Mm-hm."

I take another bite.

"They're really good," I say.

He raises his eyebrows and nods. "I know."

We're sitting on two lawn chairs, next to a hard, dirty patio table. He puts his bowl down on the floor at his feet and looks up into the sky. You can squint and pretend to see enough stars to make you at one with the universe, but I try not to pretend. I'm just glad to be here, I guess.

"I wish someone would fucking blow up that fucking lamp-post," I say.

Charlie shrugs and puts his hands behind his head.

PART THREE

VILLAINS AND MARTYRS

20

SO THERE WAS FIRST
the hurricane!

with me saying

"My parents are out of town and I didn't feel like making anything."

and Becca saying

"Really, your parents are out of town?"
"Yeah, you know they've been out of town all the time lately. Just this year."
"Yeah, but still, during this storm. Do you want to come here or something? I'm sure my mom wouldn't mind."
"I'm sure I'll be fine."

and then the world ended and I said

"I could have died."

and Rachel barely even said a word.

(four reactions)

I. Rachel

Then I abandoned Rachel and everything. She would
    "Henry? Are you busy?"
    "Actually, right this second I am. Call you back later?"
    "Okay."
    call and call and call and it was so
    FUCKING SUFFOCATING
    that I said
    "Listen, Rachel. I'm really, really . . . It's just. I'm sorry. I
have. I have a girlfriend, you know?"
    "Oh, my God. I didn't . . . I didn't have any . . ."
    "Yeah. So. I don't know, I guess I got caught up in the, um,
the moment and everything and . . ."
    "No, it's . . . I understand."
    "Are you sure?"
    "Uh-huh." But I could tell she was crying. I hung up the
phone and looked at myself in the mirror and didn't even feel
good that she liked me.
    I thought of her hair, orange-red, the color of ripe, ripe
Florida tangerines.

II. Bill

And Bill — he said, *"Jesus!* Thank God you're okay."

"Yeah, I'm all right."

It would have been easier if he'd asked, "Is this due to some manifest psychological response to a recent traumatic experience?"

Then I could have just said yes and have been done with it. Things are never that easy, though. After I started taking the pills, I told Bill what had happened, everything. Every little detail besides one. Bottle after bottle appeared in the pantry until the prescription orange tubes in their various columns turned the shelf into a treasure chest, right down to the fiery glow. It was a little city of the future, cylindrical towers of commerce and discovery, packed in with little film-sealed fifty-milligram men.

"I hope you're not full of shit," he said, "about being okay. Because if you are, I want to know."

III. The Doctors

And you *try* to be good! You tell your body, "No!" Like a bad dog. You tell your mind. Because this, this is all re-experiencing — the first group of symptoms.

Well, who *wouldn't* this happen to?

Because the doctors TELL you about how it's a real live illness and everything, and that you aren't crazy, but that's not what they're saying. They're saying you have a DISORDER. A *mental disorder.* This hurricane might irk some people, sure, but you went fucking nuts. Off-the-deep-end crazy, so take some medicine for your overreacting disorder. For being a big fucking baby. And isn't that what I am? Isn't that what I'm doing — overreacting?

Yes. I say yes. I am overreacting. I acknowledge it, now please make me a person again. What more do I need to say? I'll apologize. I'll grovel. Just make it stop.

And they make it stop. They put you on pills, make you dependent, needy, a child. This is your pacifier. To pacify you, and make you just shut up. This is your painless lobotomy.

IV. Becca

And let's not forget Becca. *Becca* wanted to know *everything* about the hurricane, because she wanted to torture me when I didn't feel like speaking about it. My parents were good. They didn't bug me about it. They just got back, asked if everything was cool, threw around a few words of compassion, and went back about their business. Why couldn't Becca take a few lessons from that?

Oh, but that's just total bullshit. Of course, I preferred Becca's response — of course — because I wanted everyone to WANT to know, and I couldn't very well just *tell them*. For God's sake.

And she said, "I'm sure it was really scary to be alone out there, Henry. It's nothing to be ashamed of or embarrassed about."

Right, all alone except for Rachel Flagler.

AND — the situation with Becca, reactions and so forth, it didn't end there. The hurricane dug and tore at me, I couldn't even function. Becca knew, and I guess she tried to make it work, but eventually . . . everything sort of went like . . .

There was a long silence on the phone.

"Henry?"

She lost because she talked first.

"Henry?"

"Hm?"

"What are we doing?"

"Talking."

"No one's saying anything."

"What do you want me to say?"

"I guess I don't know." She stopped. I expected another trapeze of silence. "Has it always been this way?" Her voice was soft. And God how I wanted to be cold.

"I guess not," I said.

"What are you getting out of this?"

"I still like you," I said. "I still care about you. I mean, I love you, Becca. You know that." I looked at my feet and my wall.

"What are you getting out of this?" she said again.

And every time she was mature, every time she acknowledged reality, I poured buckets of shit over this reluctant little candle. Lines lifted from screenplays, stolen poetry, just utter garbage, flowing like sewage. I threw every nice memory in her face and asked her if she wanted to throw it all away. Because that's what happens. Everything becomes nothing.

21

RACHEL STANDS BEFORE ME. Her bottom lip is low. It looks like it shakes, but it doesn't. Cheeks flushed, freckled, wet bottom gums, her eyes, piercing and green.

It's Monday. History repeats itself. After the storm, after the hurricane, Rachel called and called, and now, after the party, she's been calling.

The halls are emptying, classes filling up as the late bell hangs over us.

"Did it mean anything to you?" she asks. "It's okay if the answer is no, I just want to know."

"What do you mean?"

"Henry, I'm not an idiot. Don't pretend you are."

"Oh . . . the party."

"Yeah, the party. I guess it didn't." She shrugs. She looks at the floor. "Really, I honestly don't know why I bother."

"Rachel, it's just that, I don't know. Maybe it's something —"

"It's kind of funny," she says. "I mean we barely knew each

other before. But you were good to talk to — I felt connected to you in some way. And I still do."

"The connection, I think maybe that's it. Maybe I'm afraid or something. Of the power that you had, that you . . . pretty much saved my life. That I was so vulnerable in front of you and —"

"Henry."

"What?"

The bell rings distantly.

"I've always liked you," she says. "I've always thought you were smart and confident. I was attracted to you. And for a long time, I had trouble getting over it. But spare me your psychological power bullshit. Friendship isn't about whatever abstract idea you're trying to make it. You were just being a jerk. Rationalize that however you want."

And suddenly, it's so obvious. Rachel's eyes burn with intensity, with understanding and compassion. She is brave and fragile and so *human*. For her, right and wrong are nothing short of obvious. And it's always been there with her as I floated around in my ambiguity.

It's so clear: She *should* be with Bill.

"I hope you're doing what makes you happy, Henry," she says, clutching the straps of her bag, turning.

"Wait, Rachel. I miss . . . I miss something. I miss how things were. Before."

"Before?" she says. She gives me one last look before gliding through the empty hallway and slipping into class.

Before I was like this.

I stand there trying to figure out what to do. But it all floats away.

Do I want Rachel? Is this realization that she should be with Bill just some nice-guy TV fantasy? No. At least, I hope not.

Rachel is good-looking.

She is smart and sensitive.

But I know what I want.

I know that all I could ever do to Rachel is avoid her and ignore her. Because that *thing* isn't there. That Becca thing. Where no matter how much a person upsets you or abuses you . . . no matter what, you're stuck.

So could I ever get over Becca? Of course. And I don't think Rachel is stuck on me the same way. It would feel good to get with her — to exploit her kindness and make me feel good about myself. But wouldn't it sort of feel good to see Bill get with her?

(yes/no)

I guess it would. But the last thing I'd want is for this to be *altruism* or something stupid like that. I want Bill to get with Rachel. But this is NOT me finding my inner-charity or growing or whatever. I just want my friend to get some ass.

In fact, maybe getting them together would even *feed* my narcissism and selfishness and desire for power. By knowing I can, whatever, *control* other people's lives. It's still all about me.

Anyway, I know I ought to call Rachel . . . just to see. Just to ask her a couple things. Because she really needs to be with Bill.

It's interesting in class. You can agree with someone ideologically and wonder how they can be such a moron.

"But, Mr. Evans, how can that *be*? Church and state are *separate*!" she says.

In history, teachers like to throw current events in your face to pretend that high school deals with topics of relevance.

Mr. Evans grins knowingly and shrugs. "A very good point," he says. Like there's a little secret between him and the girl in the first row. She thinks she's a genius and he thinks he's Socrates.

I want to say, EVERYBODY KNOWS THAT! YOU DIDN'T TAP INTO SOME HIDDEN ARTICLE OF THE CONSTITUTION! WE *ALL KNOW* CHURCH AND STATE ARE SEPARATE, YOU SELF-SATISFIED, PSEUDO-INTELLECTUAL FUCK! AND YOU! YOU'RE SUPPOSED TO BE A TEACHER! DON'T YOU FUCKING PAT HER ON THE BACK FOR POINTING OUT THAT 2 + 2 IS 4! IT'S NOT A VERY GOOD POINT!

"I'm glad *someone* is paying attention," he says.

Bill is sitting behind me, and I think about teen movies and coconuts. What did Charlie and Bill talk about on the car ride home? How can they be alive without me? What could they say?

Hi, I am cool and I break the law and I have a cool car.

Hi, I have poker games and I am unsuccessful with girls and I play video games.

What's funny is Charlie's side of the conversation probably was like that. Just — *hey, check me out, I rock.* But Bill isn't propagating any myths. He's just existing. He's an actual human being. Not just some *loser, asshole, cool person* plate illustration. He is real.

Bill hovers a note over my shoulder.

They were probably just jealous, it says.

What the fuck are you talking about? I write on the back.

I guess it's a joke about the lecture.

Nothing, he writes. New paper.

I write, *This is hell.*

Yeah, lunch is soon.

There's more school after.

Eh, it's not so bad. At least, there are friends and everything.

Whatever.

Okay, I think Evans sees us.

The faint blue horizontal lines seem cold beneath my pen.

Do you still like Rachel Flagler?

I'll talk to you about it later.

Do you?

I guess. What's the difference?

No difference.

OK.

I look around the room. The walls are white, with motivational posters and photos of birds.

SHOOT FOR THE MOON! EVEN IF YOU MISS, YOU'LL LAND AMONG THE STARS!

THE MIND IS LIKE A PARACHUTE! WORKS BEST WHEN OPEN!

Who makes these things? I imagine a large sweatshop in Taiwan, whips and chains, skinny little women and children and angry, burly men with Viking hats. Rows and rows of laminating machines, pressing out glossy reproductions of animals with funny expressions. Monkeys with crazy hair or the clever witticisms of an arm-folded Garfield. Cats dangling from ropes, with a warm *Hang in there, baby!* across the bottom.

The clock ticks backward.

We get to lunch and Bill says, "I shouldn't have said that."

"What?"

"That I still like Rachel."

"Why?"

"Aren't you guys, like, together?"

"Who said that?"

"I thought you guys hooked up at that party."

"And?"

"And nothing, I guess."

He takes out a sandwich.

I say, "I'm pretty sure that was just a one-time sort of thing. I mean, I told you about Rachel and the hurricane and everything, didn't I?"

"Vaguely, I guess."

"Yeah — it's not really important. But I guess we sort of, I don't know, I guess there was some sort of connection there, and that night at the party it came out or something."

"Hm."

"Maybe you could try getting in a plane wreck with her or something."

"I'll consider it."

"If nothing else."

Bill drinks some Coke. "If only it were that simple."

And I'm not sure why, but I say, "Y'know . . . I did sort of get the vibe that she was into you."

He laughs. "What the fuck are you talking about?"

"I don't know. Just talking to her and stuff, she sort of gave me that impression."

"You talked to her about me?"

"I guess. Nothing specific, and maybe I'm just misinterpreting . . ."

He takes a bite of his sandwich. "Dude, there's no fucking way. When I asked her out like a month ago, she gave me that 'I don't wanna ruin the friendship' crap."

"Well, maybe she changed her mind."

"I don't think so. I even thought she was being sincere for a while, but I don't want to lie to myself about it anymore. I've been fed that line before. Girls *love* being good friends with me. I must be the friendliest fucking guy in the world."

"Well, there are worse things than being good friends with lots of girls. Some guys barely talk to any girls. Being close is pretty much one step from being together."

"No, it's not, dude." He shakes his head. His eyelids, his eyebrows, the top of his face are concise with logic. With confidence.

He says, "Question: What is the opposite of love?"

I know the obvious answer is hate, and that it can't be hate, but I say, "I don't know — hate."

"Wrong. Indifference; friendship." He leans to me across the table and says, "You know how many girls have told me about some guy they hate — some total asshole — and then a week later they're hooking up with that guy at a party? More than one. So, yeah, friends? That's pretty much the worst thing you can be to a girl. I used to think a lot about it."

Bill looks off and puts his elbows on the table. "I mean you know I've always been able to talk to girls — I was dumb enough to think that was a good thing. But seeing everything over the last couple years, it's just become sort of obvious. But there's nothing really you can do about it. They can be like — *wow, you're like a brother to me* — or *wow, you're like a teddy bear* — or *oh, my God, I feel like I can talk to you about anything!* That means *wow — I will never, EVER have ANY feelings for you. Sure, I'll talk to you about my feelings, about how other guys are such jerks and about how oh, Bill, you really DESERVE a great girl and one day you'll get her and she will be so lucky, only she can't be me, because that would ruin our super-wonderful friendship.* I'll give you a great, big hug and then go hook up with Charlie Brickell. Or even with you, Henry. That's the great phenomenon of being friends with girls. It's a blast."

Whoa. Bill totally knows. And it makes me realize why I'm friends with him. Not because of history or because I'm trying to control him or use him. It's because somewhere down there — beneath that friendliest-fucking-guy-in-the-world skin — is a person who understands. He understands that he is being fucked over and that it's unfair and he's accepted it. What can you do? Sometimes all you are is who you are. Girls know who he is. He's Bill. And they don't think of Bill "that way."

"Well, maybe Rachel Flagler is different."

"No one's different," he says.

It's so hard to fight him, when everything inside of me is saying he's right. But maybe Rachel Flagler really is different. Maybe I'm not full of shit.

Rachel's voice is like pillow feathers and vast cumulus clouds.

(This is for Bill. You are a good friend.)

And Rachel says:

"What do you want, Henry?"

"Well. The first thing I want to do is apologize."

Her breath hangs on the line. "But you're not actually sorry, are you?"

I think about it.

"Listen, this isn't about that," I say.

"What?"

"Tell me your idea of the perfect guy."

She laughs, a loud exhale of self-contempt. "I guess it used to be assholes with mental disorders."

"Okay, okay. Maybe I deserved that." It *is* a little harsh though, bringing PTSD into it. Everyone is so cruel sometimes.

"Maybe you deserved more."

"Okay, maybe, whatever. But your perfect guy."

"I'm not playing this game."

"Fine," I say. "*I'll* tell you your perfect guy."

"Oh, my God."

"Just bear with me."

"I'm listening." She sighs.

"First, let's start with who *isn't* your perfect guy, although he is *most* girls' perfect guy. Most girls' perfect guy — whether they admit it or not — is a bastard. He's someone who isn't going to give a shit about — much less understand — their feelings. He's insensitive, because society says being a guy is about being insensitive and girls are attracted by that sort of stony stoicism of masculine insensitivity that society says is good. And maybe on some evolutionary level it used to work — I mean, who's going to hunt all those great big prehistoric mammals if guys are wasting all their time sitting around crying? So if you're most girls, your perfect guy thinks crying is something you do because you're a chick, and if you're most girls, you dig that about him. Because he's *above* that — emotions are something he has to transcend. Your perfect guy — well, not *you* because of course this isn't *your* perfect guy at all — but anyway, most girls' perfect guy *definitely* isn't going to want to talk to you about whatever bullshit you happen to be bitching about on a given day. Because if he did, wouldn't he pretty much just be a girl? He's gotta smoke a lot, drink a lot — I mean, that's hot. He doesn't give a shit about lung cancer, liver failure, because you only live once — live fast, die young, and leave a pretty corpse. Because goddamn, that is *so* sexy. But that's not *your* perfect guy, is it, Rachel?"

"No!"

"Because there are some guys out there who are *not* like this — and they're pretty lonely."

"No — that's *not* my perfect guy. And I *seriously* hope you're not about to tell me that that guy *isn't* you! Because you're totally like that! You're totally afraid of your emotions! You totally think crying is weakness! You do drink, you don't give a shit about what's on my mind —"

"Listen, Rachel, this isn't about —"

"That asshole guy pretty much describes every ideal you've probably ever held!"

" — come on, this isn't really about —"

"I mean, Christ, Henry — I knew you were an asshole, but this is ridiculous. You're totally *aware* of all of these things. It's probably clearer to you what an asshole you are than it is to me!"

"Yeah, maybe . . ."

"So, yeah, go on — tell me about my perfect guy. The real one — my for-real perfect guy."

"The opposite of that."

"You're fucking right it is."

"A guy who *wants* to talk to you, to listen to you, to be there for you. Who actually listens because he *wants* to know, and helps because he cares about you, and wants you to feel good."

"Right."

"A guy who isn't just trying to get some ass, but who wants an actual satisfying, stimulating relationship."

"Right."

"A guy who doesn't just use you in some power struggle."

"Okay. Great. That's true. But that guy obviously isn't you, so I really don't know what the hell you're talking about."

"But you don't know who he is."

"No. No one's *really* like that."

"No one?"

"If someone is, I've never met him."

"Or maybe you have. Maybe you just don't think of him that way."

We sit on the phone for a little while.

"Is he not hot enough?" I ask.

"He's cute," she concedes.

"But?"

"I just never . . . the friendship."

"Do you believe that?"

"I don't know."

"It's okay if you're not attracted to him. That isn't shallow. It's important."

"Well . . ."

"Unless what I described isn't your perfect guy."

She stops for a little bit. It feels good. Maybe to put her in checkmate or maybe to do the good deed for my friend.

"It is," she says.

I feel myself smiling. This is *not* altruism.

I call Bill and ask him if he wants to hang out. Play video games, order pizza. He says definitely. I head over to his house.

On the way out, Charlie calls and says there's something I might want to know, but I say save it for tomorrow. He says that's fine. There isn't any kind of a rush, he says.

22

I STAND UP AND SCREAM fuck until my throat crackles and burns and my voice turns to hacksaws against iron bars. The phone sits echoing on the receiver.

I look at my fists and I want to destroy something, to burn down this house, to kill a man, and for everyone to see. I want to fucking smash every vase, every mirror, everything, until my muscles burn and I cannot move. Until I'm paralyzed on the floor, lying in a happy little heap of skin and muscle.

I drag myself into the hall, but I don't feel like going anywhere.

Today is Tuesday and I am pumping adrenaline.

My knuckles need to make contact with something. The hallway closet or the solid, white wall. The closet is painted white, with angled, horizontal planks of wood. Break the closet or break my hand. I don't want my parents to know, and they'd only notice it on something they paid for. I was free.

The first punch is horrible because I am too scared.

I scream "Jesus Christ" and "Charlie, you fucking piece of

shit" and let myself go, my arm, my shoulder to my elbow, and my elbow to my hand. I force my fist into the wall and I feel it, and it feels so good to feel something. The pain is sexual and incredible, and I look to my hand for proof. The knuckles are like jagged boulders wrapped in taut, thin leather. White paint on the ridges and I bleed. Pink and red around a small cut, a slit.

I punch it again and the sound is absorbed in the plaster, quieter than the shattering in my brain.

"Tell me you're fucking kidding," I said.

"I'm not kidding," he said.

"Well, at least have the fucking courtesy to tell me you are."

"Stop overreacting."

My fist pumps itself until there's nothing, until my arm aches from the motion. The wall remains intact, which is so fucking perfect and metaphorical. You can kick and scream until your hand is a fleshy pulp at the end of your arm, and nothing changes. You can vandalize a fancy FOR SALE sign development, smash windows, spray philosophy on the walls, and you know within a month, within a week, it will all be cleaned up, redone, and ready to go. You're an ant under a microscope, scuttling your little arms, swimming, gasping for air, lusting for motion, protesting against what you can never change.

"Overreacting?"

"Yes, overreacting."

"Fuck off and die."

He laughed.

"Laugh, laugh all you want, you're a fucking piece of shit. How could you do this? You knew how I felt, you don't fucking do that!"

"You told me you were over it."

"Oh, fuck off with your technicalities."

"Just calm down."

And I hung up on him.

Now I'm on the floor against the wall, my knees up and my feet flat against the parallel concrete of the hallway, cradling my hand like a deformed infant.

I scoop myself up and toss my body onto my mattress. I throw myself around. I want to pass out, but I can't sleep like this, with my mind like this. I'd never wake.

Fucking Charlie and Becca — it's so perfect, so utterly perfect. I should have seen it coming for its sheer beauty.

It's three and the sun is bright through the windows, laughing. I barrel through the house to the kitchen pantry, the medicine cabinet, where problems are solved. Oh, all those little orange prescriptions, those little tubes with their block-letter directions. My arms knock through the chamber like a torrent, a thunderstorm of bottles spreading onto the tile, rolling like heads.

I press down and twist the caps against my palm, child-safety locked but second nature by now. I empty the tablets into the garbage disposal and throw the bottles across the room. They spin and swerve like bumper cars. The caps lay scattered, and a few saved pills rest like capitals on a map.

The phone rings. My tantrum is ruined.

"Hello?" I say. I am unable to find a tone.

"Henry, I've been thinking a lot about what you said. About Bill and everything. And I think you're right. But I really want to talk to you about it, because I don't know — it's just — it's just, like, I'm afraid. Like, that . . . I don't know, that I'm going for all the wrong things — in my life, like throughout everything. I was thinking about the attractiveness thing and, y'know, I don't want to go for him just 'cause it's like the 'logical' thing to do or whatever — because that's not, y'know, it's not how relationships *work*. But at the same time I feel . . . I feel it would be a really *good* thing, definitely. It's just that I want to do what feels right and I want to do what *is* right. And I think they might be the same thing this time. I mean, I really think they might."

BLEGH! I DO NOT GIVE A SHIT!

Whoa. Get a grip.

Okay. But really: Does it have to be right now, Rachel Flagler? Does it have to be right, right now?

"Henry?"

"Yeah?"

"Is something the matter?"

I hate you. I want to tell her that I hate her.

I want to say . . . Rachel Flagler. Here's the thing, Rachel Flagler:

I did my Nice Guy Saintly Thing, setting you up with Bill, my nice friend, who was seriously deserving of some saintliness directed his way, and now you can go talk to him, call him up, then he can talk to you, you guys can love each other, maybe get into a little misunderstanding, have a nice romantic comedy arc, realize you belong together — and *bam!* — nice work, happy lives. Good. See? I'm good.

Okay?

But right now I am a little preoccupied because my *other* nice friend accidentally did some fucking shit with my vulnerable suicidal ex-girlfriend who I still am and have always been in love with. Nothing personal against you, Rachel Flagler, but that's kind of how it is. So please — if it's not too much — please do not make me *talk* to you now, Rachel Flagler, okay? Because if I talk to someone, I will probably kill them, and then I will have to find an all-new person to send Bill's way.

"Henry?"

"No, nothing's the matter. Everything's great, ha-ha-ha!"

"Are you sure, you sound sort of —"

"Ha! Well, yeah, now that you mention it, I actually do feel a bit under the weather — must be, ah, something going around, y'know. Okay, well, see you later, go for the gold, Bill's a great guy, okay, 'bye now."

I hang up the phone.

Charlie and Becca at the party, at Keith's. While I was with Rachel. *Fuck.* Charlie and Becca, and I can't fucking believe it, except it's the most perfectly obvious thing that's ever happened since the dawn of time.

At night, I lie in bed and I imagine his lips on her. That he could never appreciate her lips is why she will love him. No one wants to be appreciated. Only abused. His stubble will scratch at her, and she will place the back of her hand against her forehead in mock admiration and giggle over his manliness. Their legs intertwine on a bed, hers like a bleached plastic Barbie doll. His eyes will sloth from wall to wall until he is bored, and then he will go.

But when I fall asleep, Charlie and Becca are still fucking in my head.

In English, Mr. Englewood talks about a party we are having. People are going to bring food. Cookies. Chips. So far, I have missed the eight o'clocks.

"I could bring brownies."

"Oh, yeah, bring some *special* brownies," a boy says, and the class just can't get enough of it.

Mr. Englewood folds his arms, as if to say, *Oh, you cheeky thing.*

Oh, that is so cool that you mentioned marijuana. Tell me of other drugs, you cool, cool kid.

The boy sits smiling and I want to murder him. I wish I could shrug it off and call him amusing or entertaining. It would be more demeaning to him. But I want to murder him and everybody, because Charlie and Becca did something. I don't even know what, exactly.

I want to punch Mr. Englewood in the face, but Charlie beat me to it a full year ago.

My bag feels lighter without the weightless Ziploc bags of medicine. I am nervous. I am waiting.

Some nerdy kid makes a joke, so no one laughs. Some cool kid says "awkward silence," and everyone is laughing again. Mr. Englewood loves every second of it.

I want a fishhook fed into my mouth and pierced through my intestines and I want to be dropped until my insides hang like a mobile.

I don't know how I get from English to math or how the clocks disappear. Letters and numbers and symbols pencil their way to my paper. I look at my hands. Mrs. Page is squeaking on the white board, and I think she made a joke. Then back to math.

"Mrs. Page," a kid in the front says, "I mean . . . I don't want to be disrespectful or nothing, but how, I mean, how will we ever *use* this, how will this ever affect our *lives*?" He is smiling, a proud revolutionary standing up and calling out against the tyranny of arbitrary authority. The months he spent formulating the question, analyzing it from every angle until he found the right instant to spring his trap, to catch the oppressor during a state of vulnerability and expose her for teaching irrelevant material. Would she break under the heat of the moment? Or is she merely a victim of an intricate system which controls even its oppressors — living day to day, oblivious to the vice of her own "noble" task? Surely, she would step back twice and move her hand slowly to her mouth, muttering softly, eyes glazed in disbelief. Surely this question would ensure none of us ever have to pick up another math book again.

Or maybe she's heard it a billion times.

And Mrs. Page goes on to cite the multitudinal examples of the everyday uses of calculus, such as all those times when we want to find the rate of acceleration for a particle floating vertically along a plain at a velocity of three centimeters per second. And so forth.

Somehow I don't think it's the answer the kid in the front wanted. But he got his moment of anarchistic system smashing, and Mrs. Page has returned to squeaking marks on the board.

In the middle of class I am overcome, noise and rain, and I am afraid I will have an episode. I spend the second half of math in the bathroom.

Sitting on the closed lid I breathe in and out. In and out. And I remember this is life without pills.

When I get home I let sleep creep in and out through my ears until the day sinks into night. I try to think as little as possible. Under the sheets, cold, the lack is physical. It is like I have lopped some chunk from my brain — I know it needs to be there for me to function. It is not in blasts, or shots, but in one long monotonous vacuum of pressure in my throat, of goose bumps. I feel the sweat as it glues me deep in the mattress, and I hear the rain, in the deepest trenches of my ear, a hearing not of the world outside, but of this internal, ongoing thunderstorm.

The hours glide like ice-skaters on a frozen lake, right into a fishing hole.

This is the first day I have not taken pills in a very long time.

23

IN FRONT OF THE SINK, I am so not on pills right now. The water runs around my hands, my purple knuckles, my palms and my wrists.

My face in the mirror — bony, twisted, a caricature. I have been forgetting about food a little bit.

The bathroom mirror is so big, it is actually as big as the world. Everything vaguely backward, through the looking glass and nauseating, reversed.

Off the pills, the first day off, I was in school. There are sort of these two psychological things I know about, because I know *all* this shit — one's called systematic desensitization and the other one's called flooding.

Systematic desensitization is — say — if a guy was in a hurricane and he became phobic of water, they would start by giving him water to drink, then to pour on his hands, then to bathe in, then he'd go into a swimming pool, then a lake and so forth, until he isn't phobic anymore. Something like that.

Flooding is where you're phobic of water, so, day one, they throw you in the ocean.

Maybe that's a bad example, but anyway, say a guy is phobic of *not* being on pills. Flooding would probably be something like what happened to me. What I did to myself.

But the rest of the world walks around without pills every day. (Well, most of it, at least.) Was I so pathetic that I needed some supplement to function? Didn't other people get through hurricanes, without any kind of accompanying disorder?

I call Rachel today. Thursday.

And I say, "So . . ."

And she says, "So . . . ?"

"Did the hurricane fuck you up pretty good, too?"

"Wow."

"What?"

"Repeat that."

"Did the hurricane fuck you up, too?"

She inhales the receiver and says, "My, my, Henry Fuller, I think you may be growing up."

"Why?"

"You want to know how another human being was affected by something."

"No, enough of that! I want to see if it affects ME because *I* am on pills, and *I* just took myself off of them, and I want to see if someone ELSE who was in the hurricane had . . ."

"Yes."

"If someone else who was in the hurricane had a similar experience mentally afterward. But anyway, it's still totally selfish and I still don't really care, all right?"

"Mm-hm."

"At all."

"Right."

But she knows and it's true. Rachel's eyes with their shattering honesty, I think of the small handful of quiet afternoon talks in the den, one, two, three days after the storm. We didn't mention the rain. We spoke about life, school, being a person. I pushed her away. "Okay, fine. I feel bad."

"I know."

"It's just like . . . I should've at least asked you about it. Or talked to you about it."

"But you were with Becca."

"Yeah. I mean I was. And the doctors told me to avoid stuff that made me think about it. And obviously, you did. And I just . . . I don't know."

"I was so jealous of her."

"Remember those couple times in your house? Right after?"

"Of course, I do. That's where the whole crazy idea I had in my head of how great you were *came from*."

"Have you ever talked to her — to Becca?"

"No. I had a class with her at the beginning of last year, but she ended up switching out. I mean, no offense, but I always thought she seemed like kind of a bitch."

I smile. Yeah. That's my Becca. Not *my* Becca, though. But goddamn! *I* was hooking up with Rachel: totally inoffensive, totally symbolic, the nicest of nice girls. But *Becca* — on the very same night at the very same party — was with Charlie: the pinnacle of all that I thought I probably ought to be. I mean, she *had* to be searching for a way to give me a complex. Bah, but this is not for now. Now, hurricane, Rachel, how did it feel, how did she feel?

"All right. So did it fuck with you?"

"Of course, it did. I mean, my dog fell into a gutter."

"Yeah. I always wondered why you went out to get that dog."

"To be there to save you, obviously."

"Yeah, you were all guardian angel."

"I couldn't save Fluffy; I had to save somebody."

"I wonder . . . if that dog hadn't run out, if I'd be dead."

"Hardly seems like a worthy trade-off. That dog was loyal."

"Ouch."

"It's true."

"Yeah, well. How'd you take it? The actual storm, I mean."

"Not too, too bad. My parents talked to me a lot about it. I was fine, though. Everything messes with people in different ways. I mean — you told me yourself you felt sort of . . . y'know, with your parents."

"Abandoned?"

"Yeah. So I don't know. I don't know how much that has to do with everything about your situation with the pills and everything. But . . ."

"Yeah. Anyway. You have more people to save, yet."

"Bill?"

"I mean — worth a try."

"Yeah. Maybe I'll be in love with Bill."

"Yeah. But still be secretly in love with me."

"Always."

"But don't tell Bill about it. You know how he gets."

"You're a fool."

"Maybe."

"Are you still all stupid in love with Becca?"

Oh, God. I ask her if she knows Charlie Brickell.

"I know *of* him."

Oh, perfect. "What do you think of him?"

"I don't know. He seems like an asshole."

"He is."

But it's bad, her thinking he's an asshole. That plays into his hands. Because, like Bill said, hate is just a conversation away from love — once you get their emotions going in one direction or another, it's just a matter of playing your cards.

I think of her word choice: asshole. What Charlie says about losers, assholes, and cool people isn't what he really thinks. What he really thinks is, there are predators and there is prey. And *that's* all there is. Losers, assholes, and cool people are just terms he throws around. To be clever and to have doctrines and so I'll think he's cool. Because he needs me. He needs others to exist. Alone, what is Charlie?

you go through existence as
your own audience
yeah, exactly

"You think Charlie Brickell is an asshole because he wants you to think he's an asshole."

"I guess," she says. "What's this got to do with Becca?"

"Just bear with me."

"I don't even know him, really."

"There's not much to know." I don't know if I believe that. I'm saying it to play Charlie down in Rachel's mind. But how can I play him down if he's the subject of my conversation? If

I'm centering my life around him? There's no such thing as bad publicity.

"What'd he do?"

"I don't know . . . I think he hooked up with Becca. At this party." I don't say it was the party during which she and I were together. Seems like it would be bad for my case.

"And even though you and Becca broke up —"

"Right. Even though she and I broke up, it's still making me insane, completely insane. And I don't know if it's because of Charlie and who he is, or of — of the circumstances. Or if it's just regular old run-of-the-mill jealousy, or what, but —"

"So to answer my question . . ."

"Right, yes. To question your answer, yes. I'm still all stupid in love with Becca."

I hear the words and I guess they're true. I guess it's true.

"I can't believe it's been a year," she says. "Are you still on the pills? I remember at the beginning the doctors told you it's about a year."

"Yeah. They'd been weaning me off for a while. Then I just sort of . . . thew the rest into the garbage disposal."

"What? Why?"

"Eh . . ."

"When?"

"When I found out. About Charlie and Becca."

"You decided to take it out on your pills?"

"I don't know — at that point I just — didn't want to be so dependent. On something."

I hear Becca's words echoing from the diner. And like she said — we're all bad people in different ways. Everyone is special.

Yeah.

And Rachel says, "Maybe you should just wait it out until the doctors say you can be off completely."

Yeah, maybe. But all the pills are gone.

I hang up with Rachel and then it comes just the way it's supposed to — withdrawal.

Oh, it's bad. I fall. The hurricane lunges back upon me, not in images; it comes back in the beating of my heart, in an iciness of skin and bone, in a thick, hot bile.

It is like yesterday and I resign myself beneath the covers. I should call the doctors. I should tell my parents.

I lie there in the rain. I go to the bathroom and crouch hovering over the toilet, but no vomit will come.

24

LOVE IS IN MY CHEMICALS. I don't understand it. Friday, I decide to go to Becca's house. The last Friday I can remember, she was trying to kill herself or cutting herself or whatever. But that must have been years ago.

"Henry?" Becca's voice from the door.

Last Friday, Becca was cutting herself, and the Friday before that, I was at a party kissing Rachel Flagler while Charlie and Becca were in some room secretly slobbering all over each other and laughing at me.

"Do you want to come in?" she says.

"Yes."

She flips lights on as we walk through the halls. The leather couch sits like a black hole in the living room.

"Do you want water?"

"No. Thank you."

Looking at Becca, all I can think of is Charlie.

"What's so funny?" Becca asks.

I shrug. "Remember when you said you would love me forever?"

"Oh, Jesus, Henry."

"No, I don't mean it like that."

"Well, how do you mean it then?"

"I'm not sure exactly," I say. She sits next to me on the couch. I am crouched forward and she leans back against the armrest. "Not in an accusing kind of way."

"Anyway, I never said that. You did."

"Is that right?"

"Yeah."

"Hm." I lean into the leather. "You mean you knew you wouldn't?"

"I'm not sure. I just didn't want to say it."

"Do you love me at all?"

"I guess not."

"What do you mean, you guess not?"

"I mean no."

I let my eyes crawl up the walls to the ceiling.

"Sorry," she says.

"It's okay."

"You don't love me, do you?"

"Ah, what the fuck is love anyway?"

"I don't know."

"Me, either."

I stand up to walk out.

"Where are you going?"

"Home," I say.

I'm tactful. I don't say,

"Home, so I can throw myself around my room and punch my walls until I collapse."

or

"Home, where I can lie in bed and dream of horrible ways to kill Charlie Brickell."

I wonder what my parents would say, if I had any parents.

I know what they'd say. They'd say, "You're young. Cheer up."

If they were obnoxious, they'd say, "Being with the same girl so long isn't healthy anyway."

And if they were nice, they'd say, "If it was meant to be, it will work out."

Not that any of it would help. It's just nice to know someone cares. No one cares and I want to see Charlie so I can kill him.

My parents are home for dinner.

My dad starts. "No plans for tonight?"

"No."

"How come?"

"I'm just tired, I guess."

"You gonna hit the sack early?"

"I guess so."

We eat. I hope they'll talk to each other.

Then my mom. "How's chemistry going?"

"Fine."

"You pulling up those grades?"

"I'm trying."

A fork scrapes a plate.

"Are you having any difficulty concentrating in class?"

"Yeah."

"Well. Do you think it may be related to your medication?" I haven't mentioned to her that all of my medication is gone.

"No. It's just boring."

She purses her lips and her eyes look sad and well-intentioned. "Maybe you have ADD?"

"What?"

"Attention deficit disorder. A lot of kids seem to have it."

"Oh, yeah. I hear it's going around. I've stopped sharing drinks."

My dad chuckles and says, "Can we turn on the TV?"

My mom shrugs. Soon I'll be able to slip into bed.

I wonder whether Bill and Rachel will get together and, if they do, whether they ever would've without my intervention. I'm thinking: no. And why? Because Bill is so nice? Because they're both so *nice*?

But how nice, really? Wasn't Rachel being just as shallow and uncool as anyone, giving Bill the whole "just friends" bit? Or maybe she really didn't want to ruin the friendship . . . but I doubt it.

What's funny (in some big-picture way, I guess) is that Rachel was in love with *me* for so long, and I couldn't see any of it. Because I was too obsessed with Becca. And why? Because Becca *wasn't* into me, and because she was sarcastic to me, and because she never really seemed to care. And it was the same fucking reason why Rachel wanted me but wouldn't look at Bill. Because all the fuck anyone wants is to be hurt. That's why Bill wanted Rachel. It's like the food chain or the pecking order or whatever it is. People only want someone who can crush them. And you know how it works? Whoever hides the most is at the top of the animal kingdom. Because Charlie hides *everything* and he gives you *nothing*. And Bill's a fucking raw, open wound, waiting, vulnerable, for anything that wants to dip in and rip him apart. And Charlie's a fucking steel wall, because he's a fucking *liar* and he couldn't care less. He doesn't mind being alone, and he really doesn't even *think* he's alone, because he has himself convinced. But he is. He's alone, and being able to be alone takes away *all* vulnerability. Putting on a show makes you invincible — even if it's a fucking lie. But what's so great about authenticity? Really? What's the big commotion? All it does is get you fucked.

But — maybe Rachel and Bill will get together. Maybe they can be a stupid, giddy gas planet of happiness. And I will feel good, maybe, hopefully. Or maybe resentful. Or maybe jealous. Or maybe it won't work out at all.

I lie in bed for days and the sky outside never changes.

Do I really care about Rachel and Bill? If they died, what then?

Do I give a shit one way or other about Charlie Brickell — about this two-dimensional dark-knight comic-book hero?

Do I even care about Becca?

Who the fuck are these people, anyway? It's so strange. You meet these animals and they attach themselves to you like limbs. But it takes so long to see. Something has to go wrong. It takes so long to really, really see that they have nothing to do with you at all.

25

CHARLIE HONKED FROM OUTSIDE and I knew it was him. It was his honk. I walked out into the night, and he stood leaning against the old Skylark like James Fucking Dean smoking a cigarette.

"Lung cancer's real fucking cool."

"You die now or you die later."

"Oh, don't give me that actor shit. It's just me here and I don't feel like being your fucking audience anymore."

"Yeah, I'm trying to impress you."

"Yeah, you are." I walk to him, face-to-face. He looks at me, doesn't say anything, looks back to the ground. He takes the cigarette from his lips.

Then he says, "Listen I didn't fucking know Becca was your Becca, all right. How the fuck would I know? I didn't realize till later. It was some girl at a party, trashed and whatever, and trust me it was no one-sided affair. Besides, you were in the other room feeling up your little redheaded treasure."

"There were plenty of girls at the party."

"Okay, and I *accidentally* ended up getting with your ex-girlfriend. Sue me."

"I think you knew." I don't know why, but in all his consciousness it seems he must have, must have known everything, must have considered every angle. In his shitfaced smirk and his blinding eyes. He bleeds omniscience.

He smiles and flicks away his cigarette. I raise my eyebrows at his coolness.

"Maybe the second time, I knew."

"You piece of shit." The heat rises in me, volcanic, and he wants this — and maybe he didn't know the first time, and maybe he was innocent, but in his voice is every reason I need. I feel the blood rushing to my limbs, warm, prehistoric.

"All right, whatever, so go fucking cry. So say you don't want to be my friend anymore or whatever fucking shit you want, man. But you know what? It's pretty fucking pathetic — you all worked up and bent up out of shape over here, and you know why? Because *she wanted me*. And she didn't want you. And it's a real fucking tragedy for you, because it means you lose. In your little fucked-up, twisted, post-traumatic mind now you lose another battle to Charlie Brickell, and it's so sad because this was at least something you had over me — Becca. So now I'm the horrible villain and you're the martyr."

"Oh, don't fucking talk about yourself like some goddamn misunderstood antihero. And anyway, you love to be the villain. Because for you, that's power."

"Right," he says into my face, "and you buy into it, so you have no power. It means you're impotent and it means my dick is fantastic, because that's all any of this shit is about. Who's the fucking sexually aggressive alpha male. Who gets to further the species and fulfill his existence."

And sometimes maybe your worst fears are all true. "You want the meaning of life?" he says. "Bam, there it is. Fucking. Fucking until you die, like any animal in the goddamn universe."

And sometimes you hear without hearing. It's all there in that movie screen of my brain, playing itself out, screaming and full of ruthless ecstasy. Everyone, everyone I know, and it's all fucked up, irreconcilably, passionately.

"Whoever has the most power and dominates, drags their cavewomen into their caves and furthers the species. And here we are, trapped in this fucking society that says no to all that shit. It's a pretty sad state of affairs."

"You didn't . . ."

He opens his eyes wide and smiles slack-jawed, holding his hands out.

"But, oh, man," he says, "you weren't lying when you said you didn't fuck her. That pussy was a death trap —"

And now my hand glides through the particles in the sky until my fist is in Charlie's face and he's on the pavement. He is much softer than my wall. His cigarette lies inches away on the floor and he is not smiling, for once.

His eyes open. And the smile creeps back across his face.

"'Bout fucking time, Caveman," he says. He is on his feet and his fist is in my stomach. I should expect he can fight, and anyone, if asked, would surely assume he could. I don't care. I stagger backward. The coconuts hide in the trees.

"Good?" he says.

I swing and miss, and he says, "Please let's not make a war of this."

Pretending I don't matter. I'm not worth the effort.

We're circling like animals.

"You're a fucking joke," I say.

"Okay." He smiles.

"You are. You're a fucking actor. What we said. Acting as your own audience. That's all you do. Putting on your little play for everyone. With your little badass games, your little con man scams and fights with cashiers. It's all so you can be this Charlie Brickell, this vigilante, above-the-law cowboy. So when people think of you, they'll think you're an asshole, which is what you want. So guys will resent you and girls will want to fuck you, with your fucking, yeah whatever, alpha male confidence. They'll *say* they don't want you, of course, but they will. So, good, you have this little game figured out, but don't barf up any rhetoric on my face about fucking being honest with yourself and being genuine because you're a big fucking phony show and you know it."

"Maybe I am. Maybe I'm just doing whatever serves my best interests and maybe acting the way I do does. What then?"

"Then nothing."

"Do you still want to fight?"

"I want to kill you."

So we stand there in the street, and I punch him again and he punches me, and our adrenaline works its way up until we pummel each other into the ground and go home, both feeling better.

26

VILLAINS AND MARTYRS?

Becca was the villain and I was the martyr.

Bill was the martyr and I was the villain.

Rachel is a martyr.

I am a martyr.

We're all martyrs and we're all villains. That's the truth for everything, because it's all subjective. It's all relative.

On Saturday night, I roll my bruised and broken body around the bed and I feel a smile on my face. This fight made my wall seem like masturbation. I do not forgive Charlie, but I will go see Becca tomorrow. Charlie doesn't want my forgiveness.

So losers, assholes, and cool people.

Or girls — with fat ones, quiet ones, and talkers.

And now this.

Predator and prey.

Things can be so cut-and-dry sometimes, so obvious.

What I don't think about is Charlie and Becca actually doing it. Maybe he's lying. Maybe he's trying to fuck with my mind.

He admitted he's nothing but a big liar anyway. Maybe he just just just just just . . .

Oh, God, I know when I'm rationalizing. I know what it sounds like.

But maybe.

Charlie's hat sits on my nightstand. I wonder when I will see him again.

TENETS OF EXISTENCE

Man desires power.
Man desires abuse.
Woman is largely the same as man,
but with a more artistic body.

First, power. The ability to control other beings. To dominate, fine. You grow bored of power.

Then, abuse. To find something greater than yourself. To humble yourself and be demeaned and reduced to nothing. To be destroyed.

You can only love that which can destroy you. You love it for restraining itself. But you have to be careful. Everything you love will turn on you at some point.

As an infant, you love your parents for not killing you and starving you.

As an adult, you love your ugly, little, newborn kilo of flesh for needing you and giving you power.

Bill calls Sunday morning.

*   *   *

As an infant, you think you have power because the big people tend to you when you cry and wail and shit yourself, but really, you have nothing.

"I think you may have been right about Rachel," he says.

The only reason the adults are keeping you alive is because once you're dead, they can't kill you anymore.

You can't have power over something that's dead.

"I'm a fucking genuis," I say.

"Did you say anything to her? Like did you put in a good word for me?"

Hm. Did I? Of course. But I don't need that. I don't get off on that. I don't need to be Bill's Charlie.

"No. Only that thing I mentioned to you before. But she pretty much brought you up then."

"I can't believe it. I mean, it was like a *month* ago that she was telling me 'no, no, I just want to be friends.'"

"Looks like she grew some . . . whatever, ovaries."

"Yeah. Looks like it." Bill's voice floats through some distant sky, some thin-aired ether.

"You sound fucking ecstatic." I look up at my ceiling. The morning hangs beneath my fan.

"I am."

"Girls will do that to you."

"It feels good."

"Always does at the beginning. Then a hurricane comes and destroys your home."

"Is that what you blame your relationship with Becca on?"

"That's what I blame everything on," I say. I crane my neck and look behind me out the window. "Speaking of which, I am off the pills."

"Wow. Since when?"

"Like Tuesday."

"For good?"

"Maybe."

"Is it fucking with you?"

"Yeah. The first couple days were the worst. I still feel — I don't know. I still feel the absence of the pills. Everything's vaguely not right."

"But life's kind of like that."

"Yeah," I say. "Life's kind of like that."

"Have you spoken with Becca lately?" he goes on. "I know it might still be weird with you guys, but she might be able to help, at least to talk about stuff with."

Yeah, unless she's too busy fucking Charlie.

FUCK. Every fucking conversation goes back to *this*.

To: Charlie fucked Becca, my virgin ex-girlfriend who I will always love.

Shut the fuck up. Eternal love is bullshit.

I always figured it would be Becca and me. My throat tightens around itself and my stomach and heart pump out of time.

Now the storm is different. Everything is. My body shakes at the angry new world, and I feel it all weighing down on the muscles in my back and my stomach. And now Charlie and Becca are not just words linked by an action, but they're real people who I loved and who turned on me and took my trust and my loyalty and used it, twisted it around and faced it at me and laughed. I want to keep it abstract, but things do not exist on a theoretical plane and Charlie and Becca really did it, and I wish it was me who had been Charlie Brickell that night and who had controlled Becca and who had the essence of life on his fingers.

"Hello?" Bill says. "It was just a suggestion. I don't know if things are still —"

"Yeah, sorry, Bill, I have to go, okay?" and then I hang up and I feel my feet walking to the door pawing at the knob fingers flailing at the knuckles and legs move into the car and the ignition and my hands shake in the car I see Becca and Charlie with their tongues on their faces and their eyes white and sweating necks and elbows and hair plastered to this side or the other side and with my hands shaking on the wheel and my right foot shaking at the pedal and my left foot down hard on the rug to balance and teeth chattering and I think back to that first afternoon I freaked out passed out and going up to the hospital and how they all decided I had stupid PTSD and my pills now hiding under the kitchen rug or down the garbage disposal and how I abandoned Rachel and Becca abandoned me and my parents abandoned me and Charlie abandoned me and I abandoned Bill and how my parents felt guilty and now I am guilty and Becca is guilty and everyone is guilty and how things are so different things are just so so different now.

27

BECCA'S MOM GETS THE DOOR. She is thin and her hair is the color of wheat. I remember the day when Becca found out her parents were getting divorced, and she thundered through the meat-freezer slaughterhouse public school hallways at the sound of the bell.

I want to kiss you.

I'm not going to kiss you.

Okay, then I just want to be your friend.

You want to be my friend?

Yeah.

All right. I'll be your friend.

. . . but she let me kiss her very soon, and I fell in love with her completely — whatever that meant.

"Well, Henry Fuller," Becca's mom says. I smile and am polite and walk through the hall to Becca's room. Okay: Keep your bearings — Becca fucked Charlie and you are off your pills.

*   *   *

THE AIR-CONDITIONING is very cold in Becca's room and
SHE SITS ON HER BED

lighting incense with a lighter, cold and quiet, knowing I
am there but saying nothing.
" ," says Becca.
"Becca," I say.
"One sec." She finishes lighting it. "Okay. What's up?"

BLACK-AND-WHITE COMPOSITION BOOKS and WOOD
FURNITURE, bedposts, nightstands, dressers.

Becca's room that I know so well. Why does it seem like it's
been so long? Every little detail slaps me across the face, jumps
out at me like a blue-and-red-paper-glasses movie.
"What's up," she says again with her MOUTH and her LIPS.
I search blindly for a piece of furniture and grab hold. My
intestines tangle themselves up in each other.
"Henry?" she says, but her voice is far away and I see BECCA
AND CHARLIE and I know know know know it's no I know
it's no big deal, and this kind of stuff happens and *what, you
didn't think you'd marry her or something for God's sake did
you?* and I realize the craving on my tongue is for pills.
I realize I am experiencing symptoms of PTSD.
*Becca lied to her parents and told them she was sleeping out
at some girlfriend's house and I was so nervous, sitting there,
waiting for her to show up that night, and it wasn't cold at all,
but I was shivering, wondering what would happen, if we would
have sex or what, and I waited at a chair by the front door for her
to come. I don't know how she got there, if she got dropped off or*

walked or what, and we didn't do much besides sit in my kitchen
and eat ice cream and lie in my bed for a little while, and then I
asked if she wanted to go outside and she said sure. We sat out-
side on the grass of my backyard and watched the sun rise and I
said something about

I wish this could last forever.

. . .or, This should last forever.

Becca didn't look up, though, much less say anything. Her
eyes were big, almost triangular, white and chocolate-colored.

When she said nothing, I hated her and wanted her to leave
and get the fuck out of my house. God, I was crazy about her.

"Henry?"

"What?"

I don't know how I look. My head is a carousel. The pills are
for natural disaster or domestic abuse or war. They're for cool-
ing you, calming you down. The pill pantry shines in my
forehead. Untimely death of a family member or a hurricane.
Fucked-up relationships and fucked-up lives.

"Do you want to —"

"What?"

"Jesus, do you want to sit down? You look awful."

"I'm fine."

"You don't look fine."

"I'm fine. I just need to sit down."

"Good idea." She's smiling, the bitch.

"You bitch." Now she's laughing.

"Sit down, psychoboy."

"Let's not resort to name-calling."

I am sitting on the couch.

My body prickles up and down.

"Do you remember?"

"Yes."

"I thought you were going to say no."

"I'm just full of surprises."

"You're a bitch."

"Oh, shut up."

I do. She looks at me medically. "Now what's going on?" she says. "Do you have a fever, what's the deal?"

I shrug with what little energy I can congregate. She is gone and I see Becca in ninth grade, hovering around like a ghost, with those long shirtsleeves and tired eyes.

She is back with a thermometer. She shakes it.

"Open your mouth."

"Do you like this?" The thermometer distorts my words.

"What?" she says.

"Do you —"

"Oh, just wait a second."

"Okay."

I stare at her and she watches the thermometer.

"Ninety-eight point six."

"Hm."

"So what is this, for attention or what?"

"You should talk."

"Ha, well at least mine was more dramatic."

"Is that a plus, really?"

I lose control of myself again. And I was just getting witty. My head jerks back and my mouth opens itself.

"Should I brace myself for projectile vomiting?"

I mutter something.

*Oh Henry no it is not if only oh Charlie oh God oh God oh
yes Charlie yes yes yes*

"Oh, for God's sake!" I say.

She looks concerned now. Now that I am screaming. Her
mom must be somewhere, must be able to hear this. I don't care.

"What?"

"Oh, come on, Becca! Charlie Brickell?"

Then she doesn't say anything.

"What the fuck is the matter with you? Jesus, you're a fucking whore."

She looks sad, but I don't care. In fact, I'm thrilled. I want it.

"How the fuck could you do that?" I say. "And at some random party. For fuck's sake."

She turns away, looking into a dark corner of the dark room.

"Jesus."

She looks back at me, and her eyes are red and the tears have
stained her white cheeks pink.

"Get the fuck out of here," she says.

"Why? Do you feel guilty about it?"

"No." She stands, and so do I.

"Well you should. It's disgusting."

"How dare you."

Oh Charlie oh oh oh Charlie oh yes

"Why did you do it?"

"It's none of your business. None at all. You're a piece
of shit."

"Yeah, well."

"Why did you come here? To make me feel bad?" She has
stopped crying. Her eyes are still bloodshot and soft.

"You were making *me* feel bad!"

"Oh fuck off. I was just kidding around."

"Well . . ."

"Well what, Henry? Are you happy now?"

Everything caves slowly, crumbles. I was angry, but there is some glowing ball of light, some rising sun beyond the horizon of anger. Am I happy?

"No," I say.

"You were just jealous."

"Of Charlie?"

"Yeah. Jealous of Charlie."

"Don't flatter yourself."

"Don't flatter yourself with the idea that your interest in me is flattery."

"Touché."

And of course Becca couldn't have known Charlie and I were friends and of course she was only trying to find what she was looking for. Of course I shouldn't be mad at her. Of course this is all the illogical raving madness of a groping, flailing world.

"This is retarded," she says.

"I'm in love with you," I say.

"So you admit you're jealous."

"I hate you."

"I can't even look at you. It physically disgusts me."

"You make me hate humanity. I never feel so much hate as I do in your presence."

"I couldn't fucking care less."

"I hope you fall off the side of the earth and I never have to see you again."

"How creative."

"Fuck off."

"You better not try to kiss me now."

I take her face in my hands and kiss her and her lips feel so good against mine, like this is exactly what I needed. I kiss her and she kisses me back, our eyes closed. Her couch is both cool and warm, black leather. We just kiss and kiss and kiss like that and for a few minutes I can be safe and forget.

28

BECCA'S MOM KNOCKS ON THE DOOR.
guys I'm going out to pick up some food
okay
everything okay in there?
yes

And we are alone.
I'm afraid doing this is going to fuck you up even worse
what could possibly fuck me up even worse?
more jealousy, suspicion
how would this make it worse?
because now I'd have basis for comparison
well don't fucking TRY to make me jealous
I doubt it would slip your consciousness
what do you mean?
you are so fucking analytical
am I?
are you kidding me?

I won't be jealous
lies
I won't be
let's get on with it
well, don't talk about it like that
I'm just kidding, come on

29

"HOW MANY TIMES did it happen?" I ask.

"Twice. Once at the party and once after. We only did it once, though."

Becca and I are sitting up against the bedpost.

"You didn't leave the party when you told me you were?"

"I was intercepted."

My body swells from behind my ribs. "Um . . ."

"What?"

"I don't know."

"What, Henry?"

"Was it good?"

"What? With Charlie? Yes, Henry, it was amazing, it was incredible. We did it for hours, screaming and moaning." She could be filing her nails for all the enthusiasm in her voice.

"Come on," I say.

"What do you want to know?"

"I don't know — just make me not insecure."

"You said you wouldn't do this."

"I know."

"Okay, it hurt and it didn't feel that good."

"Oh."

Her face says *okay, now what?*

"And with us?"

"It was better."

"Better just because it was the second time and you could deal with it now?"

"Probably."

"You and your fucking honesty."

"What could you possibly want? I just said it was better with you."

"I know, but still."

"Okay, we never *actually* did it at all — we were about to and then it turned out Charlie didn't have a penis and that was the end of it. Good?"

"Yeah, whatever. I'm sorry."

"Don't be. Just don't worry about it. Everything's fine."

"Is the fact that it hurt, I mean, isn't that in Charlie's favor, like making you want him more, giving him power and every-thing?"

"Yes, Henry, I'd much prefer painful, uncomfortable sex."

"Well, don't people seek pain?"

"No, people seek happiness. Don't be retarded."

"Why is that retarded? Isn't that why you cut yourself?"

She stops.

"Okay, fine," she says. "Maybe people do seek pain. But . . ." She looks up and off, into the ceiling. "But it's not the best idea."

"Right."

"Right," she says. "So if you're not an idiot, and if you

actually stop and think about what really makes your life valuable, it's good things, not bad things."

"Are you sure?"

"I have no idea."

Later on, she tells me that Charlie was going away, catching a plane to New York and starting up some things there. He told her that.

"With his uncle?" I ask.

"His uncle?" She tells me that Charlie is homeless.

(do you get along with your parents?

i wouldn't know

oh?

they died in a plane, i live with my uncle

i'm sorry

don't be, everyone's got to die sometime)

I must have been pretty fucking impressed at the time. Words are so simple.

But I need Becca to know. I need her to know what an act it was. I need her to know he's probably with his uncle Ralph. That all the shit he told her was just to look cool. That no one is *really* like that.

"Have you ever *met* his uncle?" she asks me.

No. I haven't ever.

"So?" she says. "Isn't it a possibility he's really homeless?"

"Whatever. Enough about Charlie — to hell with him."

"Good idea," she says.

"Are you sad he left?"

"I don't really care."

"No?"

"I don't think I was as impressed with him as you're afraid of."

"I'm not afraid — be as impressed with him as you want."

"I'm not."

I look away and try to be sane and levelheaded.

She takes my hand in hers. "It's okay. Please don't worry."

"Sorry," I say.

"And don't be sorry."

"I'm not really."

"Good."

Lying in my bed Sunday night, I take Charlie's hat in my hands. Maybe he was homeless. Or maybe not. It makes sense, though. It makes sense, the poor, abandoned, rogue hero — living life on his own, barely eighteen or seventeen or however old, left to fend for himself and coming out on top. Maybe he told Becca the truth, and to me it was all a lie.

But if he was homeless, how did he get enrolled in school? You can't be expelled from a school you've never been enrolled in. Some type of bureaucratic paperwork must prevent that.

And he tells Becca what serves his best interest. She'd be more tempted to fuck him as some revolutionary, homeless rebel. It's symbiotic eccentricity. Charlie's noncomformity feeds Becca's desire for noncomformity by having been with him.

I can't imagine what else he told her.

But Charlie? Homeless? It's so perfect that it has to be bullshit. It has to be a big fucking lie. And not some subconscious slip into movie heroism. This was a deliberate shot at characterhood. To be this week's *Tiger Beat* scruffy bad-boy pinup. Quirky and alternative. Anarchistic and smart.

It was a bunch of bullshit, plain and simple.

And I feel good. I am glad to be honest. I am glad to be genuine. And I am.

Now my mind drifts between two things. They won't leave. I know they're related somehow, but I can't pin it down, not yet.

I keep thinking about how easily Becca could have destroyed me — about sex.

And I keep thinking, for some reason, about that development Charlie and I destroyed. Well, temporarily destroyed. The development we benched for a week.

It's something about drawing a line. If it's okay to break the law here — what about there? If one scam is okay, why not all?

And I remember one of the first things Charlie ever said to me. It was the first night I met him. I'd lost the poker game because I made that stupid promise to myself never to blow the last of my money. Charlie said there are no absolutes. He said that a *never again* statement just prevents you from having to think in the future, denying yourself the responsibility of choice. Because sometimes it's yes and sometimes it's no.

I don't feel guilty, but I think vandalizing the development was probably a no.

And Charlie never heeded his own words. If x was okay, why not $2x$? Why not $1,000x$? The degree didn't matter. X was x. For him, I think.

The other thing about the development, besides crossing the line, the other thing was the painful futility of the whole thing. We were ants writhing under the microscope.

I can tell you the saddest thing in the world now.
  Why?

I'm just ready to.

What is it?

How do you feel?

(Becca's hand in mine for the first time in so long, warm and satisfying, the soft mattress beneath us, the window, the air, breathable and complete, my lungs and my arms and my neck, Becca's slow, simple breathing.)

Completely perfect.

Okay. Good. The saddest thing in the world is that one day we'll all be dead and all of this may as well have never happened. The saddest thing is that we have these small, beautiful moments, where we sit and we connect, like two human beings, united, silent, and we can keep them with us for a few decades and then they're gone, forever. That's the saddest thing in the world.

I call Becca late Sunday night and say, "Hey. I just . . ." I stumble. My neck and my throat — they're so terrified of thanking her. It's so risky. She could laugh or ask me what the fuck I'm talking about.

"I wanted to thank you," I say. "For today. I mean, I don't know if it's a guy thing or if it's just me or what the fuck psychological factors were at play. But you really helped me get through that. I really . . . really needed it."

I wish I could see her. Her expression, her reaction. "I know you did," she says.

"It was good of you. You could have had all the power you wanted."

She laughs. "Oh, I still have the power," she says. "I rule you."

"That's pretty hot."

"You're so fucked up."

"I know."

I sit up in bed, the curves of Becca's jaw sweeping through my thoughts.

"What do you think will happen with us?" I say.

"Oh, God, you know I hate this stuff, Henry."

"So forget it."

She pauses for a second. I picture her over the phone, sitting up. And she says, "Well, look: I like you. I like to be around you, and you're making me happy again. Happier than anyone else is making me, and happier than I've been in a long time. And I get the feeling that lately we've sort of, I don't know, come to some of the same conclusions about life and about what's important, maybe. Something meshes. So we'll see how it goes. I'm happy right now. I mean that whole time, for a couple weeks, everything was so relentlessly depressing. You saw me. I was so fucked. I actually just looked at my wrist right now. I can't believe how bad it all got."

I feel my fingers on the phone and say, "There's something that's sort of been on my mind."

"What's that?"

I try to decide how to tell the story. I hate having to mention Charlie in conversation (does *that* give him more — shut up). "Like a week ago, I was with Charlie and we went to some newly finished, empty, upscale residential development and, for whatever angsty reason, it pissed us off and we took a bunch of baseball bats and cans of spray paint and we just totally wrecked the place."

"Really?"

"Seems like a movie, right?"

"I guess, yeah."

"And what's the point? Even more like a movie: It was just this big waste of an hour and a half. It was so dumb. And it didn't get anything accomplished. The houses are gonna be refinished, the people are still going to move right in, right on schedule. No one will ever know except a few pissed-off construction workers and contractors."

"And?"

"Well. I'm vandalizing houses. You're cutting yourself." I put one hand beneath my pillow. "What the fuck are we doing with our lives?"

I hear her breathe in and wish I could touch her. "But I feel better now," she says. "I'm not sure why, but I do."

"I do, too. I always used to feel so agitated, like every word was part of some kind of war."

"I know what you mean," she says. "For me, I realized being a person isn't *about* being alone. Needing to sort of *exist* with other people is normal. It's not dependence. It can be, but it isn't automatically. I needed to figure that out. Being with you now, I feel happy. I'm not uncomfortable with that."

"I guess sometimes you have to be apart to be together."

"Maybe."

"And I don't mean together in the going-out kind of way neces —"

"I know what you mean."

Slowly, I realize what I think happened. Did sex save our lives? That's definitely not how it's supposed to be. It's supposed to destroy everything, because it leaves everyone jealous, suspicious, on their guard, and vulnerable.

But when everything starts off so fucked up, where do you go from there? It saved us because everyone was always jealous, always suspicious, always on their guard, and always so undeniably, gut-wrenchingly vulnerable.

Sure. Sex could have magnified it, multiplied it, brought out every sulfurous evil in our hearts. But instead, Becca was compassionate. Not compassionate like Rachel, not compassionate because being nice is nice. Becca was compassionate in a way that implied a specific understanding. Of the situation, of our lives, of everything.

She was being mature.

And the cuts and the vandalism. Maybe if there's another human being who understands, who listens, it doesn't have to go that way.

Rachel saved me from the physical hurricane. Becca saved me from the mental one.

Letting me be honest and sincere was the nicest thing anyone has ever done for me.

30

BILL AND I SIT ON THE ROOF of my house. The burning streetlight dyes most of the black sky a watery blue.

We stand up and look for big rocks on the shingles.

There was no ladder. I expected to find one in my garage, but there wasn't one.

"Can we climb up?" he said.

"I don't know."

We looked for a fold-out chair and set it up against the wall as a springboard, but it didn't work.

"In the movies, they just appear on the roof," he said. We walked around to the side of the house.

"We could jump up onto the fence and reach the roof from there."

"All right."

I said I would go first. My feet were side by side on the tips of the vertical, wood planks. I slowly uncoiled myself, extended my knees, and my hands touched the roof.

"You all right?" he said.

"Yes."

I was scared though. I didn't know why. It wasn't a big fall. I was afraid for my legs to leave the ground, to dangle from the sky and crawl onto the moon. I gripped the edges and moved my legs into the air. I hovered, my chest and arms weighing on the hard, dirty clay and my legs draping like deadweight.

"You want me to go first?" Bill asked.

"No."

"All right."

"One second," I said. "Sorry."

"It's fine."

"I'm scared," I said.

"Take your time. Don't worry."

"Should we just go inside?"

"Just go up. It will be fine."

I got my head straight and realized this was ridiculous. I pulled myself up, wormed onto the roof, and lay still for a moment.

"Nice," Bill said.

I carefully unwrapped myself and stood up. It felt fantastic.

Bill got up to the fence, and I held his forearms and helped him up.

Now we look for rocks, but there are none.

I take off my shoe and throw it at the lamppost and miss.

The neighborhood is illuminated beneath us. We stand like gods. All these little people watch TV in their windows.

"This really isn't going right," I say.

"No, it's fine." Bill walks to the side of the roof and tugs out a shingle. A second one drops to the grass below. He lifts it and holds it for a second. He throws it across the street, and I watch its soft, noiseless flight. Darkness falls with a shatter. The shingle falls and the pieces of glass sprinkle to the ground.

"Fuck you, Thomas Edison," Bill says.

We lower ourselves onto the roof.

The night is alive with stars, as it must be every night.

"So you and Becca are back together?"

"I don't know, I guess."

"For good?"

"I have no idea. What does that mean? I don't plan on ending it."

"Well, how long has it been?"

"I don't know. Less than a week. We're not really together, I don't think."

"Oh."

"She's tricky."

"Yeah."

"You guys aren't really close anymore?"

He looks up into the sky, which is dark all around us. "No. Not really anymore. We used to talk on the phone every now and then." He laughs. "She was another one who just wanted to be friends."

Speaking of which: "How's Rachel?"

"Pretty good. At first it was all stupid, I guess. I was too nervous, I didn't know what to do or say. I was going to fuck it up. But then I sort of realized like . . . what the fuck do I have to lose?"

"Nothing."

"Nothing. Exactly. And what do I have to gain? Everything. I mean, I've got plenty of friends. The worst thing that could happen is I try to do something with Rachel and then she says no. Then I say okay, whatever, and that's the end of it."

"Well, not to be a douche, but how is it different from when you asked her out before?"

"It's completely different. Before I was so scared of ruining my friendship with her or making her feel uncomfortable and this and that. Now it's like, whatever. Nothing really changes."

"Everything always turns into nothing," I say.

"Okay, cryptic voice of doom."

I laugh. "It always does, though."

"Yeah, well."

"Becca can be such a bitch. I really hate her sometimes."

"Ha."

"I really do. Sometimes I find myself in her presence muttering how much I hate her under my breath."

"I thought you like her."

"I do. It's weird."

"When do you hate her?"

"Just every now and then. For being better than me or something, or for the fact that I know we're going to end this eventually and she's going to go off and do other shit with some assholes."

"That's weird."

"Yeah."

We sit for a short while. I lower my back onto the shingles and rest on my elbows.

"I heard Charlie Brickell moved," Bill says.

"Yeah, last week."

"I heard his dad got a job in Tallahassee."

"Where'd you hear that?"

"My mom's friends with his mom."

"That's hilarious."

He asks why, but I can't stop laughing. The sky is so enormous, so endless. The whole thing has to be a little experiment. A game. An advanced species looking down at us and taking notes. Laughing. Placing their bets.

It has to be. Or else why would we have to learn things this way? Why would we have to go through all this?

I laugh at the stars and the houses and I laugh at the last month and the last year and the last sixteen years, and it's all just too hilarious to stop. It's too absurd. I am so sick and tired of trying to make sense of it. Bill just sits there smiling. I could explain it to him and I will later, but you can't explain it. You just feel it. You could laugh or you could cry, like they say, or you could gouge out your eyes with garden shears and stagger blindly in rebellion. But it seems a little impractical. So you learn to yawn, I guess. Not in blindness, but in clarity. In such lucidity that to get hung up on details is endlessly, riotously funny.

It won't last long, so you have to let it wash you out completely. You could miss it altogether. The feelings last in small exhales of cigarette smoke, swirling upward to the atmosphere, fleeting twilights of consciousness.

It all turns back to shit soon enough, and you're muttering hateful profanities for the girl you love. Go figure.

The night blankets Bill and me, and I feel like we are finally friends again, really friends, like how things used to be. Then I will leave to go to college and maybe never see him again.

See? Everything's crazy.

31

I'M ON A BOAT. The water is black like the sky, and I am alone, drifting noiselessy, peacefully through space. The universe surrounds me.

When I was seven, my parents took me to Disney World. It wasn't my first time and, since I was from Miami, it would not be my last. My mom had some meeting for business in Orlando that afternoon, and my dad and I waited in line at Space Mountain, an eternity of standing around, looking at the distractions they stuck up on the walls. It was cold. I sat in the little chair in front of my dad, and the cart took us off into the vast, fiery cosmos. At once, I was so filled by it, so curious and so satisfied. I was stupid. Of course, it was just a wood box, a machine — a lie — with small lights flickering at rickety helixes. But it felt good. It feels good to be in the universe.

It's an old, shitty little thing, the boat, little more than a raft. To the left of the old, vacant lifeguard tower, four little canoes hide behind a bush. They used to lend them out to kids, I think, until there were lawsuits. I dragged it out to the coast, the sand parting quietly against the belly of the hull.

My mom asked, "Where are all of your pills?"

"I guess they're done," I said.

"All of them?"

"If there are none left."

"There are none. Why didn't you tell me?"

"I don't know."

"Well, go pick up the prescriptions."

"Okay."

I went to the drugstore, and they wouldn't fill them up.

"The date ain't right," the guy said. "Come back when the date is right."

I drove back home and went to the shoe box in my closet. The one I hadn't looked in since the storm. Now I looked in it and it was the sweatshirt Rachel had wrapped around my knee on the day of the hurricane. Just a crumpled, folded, dirty purple sweatshirt that I saved to be dramatic. I put all the pill bottles in the box and threw the box and the sweatshirt in the garbage on the side of my house. I wondered whether throwing the sweatshirt away was just as symbolic as keeping it. Whatever. Anything is symbolic if you think hard enough, if you look hard enough for connections to make.

I decided everything had to be consummated somehow. If I could have, I would have made it rain. I would have flooded out my house again, poured water and wind through the glass windows, and looked casually up at the sky with a shrug. I would have yawned and cracked my neck, laughing at the gods, at the gambling aliens above.

But I couldn't do that, so I went to the beach. I parked the car at a meter and walked in the night air toward the wide-open infinity. I stood in front of it and shivered. It had been so long.

Lying on the boat now, on the old, dilapidated wood, I let my mind float with the tide beneath my back. I am stretched out and quiet, a simple specimen of tissue and biology. I think about Charlie.

You stand in a room with a happy man and an ugly painting.

He says, "Look at this! Isn't this just the most beautiful thing you ever saw?" He smiles and claps his hands together, then looks intently into your eyes.

So you could say, "Yeah. Very nice." And be a phony.

Or you could say, "No. Are you blind? That's the ugliest fucking painting in the world. I've produced better art on toilet paper."

And we're supposed to believe that the second response is noble — it's honest and uncompromising and on and on.

But isn't it just as much bullshit? To prove that you *will not* negotiate your integrity. That you will express your opinion, without regard for social standards and societal norms. You won't — nay, can't — conceive of any other way to exist. You are a fierce individualist, and if a painting is shit, it's shit, and by God, this asshole is going to hear about it.

The truth is it's all an act. Any way you spin it.

Even if they threw you onto a single-panel-comic-strip-deserted-island in the Pacific, you'd put on a show for yourself. Invent ways to entertain the imaginary audience, wishing all the time someone was there to record you, to watch you talking to your volleyball. To laugh at your stupid jokes.

And out there on the ever-moving, ever-changing, 71 percent of the surface of the earth, I sit up and shrug. Everyone needs someone to laugh at their stupid jokes, to nod at their stupid little revelations, to share their stupid, insignificant, little lives. I smile at the world, spreading out around me, expanding with exponential growth since the dawn of time. The little creatures beneath me, fucking to survive, eating each other, being born and dying. And everyone around me, every single person, every guy who ever sat down behind five cards at a table with me and said hey. Everything just builds and builds, draws on itself, destroys itself and starts over again. Everything just happens, stops happening, expands and contracts, like the gills of a great white shark. It's all there to see, in blinding simplicity — we are all the same and we are all nothing and it's fine, perfectly and completely, and it just feels so good to be alive, to lie on a stupid boat with your stupid movie life and to catch your breath and to laugh. Because that's all you get. You get to do it all now and you better love every goddamn minute of it and know you'd do it all again exactly the same. Every single thing.

EPILOGUE

The windows fog in the cold, dense air, and the heater is up in my car in Becca's driveway. We sit until the glass everywhere is white, until we are in a cloud, speaking as if the quiet sounds of our voices in the air could sustain this exact moment into eternity.

But nothing is going anywhere into eternity. Things just come and go. And soon giant machines will carry us all through the sky into our new lives. Soon we will forget.

The sunroof is exposed, dense with the fog, and I see finger-prints poking through. They are from before, from the last time, whenever, the last time that the sunroof was white and its inhab-itants touched the thick, cold glass.

The end is spiraling. Books and diplomas and all, and I just want to save this one little second, but it is impossible. I know this is all a crock. One day, I will be gone completely. I won't remem-ber this. It will never have happened.

But it doesn't matter. It feels good right now, that it's happen-ing right now.

Becca's eyes are so bright, so beautiful, so clear. She smiles and looks up at the sunroof as I press my finger to it, leaving the date in numbers and slashes. I draw a clock. She understands, I think. Or maybe she doesn't.

I leave it there and we sit and talk forever. And one day — all I can picture is one day — when we are all gone, moved, grown, with children maybe and with lives of our own, all I can picture is this great, metallic pyramid of cars, junked and piled, shattered windows and smashed grills, and sitting somewhere in the middle, on a foggy day like this, will be this old, scrapped Volvo, and the clock floating in through the windows, floating there forever.

Charlie and I will be standing right outside the lot, throwing a coconut with Bill, laughing and cursing, and Becca will sit and talk with Rachel Flagler, about life and politics, and the cast and crew will come out to eat the catered lunch and we will be high-fiving and joking and drinking and it will all just be so, so perfect for a second, it will all be just exactly the way things are supposed to go.

And, oh, God, how I wish it could be.

PUSH
YOU ARE HERE.
www.thisispush.com
Meet the authors.
Read the books.
Tell us what you want to see.
Submit your own words.
Read the words of others.
this is PUSH.
PUSHWT

PUSH
Just Like Life

❑	0-439-09013-X	**Kerosene** by Chris Wooding	$6.99
❑	0-439-32459-9	**Cut** by Patricia McCormick	$6.99
❑	0-439-29771-0	**You Remind Me of You** by Eireann Corrigan	$6.99
❑	0-439-27989-5	**Pure Sunshine** by Brian James	$6.99
❑	0-439-49035-9	**Tomorrow, Maybe** by Brian James	$6.99
❑	0-439-24187-1	**Fighting Ruben Wolfe** by Markus Zusak	$6.99
❑	0-439-41424-5	**Nowhere Fast** by Kevin Waltman	$6.99
❑	0-439-50752-9	**Martyn Pig** by Kevin Brooks	$6.99
❑	0-439-37618-1	**You Are Here, This Is Now: The Best Young Writers and Artists in America**	$16.95
❑	0-439-67365-8	**Perfect World** by Brian James	$7.99
❑	0-439-69188-5	**Never Mind the Goldbergs** by Matthue Roth	$16.95
❑	0-439-57743-8	**Kissing the Rain** by Kevin Brooks	$6.99
❑	0-439-48992-X	**Splintering** by Eireann Corrigan	$6.99
❑	0-439-54655-9	**Lucky** by Eddie de Oliveira	$6.99
❑	0-439-12195-9	**I Will Survive** by Kristen Kemp	$6.99
❑	0-439-38950-X	**Getting the Girl** by Markus Zusak	$6.99
❑	0-439-62298-0	**The Dating Diaries** by Kristen Kemp	$6.99
❑	0-439-53063-6	**Lucas** by Kevin Brooks	$7.99
❑	0-439-51011-2	**Born Confused** by Tanuja Desai Hidier	$7.99
❑	0-439-73646-2	**Where We Are, What We See** by Various Artists	$7.99
❑	0-439-73648-X	**Heavy Metal and You** by Christopher Krovatin	$16.95
❑	0-439-67362-3	**Johnny Hazzard** by Eddie de Oliveira	$8.99

Available wherever you buy books, or use this order form.

Scholastic Inc., P.O. Box 7502, Jefferson City, MO 65102

Please send me the books I have checked above. I am enclosing $_____ (please add $2.00 to cover shipping and handling). Send check or money order—no cash or C.O.D.s please.

Name_____Birth date_____

Address_____

City_____State/Zip_____

Please allow four to six weeks for delivery. Offer good in U.S.A. only. Sorry, mail orders are not available to residents of Canada. Prices subject to change.

Sometimes you have to break down before you can break through.

I don't want to be crazy

Samantha Schutz

A harrowing, remarkable poetry memoir about one girl's struggle with an anxiety disorder that develops after she leaves for college.

Available July 2006

DIRTY LIAR BRIAN JAMES

A spellbinding novel about a boy who must come to grips with his own tortured past—from the acclaimed author of *Perfect World*.

PUSH

www.thisispush.com

IDWTBCDL